IF YOU WERE ME

SAM HEPBURN

Chicken
House

2 PALMER STREET, FROME, SOMERSET BA11 1DS

Text © Sam Hepburn 2015
First published in Great Britain in 2015
The Chicken House
2 Palmer Street
Frome, Somerset, BA11 1DS
United Kingdom
www.doublecluck.com

Cover and interior design by Steve Wells
Typeset by Dorchester Typesetting Group Ltd
Printed and bound in Great Britain by CPI Group (UK) Ltd, Croydon, CR0 4YY
The paper used in this Chicken House book is made from wood grown in
sustainable forests.

1 3 5 7 9 10 8 6 4 2

British Library Cataloguing in Publication data available.

ISBN 978-1-909489-80-6
eISBN 978-1-910002-42-1

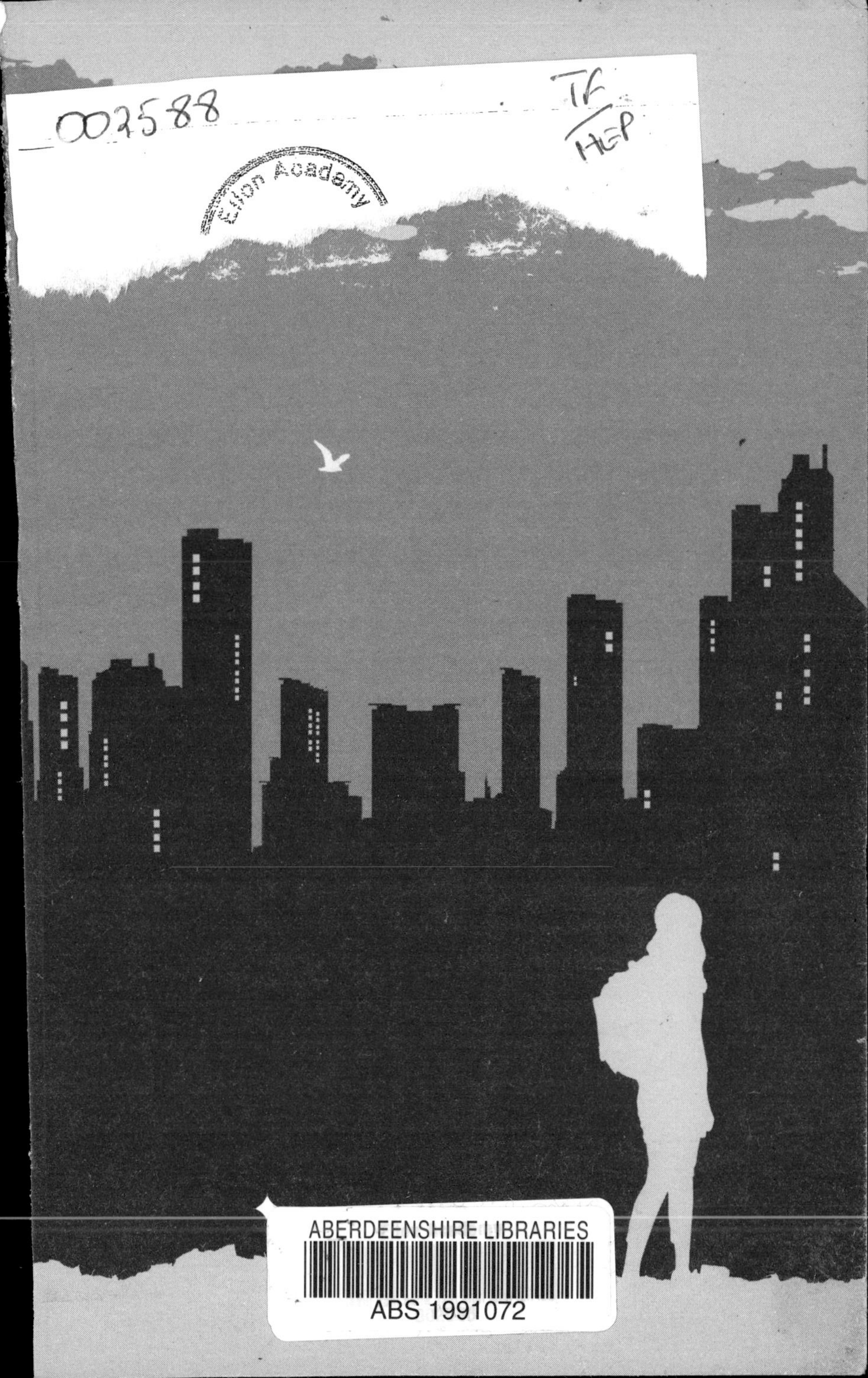

S am Hepburn writes thrillers seriously – devastating plots and brilliant characters take you places you didn't mean to go. Stories that are never what you expect, and are always hard to put down.

IF YOU WERE ME grips with a passion and a purpose. Afterwards the world feels a little bit righter, and a little bit brighter. Fantastic.

BARRY CUNNINGHAM
Publisher
Chicken House

For Beth with love

PART ONE

ALIYA

Kabul, Afghanistan

A s I jumped off the bus that night and waved goodbye to Salma the tips of the mountains circling the city were already blurring grey against the crimson sky. Salma pressed her nose to the window and waved back. But her eyes weren't on me or the sunset. They were darting across the square, following two men on a motorbike whose ragged black turban tails snapped and fluttered in the wind as they circled the fringes of the crowd. The bus rumbled away across the cobbles, spluttering puffs of exhaust into the haze of sizzling meat drifting from the brightly lit food stalls. I'd never come home this late before and I ducked into a doorway, wishing with all my heart that when I looked up I'd see my brother,

Behrouz, biting into a hot *bolani*, sucking the peppery sauce from his fingers and pushing towards me through the crush. I knew he wouldn't be there. Behrouz didn't come to meet me from the bus any more, and it was a long time since he'd wandered through the market buying food.

I peered around the edge of the wall, chewing my cuff and gazing at the mass of jostling, elbowing, shouting people. I spotted a gap and started to run, startling a cart-load of pigeons, who blinked at me through the slats of their wooden coops, squeezed myself between rickety stalls piled high with melons, fabrics, oranges, purple aubergines and bundles of mint, and dodged the swinging carcass of a freshly gutted sheep. By the time I reached the labyrinth of narrow streets that zigzagged up to our house, the sun had disappeared behind the dye works, trailing slashes of pink and orange along the jagged edges of the rooftops. I ran faster. All around me the alleys of the old town were filling with shadows and the sounds of dusk: the last echoes of the call to prayer, wheels rumbling on crusted mud, dogs barking, generators wheezing, and a radio blaring so loudly I didn't hear our phone ringing until I'd unlocked the door. The minute I picked it up it stopped.

There was just enough light to see my little sister sprawled on the rug, wagging her finger at the dolls she'd propped against the wall. I shook off my backpack, scooped her up and tugged her messy plaits.

'What are you playing, Mina?'

'School. I'm the teacher.'

'Where's Mor?'

'Sleeping.'

I know I shouldn't have felt annoyed but I did. Our generator had been broken for weeks, so I put Mina down and lit the kerosene lamps before I pushed open the door of my mother's bedroom. The curtains were drawn and she lay curled on her *toshak* with a quilt pulled up to her chin. She'd been like this for over a year, sleeping in the day, trying to blot out the world. And it was getting worse. Her glazed, puffy eyes blinked up at me through the gloom.

'Where were you, Aliya?'

'I told you this morning, Mor. A professor came from the university to judge our projects. He gave me and Salma a commendation.'

I longed for her to stroke my face, the way she used to, or smile at me with that look that said she was proud, but her hands stayed bunched beneath the quilt and her mouth grew slack. Mina trotted in, dragging a doll by its matted pink hair. 'I'm hungry, Aliya.'

I didn't want to cook. I wanted to revise for my exam but we had to eat. So I hung a lamp on the hook above the stove, propped my English book against the pans and tried to study while I stirred rice and chopped vegetables. It was hopeless. Mina was restless and wanted me to play with her. It was no wonder, stuck on her own all day while my mother slept. In the end I made a game of it, reading out sentences and getting her to repeat them while she unrolled the red plastic *dastarkhan* on the floor and skipped back and forth, spreading it with bowls of pickles and yoghurt and little piles of naan and arranging the cushions around the edge.

I was tasting the soup and listening out for Behrouz when light swept through the shutters. I looked up. A motorbike growled to a stop outside. Boots scuffed the grit. A second of silence, then the steady thump of a hammer nailing something to our door. My heart stopped beating. The lamplight seemed to flicker and dim as a sheet of paper slid on to the mat. I pulled Mina away and crept over to pick it up. Sick inside, I stared down at the crossed swords of the Taliban stamped at the top. My hand was shaking so much I could hardly read the scratchy blue scrawl that began *Asalaamu Aleikum*, 'Peace be upon you' – but there was no peace in the message.

Behrouz Sahar will be executed. Let this be a warning to all those who work with our enemies.

'No!' Choking back a scream, I ran to the window and peered through the crack in the shutters. Three men swathed in black darkened the shadows across the street; two paced slowly, watching our house, while the third leant casually against the bumper of an old pickup, murmuring into his phone. This couldn't be happening. Not to Behrouz. After my father died he'd got a job with the British army, but only because we needed money, and he wasn't a fighter, he was an interpreter. And anyway the war was over, the foreign troops were pulling out. What did it matter who'd worked for them?

I pushed my wrist to my mouth and tried to imagine what it was like inside the heads of these evil men, what they thought about while they waited to kill, what they dreamt about when they slept. My mother shuffled towards me and tugged the letter from my fingers. Her eyes skimmed the words, her jaw stiffened and her head began to twitch with panic. 'Are they out there?' she whispered.

'It's all right, Mor.' I ducked away from the window and reached for the phone. 'I'll warn him.'

'Tell him to get away. As far from Kabul as he can.'

She stood over me while I hit the buttons, twisting her hands and making soft keening noises in her throat. The line was dead. Not a crackle or an echo. I knew then that the men outside had cut the cable. I looked up at her and slowly shook my head. The letter fell from her fingers. She dropped on to a cushion, sinking deeper into the fog of misery that had swamped her since the day my father was killed by a Taliban bomb. I missed him too. The grief was like a rip inside me that refused to mend. But I could never tell her how much it hurt. How could I, without worsening her pain?

My eyes drifted across the photos hanging on the wall – my father getting his medical degree from the University of London, my parents smiling on their wedding day, our whole family at a picnic by the river. They lingered on the picture of Behrouz receiving a medal from his old boss, Colonel Clarke. He'd won it for dragging three injured British soldiers to safety in an ambush. He hadn't even been armed, and the newspapers had called him a hero, even in Britain. Was that why the Taliban had put his name on their death list? To make their own sickening headlines out of what he'd done?

I had to get out of the house. I had to find a phone that worked and warn Behrouz. I focused my mind on the layout of the rooms, picturing every door and exit. There was nothing at the back, just a carved wooden window that hung out over the sheer drop down the hillside. The roof was no good either: the taller buildings on either side cut off any hope of escape across the rooftops. The only way out was through the alley at the front, where the Taliban death squad was watching and waiting.

Mina climbed into my lap, twisting her fingers through my hair and nestling her head against my neck. I held her close for a long time and stared at the shuttered windows, feeling as trapped and helpless as the caged pigeons in the market.

Mina raised her head and looked at me. I'd heard it too. A tapping and scratching. Not much of a sound but clear enough in the silence. I lifted her off my lap and crept into the bedroom. The tapping came again. I closed the door behind me and slipped round to the window. Crouching low, I drew back the edge of the curtain. A gnarled finger scraped across the glass. I looked closer. It was a twig. Someone hissed my name. Was I was going mad? I heard it again. I couldn't stand it. I reached up and unhooked the latch, snatching my hand away as the window swung open, letting in a waft of night noises, benzine and wood smoke.

'Aliya!'

I eased my head over the sill and looked down into a face. It was all I could do not to burst out laughing. It was Behrouz, grinning up at me. The laughter died when I realized how he'd got there.

Like a lot of buildings in the older parts of Kabul, our house was built of mud bricks layered between rounded wooden beams, which jutted through the wall at the back like the prongs of a wide-toothed comb. When Behrouz was a kid, he used to get bullied by a boy called Tariq Shandana, whose father owned the bakery three doors down. One time Tariq dared Behrouz to crawl across the beams between our buildings and threatened to tell everyone that he was a coward if he didn't do it. There were wide, uneven gaps between the beams, the drop to the rooftops below was fifteen, maybe twenty metres in places, and there was absolutely nothing to stop Behrouz from falling off. I remember Tariq and his gang laughing and jeering from his balcony while I hung out of our window, scared nearly to death as I watched Behrouz make the crossing. He was grey in the face and trembling when I stretched out my hands to pull him back inside. But Tariq Shandana never called him a coward again.

Behrouz tossed the stick into the darkness, hooked his fingers over the sill and scrambled through the window. The wood creaked under his weight. I grabbed his arms, toppling backwards as he fell on top of me in a sweaty tangle of rope.

'You're crazy. You can't be here,' I whispered. 'They're outside. Three of them.'

He jumped up, slipping off the coils of rope and the canvas bag slung across his chest. 'I know. I've come to get you.'

'Don't worry about us. Get out of Kabul. We'll be all right.'

He looked at me, hesitating. 'No. No, you won't.'

'What do you mean?'

'Women, kids. The Taliban don't care. I've got until midnight to give myself up. If I don't, they're going to kill one of you, all of you, I . . . I don't know. Here.' He held out his phone.

I saw the words 'the blood of your family will be on your hands'; I didn't even try to read the rest. My eyes were locked on the time at the bottom of the screen: 23.02. I fought to steady my voice. 'What can we do?'

'Get out the way I came in.' He saw me flinch and gave me a little smile. 'Don't worry, Aliya. I'll make it safe. I've got a plan.'

It was hard to smile back, even though 'I've got a plan'

was a joke between us, the thing we always said when the other was in trouble.

'What plan?' I whispered.

Instead of answering, he unzipped his bag and with a flourish pulled out a wide khaki belt and two narrow strips of canvas fitted with spring clips at each end.

I turned them in my fingers. 'What are these?'

'Captain Merrick's army belt and the straps off the spare tyre in his jeep.'

He hauled on the rope he'd left hanging in through the window. As he tied the end of it around the casement he caught me staring at the blue dye coming off on his hands and the frayed patches where the fibres had worn away.

'Don't worry, sis. It'll work. It has to.'

Sis. That was something else he'd got from the foreign soldiers. I slipped through the door and beckoned to my mother. I tried to keep the mounting panic from my face and whispered, 'Mor, Behrouz is here.'

Mina looked up, her eyes widening in wonder. I clamped my hand over her mouth and glanced towards the shutters. 'You mustn't make a sound. You promise.'

She nodded solemnly and darted through the door. My mother followed her into the bedroom, pressing her knuckles to her thin cheeks as she watched Behrouz sweep Mina off her feet.

'You're going on an adventure,' he whispered. 'Like the children in stories.' He put her down and looked up. 'You too, Mor-jan.'

She leant against the door, breathing hard. 'What is this madness, Behrouz? They're going to kill you.'

He caught her by the shoulders. 'I have to get you out of here. The only way is across the wall to the bakery.'

'No! Forget about us.'

'I can't. We're all in danger, not just me.'

'Then take your sisters. I . . . I can't do it.' She gazed at the open window, shaking her head, wasting precious seconds. I grabbed her arm, too frightened to hold in my anger.

'Stop it, Mor! Stop being so selfish! You know we can't leave you!'

That was the first time I'd ever lost my temper with her. I felt so ashamed. But the shock of it seemed to stir something inside her. She let Behrouz take her to the window and stood quietly while he pushed a chair against the wall and whispered instructions for our escape. 'Keep as quiet as you can when you get to the bakery,' he urged. 'I don't trust the Shandanas not to give us away. Ready, Aliya?'

I nodded and lifted my arms. He pulled the army belt tightly around my waist and snapped a canvas strap on to one of the loops. I looked down into the darkness. My stomach fell away as I saw the spatter of lights glimmering deep in the valley below.

So there we were. A four-year-old child, a woman who barely had the will to get out of bed, a fourteen-year-old girl who was scared of heights and the dark and just about anything else you can think of, and a boy of just nineteen, whose escape plan consisted of a couple of canvas straps clipped to what I was sure was an old washing line he'd stolen from the back of the dye works down the street.

Behrouz went first. I watched him strap his belt to the rope and slither into the night, moving, then stopping and swaying a little as he felt for each beam with his foot, his left hand brushing the top of the rope for balance, his right shoulder pressed to the wall. Half of me was glad there was a sliver of moon to light his way. The other half was petrified that some Taliban spy would see him and shoot him down.

He got to the other end, cupped his hands to his mouth and hooted like an owl. I stepped on to the chair, relieved he'd made it across, horrified that now it was my turn. I climbed out backwards and waved my toes around, searching for the first of the narrow beams. The curved surface threw me sideways. I slipped and clung to the windowsill, scrabbling wildly for a foothold, unable to breathe. I knew then that I could never walk across. I would have to crawl like a cockroach.

I slid down the wall until my hands and shaking knees were low enough to drop on to the beams. The knobbly wood jarred my shins, scraping and bruising the skin and even with my shoulder pushed hard into the bricks there was barely room for my legs. I reached out my left hand, then my right knee, and dragged myself forward. A car door slammed. I froze, staring down into the darkness. I felt myself sway, caught up in a whoosh of dizziness. Not the sort that goes away when you close your eyes, the sort that swoops through your body in waves, shifting and blurring everything around you until you don't know which way is up. There wasn't time for this. I jerked my head back and looked up at the stars, waiting until the world stopped spinning just enough to let me push my right hand on to the next beam. I dragged my left knee forward, felt the frayed rope dip and pull, and pictured the dye-soaked threads snapping one by one as I fell. Even if they held, would Behrouz ever be able to haul me up, or would I dangle there like a swinging meat carcass till the Taliban cut me down? Don't think like that, Aliya. Think about the muscles in your legs, the sinews in your arms, the next bump of your knee against the beam. And hurry! Hurry! My calves and thighs were screaming, sweat dripped into my eyes and I didn't dare lift my hand to wipe it away. I blinked and blinked and when the dizziness came again and blood hissed in my ears, I heard Behrouz murmuring, 'Come on, sis, you can do it, just another couple of metres.' And suddenly my muscles were moving again and he was reaching down, gripping my shoulders, pulling me on to the balcony, unbuckling the belt. He gave my arm a fleeting squeeze, then he was gone, climbing back on to the beams.

I snatched a look at my watch. It was the last present my father had ever given me. The numbers on the dial glowed green in the darkness and the little silver hands pointed to twenty-five minutes to midnight. Behrouz reached the window, disappeared inside and reappeared in a flurry of arms and bodies: his, Mina's, my mother's. I couldn't make out whose were whose. A lumpy shape broke free. Anguish welled inside me. It was Behrouz, lowering himself on to the beams with Mina clinging to his back like a little monkey. He moved slowly to keep her safe and he was running out of time. There was nothing I could do except pray in my heart and watch the two people I loved most in the world caught between a Taliban bullet and a plunge to their deaths.

It was just gone quarter to midnight when I finally leant out to pull them on to the balcony. Mina's thin body was rigid with terror. I prised her hands from his neck, murmuring over and over that she was safe, but she wouldn't open her eyes and she wouldn't speak. Without a word, Behrouz turned back to fetch my mother.

Although her body was wasted by sadness, she was far too tall for him to carry, so she went ahead of him, moving like a pale, fluttery ghost in her white salwar-kameez. Suddenly her left hand was groping for the rope, snatching air. Behrouz lurched forward. I could hear him murmuring to her, gentle but urgent. Almost immediately she righted herself, searching for the beam with her flailing foot. Was the numbness helping her? Blotting out the fear of falling, as well as the pain of living? My throat was tight with tears when I finally reached for her spindly wrists and dragged her over the parapet. No time for relief. B— was telling me to lift Mina on to his back a—

mother down the sloping roof on the other side. Our feet clanged against the ridges of the corrugated iron. The noise rang out, loud as a cymbal. Somebody shouted. I turned. A shadowy figure was leaning from our window. A torch beam slashed the darkness, lighting up the rope. I ran to the edge of the roof and toppled to a stop, horrified by the dark gap running between the buildings. Behrouz's pounding feet were vibrating the metal behind me, gaining speed. I heard him shout, 'Jump!'

I grabbed Mor by the hand, her frightened fingers crushing mine as I pulled her backwards to take a run. Behrouz was up and over, crashing on to the other side, staggering forward. Mina slipped sideways across his shoulders, her skinny legs dangling loose as he stumbled on to his knees. He hitched her up and yelled again, 'Jump!'

Still hand in hand, Mor and I skittered down the roof and pushed off with our toes. Our feet rose in the air, skimming emptiness. A second of uncertainty. Then we landed on the other side in a rolling tumble, swaying, tottering, picking ourselves up. Pain shot through my ankle. Mor was limping. Scared we'd lose sight of Behrouz, I dragged her under lines of dangling washing, clambering over bins and buckets and stumbling down a crumbling concrete staircase. A glare of headlights. A jeep roared towards us, the door flew open before it had even juddered to a halt. I wrenched Mor around and hobbled blindly the other way. Behrouz was pushing me back. 'It's OK, it's OK, it's Captain Merrick.'

A soldier leapt out, big and bulky in his helmet and body armour. A voice burst from his radio. He tore Mina from Behrouz's arms, threw her into the back and flung me and my mother in after her. 'They're coming!' he hissed. 'Get your heads down and keep them down.'

He jumped into the driver's seat. Behrouz slid in beside him and rammed the door shut. We jolted forward, thrown off balance by the heavy tyres smashing through the rubbish in the alley. The smell of sweat and diesel burnt my throat. I pressed Mina on to the seat, feeling the throb of her sobs and the shudder of the chassis as we hit a pothole. Something struck the rear windscreen, cracking the glass. My mother closed her eyes, making soundless movements with her lips. Choking on panic, I jerked my head up. Merrick was yelling into his radio, his head swivelling backwards and forwards between the inside and outside mirrors. We skidded around a bend. As we swung back the other way Mina vomited, spurts of yellow shooting from her mouth, sticking to her hair and slopping across the seat. I shushed her sobs, cringing lower each time a horn beeped or a lorry lumbered past. The jeep accelerated, swerving through the narrow backstreets, cutting across lanes of speeding cars and screeching through junctions, until the lights of the city faded and the mountains loomed ahead, blacker than the night. We hit a winding track that bumped and rattled us to a halt in a boulder-strewn crevice hidden between two overhanging rocks.

Captain Merrick switched off the engine. We cowered in the darkness, suspended in silence, waiting for the roar of a Talib truck to shatter our lives. Mina lay stiff in my arms barely breathing. I held her tight, counting each second. Certain it would be our last.

A crackle from Captain Merrick's radio shot a tremble of panic through Mina's body. A voice whooped through the static. He snapped a reply, slapped Behrouz on the back and restarted the engine. My mother cried softly as he spun the wheel, bouncing the jeep's headlights over the rocks and heading down the mountain in a rattle of stones.

That's when it hit me. We could never go home. I would never sit another exam at my school and from now on Salma would always be top of our class. I leant forward and dropped my forehead on my brother's shoulder. 'Where can we go, Behrouz, where can we hide?'

I dreaded that he'd say Peshawar, the crowded refugee camp across the border in Pakistan. I didn't want to live in Peshawar. I didn't want to die in Kabul. He twisted around and grinned at me. 'England,' he said.

'We can't. We don't have visas.'

Captain Merrick shouted over his shoulder. 'Colonel Clarke's sorting all that. The lads have been pushing for Baz to get asylum and after tonight . . . well, the colonel says he can swing it. There's a plane leaving the base in a couple of hours.'

I threw my arms around Behrouz's neck, almost afraid that if I let him go, this chance of safety would be snatched away. He pulled my head close and whispered, 'It's OK, sis, it's going to be OK.'

I began to sob into his sweat-soaked shirt, loud, jerky tears that I couldn't stop. I knew Colonel Clarke was something important in the British government now and if he wanted something to happen, then it would. We were leaving this harsh, stony land full of fear and fighting and going to England. My mother and sister would laugh again, Behrouz would finish his engineering degree, I would go to school with girls who had short skirts and swishy hair and boys who put rings through their eyebrows, and we'd get to see the sights of London and the palace of the queen. Best of all, we'd be leaving the terror behind and starting a whole new life, in a place where we'd be safe. But as we skidded down the narrow track the thought of living among strangers, so far from everything I had ever known or loved, stabbed my heart with sadness. I lifted my head and glanced back to snatch a last glimpse of my mountains. There was nothing there but a wall of black.

DAN

LONDON, England. Three Weeks Later

'Get a move on, Danny. I'm going out to load up.'

I chucked my toast in the bin and followed Dad outside. I'd had plans for the first day of the holidays and helping him mend washing machines and unblock sinks wasn't one of them. I slumped into the van and slammed the door. He jumped in beside me and pulled out into the traffic.

'I'm not having you sulking all day. You know I can't manage all Jez's jobs as well as my own, not without another pair of hands.'

I glowered out the window. 'Why're you letting him skive off, then?'

'He's not skiving. He was in the pub last night and

picked an argument with the wrong bloke. Ended up in A and E.'

'What bloke?'

'Never you mind.' He flicked me a look and caught me grinning. 'It's not funny, Dan. One of these days that temper of his is going land us all in trouble.' He ran his hand over his bristly head. 'Don't tell your mother, all right? She thinks he fell off a ladder.'

'You lied to Mum?'

'You know what she's like.'

Too right. Mum had a real downer on Jez and always laughed when Dad claimed it was taking him on that had saved the business. Jez wasn't much of a plumber, that's for sure, but he was great at bringing in the work, doing the accounts and keeping the customers happy, specially the ones who went for blond hair, tight T-shirts and bulging muscles.

Dad checked his list. 'First job's at Meadowview. We'll have to pick up Jez's keys on the way.'

That was all I needed. Meadowview was one of the old tower blocks by the canal. One minute the council was going to do them up, stick a gym in the basement and sell them off to rich boys who worked in the city, the next they were going to pull them down. Meanwhile they were using the flats as emergency housing and somehow Jez had wangled the contract to keep the rotting pipework patched up. It was a lot of work but they'd divided the blocks up between them; Dad looked after Sunnyhill and

Woodside and left Meadowview pretty much to Jez, which was fair enough, seeing as Meadowview was even more of a dump than the others. It stank for a start, and there were rumours of all sorts going on behind those boarded-up doors. I hated going in there, specially when I could have been earning good money unlocking phones for Bernie Watts. Plus, I didn't want anyone I knew catching me in these stupid overalls. The in-your-face 'Abbott & Co' logo was one of Jez's bright ideas. He called it 'branding'. I called it looking like a prat.

Dad pulled up outside Jez's house and stomped through the rain to get the keys off Jez's girlfriend, Donna. She came to the door looking pretty upset, though not upset enough to let Dad inside in his work boots. Once she'd fetched the keys, she kept him on the doorstep talking. Or rather she talked and Dad stood there with his arms folded, looking shifty.

'How's he doing?' I said, when he got back in the van.

'He'll live.'

I could tell from the way he was glaring at the road and gripping the wheel that there was something going on, but he wasn't about to tell me what it was. He turned the radio on full blast and didn't say another word till he swung into the Meadowview car park. He braked hard to avoid a gang of kids who were setting fire to a tatty string of bunting draped round the play area. One of them kicked a can at the van. By the time Dad got the window down to yell at them, they'd legged it down the alley. 'Little buggers,' he muttered.

He parked round the back, on the stretch of car park overlooking the canal. Two blokes in parkas peeled themselves off the wall and came slouching towards us. Dad gave them a look, like he was warning them off. They stared him out for a bit but as soon as I got out they swerved away, muttering to each other.

'Who are they?' I said.

He shrugged. 'Dunno. Come on, eighth floor. What's the betting the lift isn't working?'

I looked up at the twenty storeys of mouldering concrete, peeling paintwork and broken windows. Some mate of Jez's was supposed to take care of the general maintenance but the rusty skip and rickety old JCB he'd dumped outside the loading bay had been there for months and the smell was disgusting. The guys in parkas were still eyeballing us but they'd gone over to lean against the rolling door and murmur into their phones. Dad wasn't bothered. As far as he was concerned, dodgy locals and stinking drains were all part of the job.

He was right about the lifts, though. I was nearly dead by the time we'd chased up eight flights of stairs, but he didn't even drop the tool bag before he rapped sharply on the door of flat 805. The door cracked open and a watery eye glared out at us through a haze of cigarette smoke. 'What do you want?'

Dad flashed one of his cards. 'I've come about the leak, Mr Brody. Council sent me.'

Brody's eyes flicked to the logo on Dad's overalls. 'Where's the other one?'

'Jez? He's off sick.'

'What's the matter with him?'

'Accident. Nothing serious.'

Brody sneered. 'Pushed his luck once too often, did he?'

'Where's the leak, Mr Brody?'

Brody pulled open the door. 'It's that lot upstairs.' He took a suck of his soggy roll-up and pointed at the big patch of damp on the ceiling. 'Look at that! Twice the size it was last week. And you should see what they've done in there.' He jerked his head towards the bathroom. 'Started last night. Don't they have running water where they come from?'

I hovered in the hall, holding my breath against the reek of fags and garbage, while Dad took a closer look at the circle of drips round the bare bulb in the bathroom. Brody edged towards me and leant close. His breath stank.

'They want to stick me in a home and give my flat to a load of scroungers.' He took a drag on his fag and started to cough. 'I told 'em, I'm not going anywhere. Thirty-two years I've been living here.'

'Right.' I pulled away and stared at the mildew creeping along his filthy skirting boards. 'Must have been a bit different when you moved in.'

'It was.' Brody picked a fleck of tobacco off his lip. 'No

dirty foreigners messing the place up.'

I was trying to think of something to say to that when Dad came out of the bathroom.

'OK, Mr Brody. Looks like it's your mains pipe leaking. We'll have to get to it from the flat upstairs.' He made a quick call to the council, who said there was a family called Sahar in the flat above. Dad picked up his tools. 'We'll nip up and see if anybody's in. Meantime, make sure you don't turn on any lights.'

Brody grunted and shuffled off down the hall, still muttering about dirty foreigners.

I slammed the door. 'Should have let the old git electrocute himself,' I said.

Dad grinned. 'You meet all sorts in our line of work. The trick is not to let them get to you.' He hoisted the tool bag on to his shoulder and headed down the corridor. 'Honestly, last week I was doing a rush job for this posh woman up in Camden who said if I worked through my lunch break she'd bring me something to eat. Anyway, lunchtime comes, I'm starving and she walks in with this big fancy plate but all there is on it is a couple of tiny biscuits. So I bite into one of them and it's a ruddy dog biscuit.'

'You're kidding? Did you spit it out?'

'No. I chewed it up and swallowed it. You can't go upsetting the customers.'

We were halfway up the stairs, still laughing, when a young skinny guy with a kink in his nose and black curly hair flopping across his forehead came racing round the corner, crashed into Dad and leapt back, flattening himself against the wall with a look of total terror on his face. For a second he just stood there, eyeing Dad's tool bag as if he thought we were going to pull out a couple of spanners and attack him. 'Hey, no problem,' I said, raising my hands and standing back to let him pass. He stared at my overalls, then at my face, his dark eyes probing mine, before he mumbled, 'Sorry,' and clattered off down the stairs.

Dad rolled his eyes. 'Like I said, you meet all sorts in this job.'

Most of the doors on the ninth floor were boarded over. Even the ones that weren't were splashed with graffiti. Dad tried the buzzer of flat 905. It didn't work. Course it didn't. This was Meadowview. He knocked hard. After a long silence we heard a croaky, 'Yes?'

'Is that Mrs Sahar?' he said.

'Who is there?'

'Ron Abbott,' Dad said. 'Council sent me. I'm a plumber. There's water leaking into the flat below.'

The door opened slowly and bumped back on its chain. The woman on the other side had probably been quite pretty when she was younger. Not any more. Her face was lined, her eyelids drooped and her dark hair was stringy and streaked with grey. Dad was ready with another of his cards. She took it slowly and stood there, staring at the writing as if she'd forgotten we were there.

Dad held out his mobile and said gently, 'Here, do you want to talk to the council? They'll vouch for me.'

She hesitated for a minute, then unslid the chain and let the door swing open. We followed her into the living room. I frowned at Dad but he wouldn't catch my eye. He kept this fixed smile on his face as we took in the rotten window frames, the scrappy bits of furniture and the damp plaster showing through the peeling wallpaper. The kitchen, if you could call it that, was through a door-way down one end, just a sink, a rusty cooker and a couple of units with the doors hanging off. It looked like someone had had a go at scrubbing off the worst of the dirt but they hadn't managed to shift the mildew or get rid of the smell of must. A little girl, she must have been about three or four, was curled up on a torn vinyl couch, watching cartoons with the sound turned down, sucking her thumb. She was so quiet I didn't notice her at first and when Dad crouched down in front of her and said hello, she looked right through him. I didn't blame her. If I had to live in Meadowview, I'd switch off too.

Dad heaved himself up. 'We'll have to take up some of your floorboards, Mrs Sahar. Will that be all right?' She flapped her hand as if she didn't much care what we did and sat down beside the little girl, murmuring to her in a low breathy voice. Dad handed me a jemmy and a torch. 'Have a look under the bath, Danny. I'll make a start in the hall.'

The bathroom was about as scuzzy as it gets: cracked

basin, rust stains under the taps, chipped tiles lifting off the walls and one of those old-fashioned Ascot water heaters. Mum would have freaked if she'd had to give up her power shower and sparkling tiles to live in a place like this. Half the floorboards were rotten and the ones under the bath weren't even nailed down. I lifted them out and shone the torch into the hole. The disc of light wavered along a length of green copper piping, picked out a few places where the drips had darkened the dust, and glistened on a water-spattered carrier bag, wedged under the pipe. Dad was always going on about the weird things he'd found under floorboards – money, dirty magazines, a mummified cat. I tugged the bag free, shook off some of the water, put my hand gingerly inside and fetched out a tobacco tin. I popped open the lid. Inside was a phone wrapped in cling film. The screen was chipped and it was too old to be worth anything. I slipped my hand back in the carrier and pulled out a bundle of sacking. My brain flipped slowly between shock and disbelief. Poking out of one end of the sacking was the curved black handle of a gun. Poking out of the other was the grey metal tip of the barrel. I'd never held a gun before and I felt a horrible sort of thrill as I unwrapped it and weighed it in my hand. It lay there, compact, deadly and not much bigger than my palm.

I was sat there staring at it for a couple of minutes, too stunned and scared to move, when I got that prickle across my scalp that tells you you're being watched. I glanced up. There was a girl at the door in a grey dress and baggy trousers, with a dark blue scarf round her head. She was skinny, fourteen, maybe fifteen, dark hair, narrow nose, high cheekbones and eyes that were this weird greeny-grey colour. For a second we just looked at each other.

Her eyes darted back to the gun and she stepped forward, reaching out her hand as if she was trying to take a bone from a dangerous dog. 'Please. Do not tell anyone. If the police find out, they will make trouble for us.'

Dad's boots thudded down the hall. I dropped the gun and the tin back in the carrier and shoved it into her outstretched hand. Dad poked his head round the door. 'What you got there, Danny?'

The girl swung round, fear freezing her face, but he was looking at the hole under the bath. I said quickly, 'Yeah . . . you're right, Dad. Pipe's split.'

He squatted down and poked around under the pipe. 'Looks like it's been knocked. It's so corroded it couldn't take it.' He stood up and smiled at the girl. 'What you been hiding under there, then? The crown jewels?' She opened her mouth. No words came out and he went on chatting and smiling as if there was nothing unusual about the way she was backed into a corner, clutching a wet plastic bag to her chest and struggling to breathe. 'We're going to have to replace the whole lot, I'm afraid.' She didn't answer and as she tried to dodge past him to get to the door the bag slipped through her trembling fingers and fell with a thud. Dad picked it up. I saw her eyes flicker with panic, so I blurted out the first thing I could think of to get her and the gun out of there.

'Hey, tell you what,' I said, 'I could murder a cup of tea.'

Her eyes flew to my face, trying to work out what I meant.

'Tea'd be great,' Dad said. 'I'm gasping.'

She reached out to take the bag from Dad's fingers and once she had it in her grasp she scuttled down the hall.

'Milk and two sugars if you've got it,' he called after her. He threw me a sideways smile. 'We'll make a plumber of you yet, Danny.'

I looked away. *In your dreams, Dad.*

ALIYA

I ran into the cramped little kitchen and fell back against the wall, with my cuff to my mouth. My mother called out in her weak, fretful voice, 'Aliya, What are you doing?'

It was a struggle to move, to breathe, to think, but I called out, 'Making tea, Mor. I will bring you some.' I took the kettle from the stove and turned on the tap but my hand was shaking so much the water bounced and splattered everywhere except into the spout. I couldn't help it. The shock of seeing that gun and that blue plastic bag had made my muscles seize up. I thought back to last night: Behrouz had come home very late and I remembered seeing him take that bag into the bathroom and come out without it, but I never dreamt there was a gun in it.

Behrouz hated guns. Only fear and desperation would make him bring one into our home. I put the kettle on to heat, leant over the sink and stared down at the black water of the canal sliding past the buildings below, wondering if the boy would tell anyone what he'd found. I wasn't sure. He'd been scared, I'd seen it in his eyes, but at least his strange talk of murdering tea had helped me to get the gun away from his father.

What was happening to us? When we arrived three weeks ago, Behrouz had fallen in love with everything about our new English life: the endless rain that washed all the colour from the sky, even when it was supposed to be summer, the cinemas and restaurants we couldn't afford, the man at the corner shop who sold us rotten fruit, the hooded boys who reared up on their bikes and scowled at us whenever we walked by, and the angry, dull-eyed men in the other flats who had no families and no work.

He wouldn't speak a word against that miser Amir Khan, who'd given him a job driving a minicab. My brother had always loved driving and always loved cars, and he said Mr Khan had taken him on as a favour because he had been friends with our father in Kabul. But making him work such long hours for so little money didn't seem like much of a favour to me. Behrouz didn't even mind living in this damp, dirty flat. He said we were lucky to have it at all and that we only got it because Colonel Clarke and his wife ran a charity that had an arrangement with the council. They call their charity Hope Unlimited.

It is a bad name. Hope is not unlimited. It is like a fire or a child. If you do not feed it, it will die.

The day we moved in, Behrouz helped me to rip out the cracked lino and the dusty curtains and we scrubbed every room until our backs ached. When we'd finished, I wanted to cry, because the whole place still made me feel empty and sad. The next day, to cheer me up, he took us in his cab to see some of the famous sights of London: the palace where the queen lives, a place called Trafalgar Square, which was full of pigeons, and the tower of Big Ben. I wanted to go for a ride on the big wheel they call the London Eye, which is so huge I can see it from our flat, but the tickets were too expensive. Instead Behrouz bought us fish and chips. He said they were typical English food but the chips were so grey and floppy they made us laugh when we held them up and in the end we fed them to the pigeons.

That evening Colonel Clarke came to visit us. He brought us a television, some books and chocolates for me and Mor, a doll for Mina and a signed photo of him giving Behrouz his medal, to replace the one we'd had to leave behind. The colonel was very tall and I was a little scared when he walked in, but he was kind and easy to talk to and he made us laugh, even my mother, although Mina wouldn't come out from behind the sofa. He told Behrouz that in a few weeks' time there might be a chance of some work for him at Hope Unlimited. When he'd gone, Behrouz put his hands on my shoulders and said that with two jobs it wouldn't be long before he'd be able to get us a house with a garden for Mina to play in, the best doctors to make Mor well again, all the books I could ever want and a computer of my own. I smiled up at him, and just for a second I believed that in a country like England such things could be possible.

Then, a week ago something happened to Behrouz that changed him, something bad that dried up all his hope and laughter and stopped him eating and sleeping. It was the day some women hung flags across the doorways and put up stalls, selling things to raise money to mend the broken swings. I remember it because he went down early to help them set up, and when I took Mina down later to see the clown, we found Behrouz standing on his own behind the skips. He looked very pale and he left quickly. When I saw him later, I begged him to tell me what was wrong but he said it was nothing.

Over the days that followed he started to act like a stranger, and I've felt his fear getting worse and worse, infecting everything, gnawing at our nerves like the rats in the walls. My mother has stopped taking the tablets the doctor gave her and Mina is getting thinner and has started to cry in her sleep, although she still won't speak, not a word since we left Kabul. And then this morning, just as I was getting her to drink some milk and eat a little piece of toasted naan, that mean old man from downstairs frightened her by shouting at us and beating on the ceiling with his stick. I didn't go down to see what he wanted, because he's been shouting at us from the day we arrived. He complains about everything: the smell of our food, the money the government gives us, even the sound of our footsteps. I don't understand about the footsteps. Whenever my mother gets up, which isn't very often, she drifts around like a ghost, Mina sits on the couch all day watching cartoons and Behrouz works so many shifts he is hardly ever at home. I'm sure it isn't my footsteps he can hear. In fact I'm beginning to feel as if I don't exist at all, even though there is food on the stove that I have cooked, forms on the table that I have filled in, and suspicion in that boy's eyes when I begged him not to tell anyone about the gun.

I left the kettle to boil, crept into the narrow bedroom I share with Mina, opened the grocery bag and looked at the gun. There were bad people on this estate, thieves and crooks, people Behrouz had warned me to stay away from. Had he got involved with them? Had he done something terrible to get us the things he'd promised? I hated myself for even thinking these thoughts. I dropped the gun back in the bag and opened the tin, bewildered when I found what looked like Behrouz's phone tucked inside it, wrapped in cling film. I picked it up. Why would he hide it? He hated to be without his phone. Cold darkness crawled up my skin as if it was trying to creep into my head. I wouldn't let it in. I pressed the keys. The battery was too low to get a signal and there was no credit. I shut it back in the tin, dropped it in the bag, pushed it under the mattress and rumpled the sheets to hide the bump. As soon as Behrouz came home I'd make him tell me what was wrong and, however terrible it was, I'd smile and tell him that I had a plan and we'd work out what to do. The way we always did.

We didn't have any English tea or any milk, so I made green Afghan tea and carried it to the bathroom. My hands were still shaking and I spilt some on the floor. The boy poked the curly leaves floating in his cup and pulled a face. His father made a tutting sound. 'Come on, Dan, it's good to try new things.' He took a big sip and smiled at me. 'Not bad.'

The boy tried his and pushed his cup away. His father looked embarrassed. 'If you're not going to drink it, you can go and see if Jez has got any replacement pipe in the basement.' He threw him a heavy bunch of keys. 'I'll need about four metres of twenty-two and a box of connectors. He keeps his spares in a cage by the door, but watch yourself, there's building work going on down there.'

The boy hurried out, jangling the keys. He didn't even look at me.

DAN

I couldn't get out of there quick enough, though the dark landing and the stink of pee in the stairwell were nearly as bad as that manky flat and the fear on that girl's face.

The Meadowview basement was a lot tougher to get into than the ones in the other blocks. There was a tangle of shopping trolleys and broken wheelie bins chucked across the entrance, which had bright-yellow 'Danger! Building Work in Progress' signs stuck all over it, and instead of flimsy metal panels and a wobbly lock that gave way if you kicked it hard enough, the doors were reinforced steel, fitted with heavy-duty bolts and thick new padlocks. I rifled through Jez's keys, trying out three or four before I found the right ones and got the doors open.

I fumbled around for the light switch. A couple of fluorescent strips flickered on, leaving the outer edges of the vast space in gloom. The place was a bomb site. The floor had been hacked into rubble and piled up all over the place, and I had to duck to avoid flapping strips of foil and loops of cable dangling from the ceiling. I looked around for the metal cage where Jez stored his supplies. Wouldn't you know it? He'd dumped it right down the other end with a load of builders' junk. I picked my way across the debris, tripping on lumps of concrete and stumbling into craters full of scummy water. I turned on my phone and flashed it across the cage. It was big, maybe two metres high by one across, and full of lengths of pipe and boxes of taps and fittings, all covered in gritty dust like they hadn't been touched in months. No surprises there. Jez wouldn't bother replacing anything if he could get away with botching up a quick repair. The lazy jerk hadn't even left the door facing outwards.

Annoyed, I shoved my fingers into the mesh and shunted the cage to one side. A stash of planks and scaffold poles came crashing down, slammed into a wobbly stack of oil drums and set off an avalanche of junk. I wrenched my fingers out of the cage and dodged back but I still got bashed by a falling pole. I dabbed my bleeding scalp and kicked the pole across the floor. It could have killed me. I flashed my phone across the mess. Why hadn't Jez and his stupid builder mates dumped all this crap in that skip I'd seen outside? It's not like it would have taken much effort. There was a big double door right there where they'd stashed the oil drums. In fact it'd be much easier to take the spare pipe out that way than kill myself hauling it back across the building site. I shone my phone at it. The pale light bounced off three heavy bolts fastened with shiny padlocks, identical to the ones on the outer door. I clambered over the fallen planks, battered oil drums and coils of wire and fetched out Jez's keys. Three of them fitted. Wiping the dust off my face, I kicked one of the doors open and squeezed through on to the raised platform of the loading bay. As my eyes adjusted to the gloom I could see a fork-lift truck parked next to a pile of large polystyrene boxes stacked on pallets. I ran the phone light across the labels – dishwashers, washing machines, tumble driers. All top of the range. I knew that, because they were exactly the same as the ones Dad had just got for Mum. The ones he'd installed as a birthday surprise, telling her, 'Only the best for my Debs,' the ones she never stopped bragging about to her mates.

All knock-off.

Had to be. Why else would they be hidden away in an unused loading bay?

I staggered back, feeling sick. So this was how Jez had helped him to 'save the business'. I knew Dad was no angel, he'd done a bit of time when I was a little kid, but he'd sworn to Mum that he'd gone straight ever since. I'd seen him do it, look her right in the eye and tell her she'd never have anything to worry about on that score ever again. What a liar! She'd go mental if she found out. My eyes flitted round the loading bay like a camera, taking it all in bit by bit. It looked like they'd got a system going for stripping the original wrapping off the boxes and rewrapping them using the heat-sealing equipment and jumbo-sized rolls of polythene set up at one end.

I squatted down in front of one of the unsealed washing machines, opened the glass door and pulled out a bundle of leaflets and a freebie pack of washing powder. I'd have shoved it straight back if I hadn't noticed a glob of glue on the bottom of the box. I stared at it for moment, then I slid my finger under the flap, plunged my hand into the soapy granules and pulled something out. A handful of little plastic bags filled with white powder.

For a second I was baffled – then, like a slow-motion wrecking ball, it hit me. I'd watched enough cop shows to be pretty sure what it was. Drugs.

I stared around me in shock, not wanting to believe that Dad would ever get involved in something like this. But the evidence was right there, staring me in the face, and it looked like a big operation. Nice little loading bay with nothing overlooking it except the canal, where they could unload and load up out of sight, and plenty of room for storing the appliances, packing them full of drugs and sealing them up again. And who was going to think twice when they saw a couple of plumbers delivering a washing machine or dropping off a few free samples of washing powder? But if they got caught, they'd be looking at years and years inside.

Thoughts crashed round my brain. I tried to separate them out, make sense of them, think what to do. My phone rang. It was Dad.

'Yeah?'

'What's taking so long?'

'Nothing.'

'Have you found the stuff?'

'What?'

'Spare pipe. Did you find some?'

'Oh . . . yeah . . . plenty.'

'Well bring it up, then. I haven't got all day.'

'All right. I'm coming.'

I shoved everything back and slipped through the doors, giving the pile of appliances a last swift glance before locking the bolts and stacking the oil drums back into place. The cut on my head throbbed, my heart pumped and I felt sick. Worst of all, I had no idea how I was ever going to look my dad in the eye again.

ALIYA

tried to stay busy. I swept floors, scrubbed pans until my knuckles hurt and sliced aubergine and onions to make *banjaan*. Outside in the hall the boy's father banged and sawed and clanked in and out with pieces of pipe. After a while I heard him phoning the boy. He was annoyed. He told him to hurry up.

My mother called out, asking for her tea. I poured her some, sprinkled it with sugar, the way she likes it, and took the cup to where she lay on the sofa. One of her fists was clenched against her chest as if she was holding something precious.

'What's in your hand, Mor?'

She opened her fingers. In her palm lay a crumpled card printed with the words 'Abbott & Co Plumbing. Prompt,

Fast, Local' and a scrap of paper with a number written on it.

I took the paper. 'What's this, Mor?'

She frowned, searching for an answer, then almost smiled as the memory drifted back.

'Behrouz came home. When you were at the shop. He said to be sure to give it to you.'

'Why?'

'He has a new phone. This is the number.'

The cold darkness made my voice tremble. 'Why did he change it?'

My mother blinked at the floor and I knew she hadn't even thought to ask him. I stuffed the card and the number in my purse and went back to the onions, as if cooking Behrouz's favourite dish would solve the mystery of the gun and the phones and make everything all right. The boy came back to the flat. I saw him go up and down the hall at least twice. He didn't look at me and whenever his father spoke to him he grunted or didn't answer at all. His disrespect surprised me very much. I was frying the onions with garlic when his father poked his head around the door and handed me back the cups.

'Smells good,' he said. 'Thanks for the tea. All fixed now. Any problems, just give us a ring. Your mum's got one of our cards.'

'Thank you,' I said.

He walked down the hall and called over his shoulder, 'Bring the rest of the tools, will you, Dan. I want to have a look at those drains before we go.'

I slipped into the bathroom. The boy was kneeling on the floor, dropping tools into a bag. He looked dazed and troubled and he had a cut on the side of his head. I could see where the blood had soaked into his hair. Dan. That's what his father had called him. I wanted to say his name and make him look at me. I didn't dare. Instead I touched his sleeve. He pulled back, startled, as if his thoughts had been far away.

'Please. Don't tell anyone about the gun,' I whispered.

Still avoiding my eyes, he zipped up the tools.

'Swear to me you won't say anything.'

He gave me the tiniest nod and walked away. The front door slammed behind him.

The flat felt very empty when he'd gone.

The rest of the day crawled slowly. I tried to fill time by reading the book I'd borrowed from the library. It was *Oliver Twist*, one of my father's favourites. But the story was sad, about an orphan boy lost in London, and my thoughts kept slipping back to Behrouz and all the things I'd say to him when he got home. When it was time for our evening meal, I ate only a small piece of naan dipped in yoghurt and stood at the window watching for Behrouz while my mother and Mina picked at the dish of *banjaan*. Night was falling, studding the view from our flat with glimmering lights as if someone had spilt a basket of jewels across a dark carpet. I watched the lights gleam and twinkle until they merged into a shimmering blur. I was still there long after Behrouz's food had gone cold and my mother and sister had gone to bed.

At midnight, when Behrouz still hadn't come home, I threw my mother's shawl around my shoulders, took my purse from the drawer and crept out of the flat. The lights on our landing were broken and the yellow glow from the street lamps threw long jagged shapes down the stairwell that seemed to follow my footsteps. I wanted to turn and run back inside but I shut my ears to the voices in the shadows and hurried across the car park to the all-night garage on the corner. There was a phone booth on the forecourt that I used when I had to call the doctor about my mother or speak to Mrs Garcia from the refugee centre. I took out the piece of paper and dialled Behrouz's new number. It went straight to his voicemail. I hung up and searched in my purse for the card for the minicab company where he worked. I held it to the light and dialled again. A woman answered.

'Khan's Cars. How may I help you?' She had a deep, throaty voice and an accent I didn't recognize.

'My name is Aliya Sahar . . . please, may I speak to Behrouz?'

'No private calls on this line . . .'

My words tumbled out. 'Please, I am his sister. He hasn't come home and he doesn't answer his mobile. I need to know if he stayed to work a night shift.'

'I've just come on, but I'll check for you.' Her voice was kinder now and it got fainter as she swung away from the speaker.

'Hey, Liam, is Baz on lates tonight?'

I clamped my hand over my other ear, straining to hear the answer.

A man's voice said, 'Nah, he came in early, dumped his car and buggered off.'

'Was he sick?'

'Don't think so. I reckon he's got himself a bird.'

I heard other men laugh. The woman snapped something I couldn't make out and came back to the speaker. 'Sorry, he didn't work today.'

'Oh . . .'

'Are you all right?'

'Yes. Thank you.'

I hung up. But I wasn't all right. Not at all. Why would Behrouz take the day off when we needed all the money he could earn? Where had he gone? Where was he now? The flickers of doubt were taking on life, turning into a monster in my mind that was feeding on the thought of the gun beneath my sheets. I knew what I had to do.

I crossed the road at breakneck speed. A taxi blasted me with its horn. I hurried across the car park, keeping my head down. Doors slammed, an engine revved and a pair of headlights snapped on, blinding me as a van shot out between the cars, swerved towards the exit and screeched into the traffic. I ran upstairs and let myself into the flat.

Moving quietly so as not to wake Mina, I took the grocery bag from under my mattress and ran back to the landing. There were people on the stairs. I pressed my back against the wall and waited until their voices and footsteps had gone before I dared to run downstairs. I crouched behind the skips and made my way around the edge of the car park, darting from one patch of shadow to the next until I reached the muddy alley that led down to the canal. I'd taken Mina there once to see the ducks and the painted boats but the burnt-out warehouses by the water had made her cry. I think they reminded her of the bomb-blasted buildings in Kabul that people said were haunted by djinns. The warehouses looked even eerier by moonlight. Tattered posters flapped and whispered from the blackened walls, and behind the broken windows there was nothing but hollow darkness. My feet slithered on the muddy path, I lost my balance and fell, smashing my knee on a sharp stone. I cried out, I couldn't help it. Shadowy figures ran from beneath the bridge, where a small fire flickered on the path. I tried to limp away, frightened they would hurt me. When I turned around, they had slipped into one of the darkened doorways.

Something rustled the rubbish along the path. I jumped back. A fox bounded out, shaking a rat in its jaws. Its eyes glinted at me for a second before it loped away. I was hobbling and sliding but I forced myself to keep searching until I found what I was looking for: an old wooden boat called the *Margaretta*. The first time I saw it,

I'd felt sad that a boat with such a pretty name had been left to rot. Now I was glad it had been abandoned. I pulled on the rope, bumping the slimy hull against the bank. With a quick glance along the path to make sure no one was watching, I pushed the bag through a tear in the tarpaulin. The heavy thump of metal on wood echoed along the water. I heard a footstep. I spun round. An old man with long white hair and a dirty white beard staggered out of the darkness with a bottle in his hand. The smell of him made me choke. He swayed towards me, holding out his arms and making a gurgling sound with his mouth. I pushed him away and I didn't stop running until I was back in our flat. Even then I didn't feel safe.

DAN

What a nightmare, knowing what I knew and having to trail round after Dad all day when all I wanted to do was yell at him for being a liar. Thankfully we were so busy we didn't stop for lunch, just grabbed a sandwich in the van, and the rest of the time I managed to avoid talking to him by putting on a sulk whenever he opened his mouth. By the time we got home I thought I was going explode with the strain so I decided to ring round a few mates and see if anyone wanted to meet up. I reached in my jeans pocket – no mobile. I couldn't believe it, not after the day I'd had. I dug through all my other pockets, rang the number from the house phone, ran outside to check Dad's van. Nothing. I must have left it at one of the jobs. I'd just have to think which one. When I got back inside, Mum was in the kitchen dishing up shepherd's pie.

'I knew you'd be hungry, so I've done your favourite.'

Hungry? Was she kidding? After stumbling across Dad's little sideline I never wanted to eat again.

She hollered up the stairs, 'Tea's ready, Ron!'

Dad came running down, rubbing his hands like a bad actor in a sitcom. 'Looks great, love. I'm starving.' He sat down and attacked the mound of food on his plate as if he didn't have a care in the world. 'I was just checking out some holiday deals in Turkey. What do you think, Dan? We thought it'd make a nice change from Spain.'

I stared at the table, not trusting myself to speak. How could he sit there shovelling down mounds of mashed potato, helping himself to gravy and going on about holidays? *How were you thinking of paying for it, Dad? With your share of the drug money, or by selling off a few more stolen washing machines?*

Mum frowned at me. 'What's the matter, love? Don't you fancy Turkey?'

I shrugged. Dad rolled his eyes. 'Ignore him, he's been in a strop all afternoon. I've hardly had a word out of him.'

I played up the sulk, hunched my shoulders and picked at my food, trying to remember where I'd left my phone, only my brain was so churned up I couldn't think straight.

Mum kept looking at me, wondering why I wasn't eating, and her eagle eyes homed in on the cut on my head. 'What's this?' She pushed back my hair and inspected my scalp.

I'd done my best to clean off the blood but I should have known she'd see it. I scowled and shook her hand away. 'Nothing.'

'That looks nasty. How did you do it?'

'Stop fussing, Mum.' I didn't want to think about hitting my head or what had been hidden behind the falling junk in the Meadowview basement. But even as I mumbled something about bashing myself on a bathroom cabinet it dawned on me in a horrible rush of panic exactly where I'd last used my phone. It was at Meadowview, when Dad called to tell me to hurry up with the spare pipe. I'd been in the loading bay and I put it down so I could shove the drugs and the washing powder back in the washing machine. I must have forgotten to pick it up. Picturing Dad or Jez walking in there and finding it made me feel sick. That couldn't happen. I'd sworn to myself I'd never set foot in that place ever again and now, just when I thought my life couldn't get any crappier, I'd have to go back there to get my phone.

But I wasn't going to risk doing it in daylight. After tea I took my skateboard down the park till it got dark, then I hung around in my room, playing half-hearted games on the PlayStation, waiting for Mum and Dad to go to bed before I nicked Jez's keys out of Dad's jacket, snuck out of the house and biked it over to Meadowview.

The car park was even creepier at night. It looked deserted but you could feel there were people around, hiding in the shadows, watching from the darkened windows. I walked fast, trying to make out I was a kid from one of the flats, coming home late. I crept down to the basement and as I let myself in something rustled the litter in the stairwell. I swung round, peering into the darkness. What if I'd been followed? What if Dad turned up when I was in the loading bay? It was weird. There was this big black hole in my mind sucking in everything I thought I knew about him and twisting it into something dark and distorted.

At least I'd brought a proper torch with me this time so I wouldn't break my neck tripping over. I fumbled my way across the rubble, beginning to wonder if the mess was just a way to keep people out.

Shifting all the scaffolding and oil drums again took ages, because I was trying to keep the noise down, and I was sweating hard by the time I stepped into the loading bay. Get in. Grab the phone. Get out. That was the plan.

But where was it? I flashed the torch around, peering between the boxes, feeling inside the washing machines, going crazy. Come on, Dan. Start by the door. Do it methodically. I was on my knees, sweeping the torch around, inching backwards, when I heard a noise. A wheezy engine turning over, tyres crunching tarmac, and voices. Hushed. Urgent. It sounded like someone was moving the JCB I'd seen outside. My skin turned icy. I flipped off the torch and squeezed behind the pile of appliances, holding myself against the wall of boxes. A pinprick of light winked red in the darkness. My phone. Just out of reach. Footsteps were coming nearer. I willed them to go away. Fear exploded through my body as I heard the jangle of keys and the electric hum of the rolling door sliding up. Through a gap between the boxes I saw a red van back in and made out something that looked like '—tal Meats Ltd' written down the side. Two men jumped out. Outlined in the glare of the headlights, the driver was tall, thin and stooping, wearing a woolly hat. He used a key to lower the door and as he turned round I caught a glimpse of a face I wouldn't forget in a hurry. Thick eyebrows, sunken cheeks, hooded eyes and skin like badly mixed cement. The other man flung open the back doors of the van and the two of them sat on the tailgate, lighting cigarettes, checking their phones. Waiting. For what? My muscles burnt with the strain of keeping still. The slightest twitch would crackle the plastic. Give me away. I bit down on my lips to stop my teeth chattering and glanced at my phone, poking out from under one of the boxes. If it rang, I'd be dead.

I heard something outside. Muffled cries, scuffling, an angry shout, then footsteps coming across the car park, getting louder. Cement Face switched off the headlights. Dropping his cigarette in a shower of sparks, he raised the rolling door. Three more people ducked under it, and as he turned the key to lower it again I fought a crazy urge to dash out, wriggle under the slowly narrowing gap and make a run for it. I knew I'd never make it.

The headlights flicked back on. One of the new arrivals, a big fair-haired bloke, was dragging a hunched-up woman who had a black shawl over her head. The other man, a weaselly-looking creep, had a gun wedged into her back. When he snatched off the shawl, I nearly gasped out loud. It wasn't a woman. It was a young dark-haired guy, blinking and shaking his head. Despite the blood and the bruises, I recognized him. He was the man I'd seen that morning on the stairs. He was trying to speak, hissing bubbles of blood through broken teeth. 'Please . . . don't hurt my family, they don't know anything . . . please . . . please don't hurt them.'

'Shut up.' Cement Face had a voice that made my hopes sink for the bloke they'd just dragged in. He held his hand out to the weasel with the gun. 'You get his phone?' Weasel tossed him a mobile.

They pushed the young guy towards the back of the van. As he stumbled forward his head shot round in a last desperate hope there'd be someone there to save him. There wasn't. There was just me, cowering in the dark, nearly wetting myself. Weasel flipped the gun, caught it by the barrel and thwacked him hard on the side of the head. With a dull crack of metal on bone the man slumped forward. They caught him as he fell and threw him inside.

'What you going do with him, boss?'

Cement Face gave a short, grating laugh. 'I'm going to make him famous.'

He slammed the doors. As he got in the driver's seat he jerked his head at the pile of appliances. 'Get that stuff out of here. Before it all kicks off.'

Weasel slipped his gun in the back of his trousers and got out his phone. 'No worries. I'll get Jez and Ron on to it.'

Jez and Ron. The names slammed round my head. Jez Deakin and Ron Abbott.

The rolling doors hummed shut and after couple of minutes I heard the JCB rumble back into place outside. They'd gone. I crept from behind the appliances, grabbed my phone and stumbled back to the basement, the freeze-frame of that bloodied face seared into my brain. I wanted to call the cops but how could I when my own dad was involved? Somehow I managed to lock the padlocks and sling a few oil drums across the door before I slid to the ground and lay there, hunched over on the cold concrete, my thoughts flipping back to the night of my fifth birthday. We're in the crummy flat we had back then. I can hear Mum on the phone. She's crying. That makes me angry. I'm the one who's upset. I'm the one whose birthday Dad has missed. I run into the kitchen. She turns round, her face is red and blotchy and she squats down, opening her arms to me, smothering me in kisses. When she speaks her voice is jumpy, as if she's struggling to breathe, and she says, 'I swear to you, Danny, your Dad's never going miss your birthday again. Not ever. And when he comes home, we'll have a special day out to make up for it. Just the three of us.' Then she gets down the calendar and we count the days till he'll be back. Every single one of them, and I'm feeling proud because it's the first time I've ever counted to one hundred and twenty-two. That's what he's got left of the nine-month sentence he's serving for receiving stolen goods. They'd gone easy on him because it was a first offence, but it seems like a lifetime to us, and when Mum hugs me again, her tears wet my cheek.

Only they weren't Mum's tears I could feel – they were mine, and I wasn't sitting at the table holding a chunk of birthday cake and looking at a calendar. I was lying in a freezing basement staring into blackness and wondering what the hell Dad had got himself mixed up in. He'd be setting off, any minute, him and Jez. I had to get the keys back before he discovered they were missing. I picked myself up and started to run.

PART TWO

ALIYA

They came while we were sleeping. An angry swarm of policemen, smashing the door down with a bright-orange battering ram, pointing their guns at us and ordering us to 'Freeze!' Black boots, black gloves, black helmets and angry eyes staring through plastic visors. My mother didn't make a sound. She just stood in the middle of her bedroom, wrapped in her long white shawl, looking more like a ghost than ever. A video camera swung past my face. Someone jerked my hands up my back and clamped my wrists with tight metal cuffs. They were doing the same to my mother, leading her to the door. Mina ran to me and clung to my legs. I couldn't reach her, I couldn't move my hands. I shouted at the men in black, 'What do you want? What do you want? Where are you taking my mother?'

They acted as if I was invisible, kicking open doors, pulling food from our cupboards, tipping out the rubbish pail from under the sink. There were dogs with them, straining on leashes, scrabbling down the hall, sniffing and whining at the floorboards in the bathroom. The relief of knowing the gun wasn't there was swallowed by a terrible certainty. They would never send this many dogs and this many people to look for one small gun. They were searching for something else. I told myself over and over it was all a mistake and everything would be all right once they'd spoken to Behrouz. So why was the dark coldness squeezing my throat so tightly that I couldn't even scream when they prised Mina's arms from my legs and carried her away?

One of the figures in black was a woman. She threw a blanket around my shoulders, dropped my sandals at my feet and hustled me downstairs, fingers tight on my arm. My feet slapped on the damp concrete. The blanket smelt bad and I felt ashamed to be outside in my nightclothes. She wouldn't answer my questions. I felt her hand pressing on my head as she pushed me into a waiting police car. The car roared away. I looked back, trying to see what they'd done with Mina. I told myself this was England. That we'd come here to be safe, to get away from the terror, and that nothing bad could happen to us here.

They drove me to a big ugly police station and put me in a room without windows. Half of one wall was made of darkened mirror. The rest of it was empty except for a camera on a metal stand, four plastic chairs and a metal table with a tape recorder on it. Another woman came in. She wore a creased blue suit; her hair was short and brown with ragged orange tips. She said her name was Detective Constable Audrey Callhoun. She unlocked my handcuffs and asked me very slowly if I wanted an 'in-ter-pret-er'.

'I . . . I don't need one.' I struggled to breathe. I was used to fear: the dull ache that had always been with me when Behrouz was on patrol with the British soldiers, the fierce panic I'd felt when we were escaping from the Taliban, and the shuddering sweats I get when I'm up high or in the dark. But the fear I was feeling then was thick and paralysing like the terror in a dream. I pushed out the words, trying to keep my voice steady. 'Please. Why am I here?'

She was watching me closely and her voice was firm but low. 'You're not under arrest. We've brought you here as a witness. We think you can help us.'

I didn't believe her. 'A witness? I can't help you. I haven't seen anything.'

'Can you tell me your name?'

'Aliya Sahar.'

'How old are you, Aliya?'

'Fourteen. Where is my sister?'

'She's all right. She's upstairs with a social worker.'

'She doesn't like strangers. She needs to be with me.'

'She'll be fine. The social workers are specially trained to deal with distress. We just want to talk to you. But first,

I have to search you.'

I backed away, pulling the blanket tighter. 'Why? What are you looking for?'

'Please, Aliya. This is important for you as well as us.'

I let go of the blanket and slowly lifted my arms, burning with shame as she patted me and prodded me through my thin nightdress. When she'd finished, she handed me a bundle of clothes. 'Here, we brought these from your flat. You can put them on in the ladies.'

She led me across the corridor to a cold bare cloakroom that had green and black tiles on the walls, a lock on the window and a chipped mirror nailed above the sink. She waited outside. I could see the shape of her body darkening the glass in the door. I went into a cubicle and pulled on the salwar-kameez I'd been wearing the night we left Kabul. It was clean. I'd washed it many times since then but to me it would always smell of fear and diesel and Mina's vomit.

A young policeman with a freckled face and hair the colour of sand followed us back, carrying a tray with tea in a paper cup and a cheese sandwich wrapped in plastic. When I caught him staring at me, he looked away.

'Thanks, Mark.' The woman detective took the tray.

'That's OK. Give us a shout if you need anything else.'

Her voice was sharp and easy to understand, whereas his was soft and he drew out the sounds in a way that made words sound strange. I didn't want the sandwich and I only took the tea because I thought that holding something would help me keep my hands still. As we sat down at the table a tall, angry-looking man came in, pulling a jacket over his crumpled shirt. There was stubble on his chin and he smelt of sweat. He switched on the tape recorder, then leant back, pushing his fingers through his dark greasy hair.

'I'm Detective Inspector Terry McGill. I need to ask you some questions.'

'I'll try to answer anything you ask,' I said, respectfully. 'But first, please take my sister home. My mother too. She's sick. She takes tablets. She shouldn't be here.'

'I've just spoken to your mother, Miss Sahar. My colleagues will be finished with her soon.' His eyes were accusing, as if my mother had told him something bad about me.

'Why are we here? Please, you have to tell me.'

'We'll get to that.' He tilted his head to one side. 'Where did you learn such good English? I understand you only arrived here three weeks ago.' He said this as if speaking English was a crime.

'My parents taught me. My mother used to teach languages at the University of Kabul. English and French.'

He frowned. I think he was surprised that my mother hadn't always been the blank, staring creature she was now.

'And your father?'

'He studied to be a doctor in London.'

'When was that?'

'In the 1970s.'

'Where is he now?'

'He died. A year ago.'

'How?'

Tears burnt my eyes. 'Why do you want to know this?'

Detective Callhoun leant forward. 'Please don't get upset, Aliya, we just need to establish—'

He silenced her with flick of his hand. 'Answer my question, Miss Sahar.'

'There was an explosion near the hospital. A Talib suicide bomber . . . my mother has been sick since that day. She has to go home. She's not strong. She's –' I searched for the right English word – 'depressed.'

'I've told you. Your mother will be released as soon as we've finished questioning her. So your father wasn't killed by Allied action?'

'No. It was a Talib. I told you.'

'What about the rest of your family? Any of them killed or injured by British forces?'

'No. Everyone we have lost was killed by Talib fighters . . . or Russians. My grandfather was killed by the Russians, but that was before I was born.'

'You have a nineteen-year-old brother, Behrouz.'

The dark coldness crept up my throat. I swallowed hard to make it go back. 'Yes'

'Are you close?'

'Yes.'

'When did you last see him?'

'Yesterday. In the morning.'

'Where did he go?'

'To work. He drives a minicab.'

'Did he come back to the flat that day?'

I knew he was testing me to see if I would tell him lies.

'Yes.' I fixed my eyes on his. 'He came back in the morning when I was at the shop.'

'Why?'

'He gave my mother his new telephone number.'

Something passed across his face. 'Do you have that number?'

'It's on a paper in my purse.'

He glanced at Detective Callhoun. She nodded and made a note.

'Why did he change it?'

'I . . . I don't know.' *Please don't ask about his old phone. Please don't make me lie.*

'Is that the truth?'

'Yes.'

'Where did he go after work last night?'

'I don't know. He didn't come home to eat and he didn't answer his phone. I called the cab company where he works and they said that he –' I felt his eyes boring into me – 'that he brought his car back early in the morning and didn't work that day.'

'Did that surprise you?'

'Yes. He tries to earn as much as he can. He is proud. He hates taking benefit money.'

'Do you have any idea where he went?'

'No. I was worried in case he'd had an accident.' The policeman's face was like stone. The darkness filled my mouth and made my words into a muddle. 'Why? I don't ... Where is he? What's happened ...?'

His voice didn't change. His eyes didn't blink. 'At four a.m. this morning there was an explosion in a lock-up garage in Kilburn. When the fire brigade arrived, they found your brother inside.'

'No!' I jumped up. The room swam around me. I reached for the table.

'Is he ... dead?'

'No.' Detective Callhoun reached over to touch my hand. I pulled away from her. 'He's concussed and badly burnt. He's in intensive care.'

'I have to go to him.'

Inspector McGill was still staring at me, hard. 'Sit down, Miss Sahar. He won't be having visitors until he's been questioned and that can't happen until he's conscious.'

The room was still spinning. I could hear my breath coming very fast. 'Questioned? What about?'

He leant forward, his face so close I could see the broken veins on his nose. 'His terrrorist activities, Miss Sahar.'

Shock shook my body, making my voice quiver and jump. 'I ... I ... don't understand.'

He leant back, folding his arms. 'Then let me spell it out for you. That lock-up was where your brother made his bombs. And he's in hospital because one of his devices went off while he was working on it.'

'No...' Darkness closed over me. For a few seconds I sat there gasping, my hands opening and closing as if I might catch the right words to explain the terrible mistake this hard-faced policeman had made. But all I could whisper was, 'He is not a terrorist. Please. You must believe me.'

His eyes were drilling into mine, searching for something I hoped wasn't there. 'He studied engineering,' he said.

This was madness. He was taking something good and turning it into evil. 'That doesn't make him a bombmaker. He wanted to rebuild our country, to make roads and bridges. Me too.'

'What?'

'I also want to be an engineer.' I said it defiantly, proud of my ambition. He made a note and from the way he glanced at the woman I knew that somehow I had made things worse.

'In addition to the chemicals in the garage, we found a number of electronic detonators with his fingerprints on them. Can you explain how they got there?'

I felt weightless, as if my mind had left my body. I didn't understand what was happening. All I knew for certain was that Behrouz was innocent. 'I...I...it's a mistake.'

'Did he resent the presence of foreign troops in Afghanistan?'

Anger snapped me back into my body. 'No! He worked

for the British army. He was an interpreter. They gave him a medal for saving three soldiers. If we hadn't come to England the Taliban would have killed him. Like they killed my father!'

'I told you to sit down, Miss Sahar. Calm yourself.' I sank back on to the grey plastic chair. 'There have been countless incidents of Afghan nationals turning on their foreign employers.'

'Not Behrouz. He would never hurt anyone. Someone else put those chemicals in that garage. When Behrouz can speak, he'll tell you what happened.'

Detective Callhoun cut in quickly. 'You need to prepare yourself, Aliya. Your brother's injuries are very bad. He may never regain consciousness.'

She was just pretending to be kind. She didn't care that he was injured, maybe dying. I closed my eyes to shut out her face. All I saw in the darkness was fear and danger and confusion.

'Have you heard of a terror group called Al Shaab?' the man said.

I looked at him, bewildered. 'I think maybe on the news. Last year. They planted some bombs in Helmand, I think, and . . . and maybe Lahore . . . I . . . I don't know.' *Why was he asking me this?*

'They contacted us. They told us that your brother was working for them.'

His words slipped into my brain like a thin sharp blade. 'No! They're lying!'

'They identified him by name at least half an hour before we'd established his identity.' The blade slid deeper, probing for doubt.

'Anyone could pretend they're from Al Shaab. Anyone could tell you these lies.'

'The caller gave us details of a foiled bombing attempt carried out by Al Shaab earlier this year.' He kept his eyes on mine.

'I don't understand . . .'

'Those details were known only to the bombers and the security services.'

'No . . . somebody is doing this to him.'

'Why would they do that, Miss Sahar? Does he have enemies?'

'Only the Taliban. He got away from them in Afghanistan. Maybe they came after him here.'

He waved his hand dismissively. 'They couldn't stage something like this. It's not how they operate. Now, we need you to tell us about your brother's associates.'

'Associates?' I glanced at Detective Callhoun.

'Friends, acquaintances, work mates,' she said.

I searched my head for names. 'There's his boss, Mr Khan, and he's mentioned a dispatcher called Corella, and some other drivers – Steve, I think . . . and Liam and Arif, and someone called Geoff, and he talks to Mrs Garcia from the refugee drop-in centre. He used to talk to some men who live in our block, but he doesn't like them and he told me to keep away from them, and sometimes he says hello to Mr Brody downstairs, but he only shouts at us.'

'Has Behrouz visited a mosque since you've been in the UK?'

'No. He's not very religious.'

He stared at me hard. 'Have you?'

'No.'

'Are you religious?'

I hung my head, ashamed. 'No. Not really.'

'Did you notice any change in your brother's behaviour recently, anything unusual?'

'He seemed unhappy, afraid . . . I . . . don't know.'

The look that passed between the two detectives made me feel like a traitor and I knew I was right not to tell them about the gun. They wouldn't understand. They would think it was proof he was a killer.

'What do you think was making him unhappy?'

'He's been through a lot. I told you, the Taliban tried to kill him, he wants to finish his studies but he can't because we have no money, he's worried about my mother and my sister. It's not strange that he's unhappy. It's normal.' My words sounded hollow, even to me.

'Did he spend time at any other properties?'

'I don't know. I don't think so. He works and he sleeps. He doesn't have time to go anywhere.'

'When you lived in Afghanistan did he go away for long periods?'

'A few days sometimes, with the army. You can check with Colonel Clarke.'

Inspector McGill dropped forward on his chair. 'Ah, yes, Colonel Clarke. How does Behrouz feel about him?'

'The colonel was his boss. He respects him. He's grateful that he's sponsoring our asylum application. We all are.' I was floundering, unsure what he wanted me to say. 'He is kind, he came to our flat to welcome us to the UK and he brought us a television.'

'Do you know why Behrouz wanted to see the colonel?'

'No.'

'The day before yesterday he called his office at the Houses of Parliament. Clarke's secretary said he was pushing to see the colonel urgently and that he got very agitated when she told him he was in New York. Then yesterday morning he called the colonel's home and spoke to his wife, demanding to see the colonel as soon as he got back from the States. Do you have any idea why he was so anxious to see him?'

'No . . . I don't know, maybe . . . maybe there's a problem with our papers.' I was pleased that I'd thought of something sensible and ordinary.

'Or,' he said, and his voice grew slow, 'perhaps Colonel Clarke was the planned target for Behrouz's bomb.'

I couldn't speak. The walls were closing in, trying to crush me.

'The colonel's an extremely high-value target. We think Behrouz was trying to exploit their relationship so he could gain access to his home and plant a device.'

'That is not possible.'

'We checked with the colonel. He gave Behrouz the numbers of his parliamentary and constituency offices but not his home. So how did your brother get hold of it?'

'I . . . I don't know.'

'I think you're lying, Miss Sahar. I think you know a lot more about your brother's activities than you're letting on.'

'My brother goes to work and he looks after us. That's all he does!'

'Did he leave you instructions? A list of things to do or people to contact if he was killed or injured?'

'No. Why would he?'

He ran his thumb down his stubbly cheek. 'We're going to let you take a rest now, Miss Sahar. While we're gone, I'd like you to think about everything I've told you. When I come back, we'll talk again.'

They left me then. With nothing to look at but my own reflection.

DAN

I was wrecked. Not surprising considering it was nearly two-thirty by the time I got home. I'd cycled like a maniac but I only just made it up to my room before I heard Dad tiptoe downstairs and slip out the front door. After that I'd stayed awake half the night, worrying about him getting sent back to prison, wondering what Cement Face had done with the man he'd kidnapped, and wishing I'd never set foot in Meadowview. You walk in there thinking you're a normal person with a normal life and you come out smeared in filth, with the stink of fear and garbage in your nose and your head full stuff off the TV you never thought you'd see in real life. It was as if that whole building was rotten, not just the pipes, and if you lifted up any floorboard or opened any door, you'd find some festering filth reaching out to suck you in. Every time I managed to drop off to sleep, I'd see that bloke's bloody, petrified face, the gun under the bath, packets of drugs stuffed in boxes of washing powder, then I'd hear that weasel saying Dad's name and I'd wake up yelling, imagining him going back to prison and me and Mum ending up in a place like Meadowview. She'd never cope.

Around four in the morning I heard the front door click shut: Dad coming back. I pulled the pillow over my head, trying to block out the sound of his footsteps padding past my room, and when he'd gone, I hurled it across the room and lay there in the darkness, asking myself over and over if keeping quiet about someone else's crimes makes you as guilty as they are. When he came in a couple of hours later to wake me up, I fixed my eyes on the wall and told him I felt sick and couldn't face going to work with him.

'No problem,' he said, 'Jez is back.' He put his hand on my forehead, like when I was kid. 'You are a bit hot, son. I'll get you an aspirin.'

For a second the comforting weight of his big rough palm made me certain I'd got it all wrong, that there was a simple explanation for what I'd seen in the loading bay and that I'd dreamt I'd heard him coming and going in the small hours.

I shifted round a bit. 'Did you go out last night?' He gave me a funny look. I stared at him and suddenly it felt like the familiar crinkles round his eyes, the scar on his chin, the crooked tooth that showed when he smiled and his short bristly hair had been stolen by a stranger. I really did feel sick as I waited for his lie. I felt even sicker when it came. He gave me that easy, hey-what-can-you-do? shrug of his. 'Yeah. Old people's home had an emergency, whole place got flooded.'

'Was Jez with you?'

'Yeah. We turned off the water and patched it up and we're going back this morning to sort it properly.'

He didn't hang around after that and I was glad. I couldn't face talking to him or anyone else, so I stayed in my room, hunched over the PlayStation, ignoring my phone. When Bernie Watts started calling, I turned it off.

ALIYA

They went over the same things again and again. The man getting angry, drumming the table, chewing his cheek and the woman stepping in, trying to keep him calm, insisting they just wanted my help. Then they'd leave me on my own in that grey, ugly room as if I was a criminal and come back a little later with more questions and cups of tea that were too weak or too strong and food that I didn't want and couldn't swallow. It went on like that for most of the day, until finally, at about eight o'clock in the evening, the woman came back alone.

'You must be tired, Aliya. Just a couple more questions, then you can go. Does your mother have a mobile phone?'

'No.'

'Do you?'

'No.'

'How do you contact people?'

'I have no one to call. Just the doctor and sometimes the refugee centre. If Behrouz isn't there, I use the telephone at the garage opposite our flats.'

She frowned a little and wrote something down.

'Are you certain Behrouz had his new mobile with him when he left the flat?'

'My mother told me so, but I was not there. Why?'

'We didn't find it on him, but it may have been destroyed in the explosion.'

Along with Behrouz. I looked down and tried not to let the tears come.

'All right, that's enough for tonight.'

'When can I see my brother?'

'We'll let you know.'

'Can I speak with his doctors?'

She looked away and shook her head, her mouth tight. 'The hospital's issuing regular press bulletins. As of thirty minutes ago, he was stable but still unconscious.'

'What is stable?'

'No better, no worse.'

No worse. This was something to hold on to.

She handed me a card. 'If you remember anything that might be of help to us, please call me on this number. If we need to speak to you, we'll contact you at the hotel.'

'Hotel?'

'You can't go anywhere near Meadowview, not until

we've finished searching your flat and the surrounding area.'

I pushed away the thought of the gun and the phone in the *Margaretta* and looked down at the floor. 'There is nothing in our flat, I promise.' It wasn't a lie. It just felt like one.

'Thank you for your cooperation, Miss Sahar. WPC Rennell will drive you to the hotel.'

I stood up. She raised her finger. 'Remember, if anyone contacts you, trying to get a message to Behrouz, you call me immediately.'

A round-faced, pink-cheeked policewoman marched me down the hallway, her swinging hips rattling the keys and handcuffs on her belt. I was so empty and tired I could hardly keep up. The only thing keeping my legs moving was the need to get away from the grey walls, the endless questions and the sour smell of people shut up for too long in a stuffy room. We turned a corner. I saw swing doors with a glimmering green sign above them saying EXIT. WPC Rennell didn't walk towards it. She turned left down some stairs that disappeared into darkness. I pulled back. She had been lying. She was going to lock me up!

'Where are you taking me?'

'Out the back way. The press have found out you're here. Someone's posted it on Twitter.'

'No!' My throat tightened around the sound.

'It's all right. Come on, quick, before the crowd gets any bigger.'

She hurried me down the steps, through a door into a gloomy underground car park and guided me towards a small red car. It was old, with a dusty plastic dog in the back window and a dent along the side. She told me to lie across the back seat while she fetched an old rug from the boot.

'Here, when I give you the word, put this over you,' she said. 'It won't be for long.'

She got into the front, pulled off her jacket and cap and shook out her curly fair hair so it stuck up around her head like one of Mina's dolls. Two uniformed policemen leapt into a van parked nearby and roared up the ramp and through the exit with the roof light flashing and the siren screeching. A burst of voices shouted my name, screaming filthy words. It made me sick inside. They were so angry, so full of hate. The voices grew louder. I wanted to shout back and tell them it wasn't right what they were saying. The shouting faded as the crowd chased after the van.

'OK. Stay down,' said WPC Rennell.

I heard the clunk of the door locks and I lay down flat, pulling the dusty rug over my head. It was itchy and smelt of dogs. My mouth was dry. My heart was thudding.

'All right,' she said. 'Here we go.'

I felt the rumble of the engine and the bump of the ramp. The car stopped.

'Don't move,' she whispered. 'There's still a few stragglers hanging around, looking for trouble.'

The car edged forward. The shouting started again. A

fist thumped the roof, we swerved sideways. I pushed my face into the sweaty plastic, fighting the urge to vomit, and I thought of Mina throwing up in Captain Merrick's jeep. Voices came right up to the car. I could feel the people out there. Hating me. Wanting to find me and hurt me. Knuckles rapped on the window. The car turned sharply and we sped away.

'It's OK,' she said after a few minutes. 'We're clear.'

I slipped the rug off my face.

'There's a lot of angry people out there.' I could see her looking at me in the mirror. 'But don't worry. We'll be around, making sure you're all right.'

'There's no need,' I said, trying to sound sure of myself. But I wasn't sure of anything. I was so lost and scared it felt as if my body had broken into pieces.

All I knew was that I had to help Behrouz, and I couldn't do that with a policewoman standing over me, watching everything I did.

DAN

It was nearly four o'clock when I finally dragged myself downstairs to make a sandwich. On my way past the living room I heard the murmur of the TV and, looking round the door, I glimpsed a grainy, blown-up passport photo on the screen. The shock made my skin burn. It was him. The man who got kidnapped from Meadowview. The one whose petrified face had kept me up all night. I took a deep breath and kept walking. I didn't want to know. My head was still urging me into the kitchen when my feet swivelled round and turned back down the hall. I pushed the door wide. A bright-eyed, smiling weather forecaster was pointing to a map predicting rain. I gripped the doorframe. 'Hey, Mum, that bloke on the news just now. What's happened to him?'

She was ironing, with her mobile clamped to her ear, gossiping to one of her friends. When I started mouthing at her and pointing to the TV, she frowned, shrugged and shook her head. I ran upstairs and checked the news online. It didn't take me long to find the story.

The man on TV was making headlines on every channel. He was a nineteen-year-old Afghan minicab driver who'd nearly died when his bomb-making equipment exploded in a lock-up in Kilburn at four a.m. that morning. I broke out in a sweat and rocked back on my chair, staring at his face on the screen, trying to work it out. Two hours before the explosion I'd seen him being whacked round the head and dragged off in a van. He'd have had trouble standing up after that, let alone getting himself to Kilburn and cooking up a bomb. Cement Face must have dumped him in that lock-up. That's what he'd meant about making him famous! I closed my eyes, feeling trapped, cornered, guilty as hell.

You could have saved him, Dan. You could have called the cops.

Then the reporter said his name: Behrouz Sahar.

I jerked my head up. Sahar! He had to be the brother of that girl in the flat! I kept hitting replay so I could take it all in. It looked like Sahar was in intensive care with half the anti-terrorist squad camped round his bed waiting for him to come round.

Shots of the entrance to the hospital and an aerial view of Meadowview gave way to pictures of tanks churning up dust in Afghanistan and a reporter saying Sahar had been an interpreter for the British army. There were photos of his time with the troops: Sahar laughing with a bunch of grimy, sunburnt soldiers, Sahar leaning out of a tank giving the thumbs up, Sahar with all these men in suits at some big meeting, and one of him getting a medal pinned on his chest by a posh-looking army officer. The picture cut to the same man pushing a trolley through Arrivals at Heathrow. A slim woman with long shiny hair was running towards him, trying to shake off a mob of reporters. They were all shouting at him: 'Colonel Clarke, did Sahar ever show any signs of instability? Colonel Clarke, did you ever have cause to trust his loyalty? Is it true you were planning to use him as a good-will ambassador for Hope Unlimited?'

Clarke leant in to the nearest microphone. 'I cannot find words to express my astonishment at this horrific news. The Behrouz Sahar I knew, or thought I knew, was a brave, upstanding young man who risked his life to save three injured British soldiers under my command. When his army colleagues discovered that he was on a Taliban death list, they urged me to intervene personally to bring him to Britain. Which I duly did. I can only assume that his decision to plan an act of terrorism against this country came about either because of some deep-seated mental disorder triggered by the traumas he experienced in Afghanistan, or because he had been subjected to inten-sive brainwashing and radicalized by Al Shaab militants intent on exploiting his youth and vulnerability. We can never condone what he has done, and he must of course be punished. But the way forward is to support all those who have been touched by the horrors of war, civilian and military alike, which is why organizations like Hope Unlimited, the charity my wife and I set up some years ago, are so important for the future peace and stability of our world.'

His wife, who'd been gazing up at him, nodded and turned a pair of soft brown eyes to the camera. That's when I recognized her. She was that actress, India Lambert, the one who spent half her time making films and the other half roaming round war zones banging on about injustice. She squeezed his arm and with a murmured, 'Thank you,' the two of them turned and walked off towards the exit.

The whole of me felt numb as I clicked on a live update of the story.

'. . . A spokesman for the Metropolitan Police has just confirmed that Behrouz Sahar's mother, Farah, forty-two, and his sister Aliya, fourteen, were taken in for questioning soon after the explosion. While they are in custody his four-year-old sister Mina is being cared for by the authorities . . .'

How was that spaced-out little kid I'd seen on the Sahars' couch going to cope with a load of strangers looking after her? As for the mother, they'd have a hard time getting any sense out of her. Which left that girl,

Aliya, facing the police on her own. I leant forward and dropped my face in my hands.

'The police are anxious to talk to anyone who has information about Behrouz Sahar's activities since he came to the UK, or who can help trace his movements over the last forty-eight hours, particularly between one and four a.m. this morning. If you have any information, however small or seemingly insignificant, please contact this number . . .'

I knew I should call that number, tell them what I'd seen, get Behrouz Sahar cleared of being a terrorist. But I couldn't. Because of Dad. Whatever he'd done, he was still my father. I couldn't risk him going back to prison.

My mind raced with shock, anger, pity, guilt.

What you going to do, Dan? What you going to do?

ALIYA

WPC Rennell drove me to a busy district of London called King's Cross. The hotel was a tall narrow building down a side street, with the name Holly Lodge painted over the door and a sign in the window that said VACANCIES in winking blue lights. She hurried me past the deserted reception desk, up to the first floor, and pointed down a narrow corridor.

'You've got rooms 11 and 12. Do you want me to come in with you?'

I looked into her scrubbed, shiny face. She gazed back as if she was still trying to work out what to make of me. 'No, thank you,' I said.

'OK. Here are your keys. I'll be back first thing. Remember, stay inside as much as you can and don't get friendly with the other guests. If anyone asks who you are, you say your family name is Tarin and you're down from Birmingham sorting out your visas. Any problems, call us immediately.'

I took the keys and walked away, keeping my eyes fixed on the worn red carpet. I didn't glance back until my fingers were on the door handle. She gave me a nod. I took a long slow breath and went inside. Mina was asleep on the bed. My mother was beside her, staring at the television. She didn't look up when I came in and just went on running her prayer beads through her fingers, murmuring that Behrouz was a good boy, her firstborn, the apple of her eye. I should have gone to her, taken her hands, comforted her, but I couldn't find the strength. I followed her eyes to the screen and kept them there, held by a strange sort of fascination. She was watching Mr Brody. He was standing outside Meadowview, telling the reporters that he'd had his suspicions about us from the minute we'd moved in and that this is what happened if you let scum into the country. Another man came on, a policeman who said that people like Behrouz 'represented the worst kind of danger to the public, because they weren't known to the police or the security services'. When the reporter asked him why the police hadn't arrested any other members of Al Shaab, he looked angry and said they were doing everything they could but Al Shaab was an elusive organization with no traceable links to any other terror group.

I looked away and gazed at the bumpy beige wallpaper, the thin green curtains, the battered brown furniture and the big plastic bag stuffed full of our things on the floor. I rummaged inside it for my purse and slipped downstairs. I didn't know where I was going. I just needed to get away, to feel free again, but the cool night air and the rush of lights made me dizzy after the gloom of the hotel, and the sight of Behrouz's photo staring from a news-stand made me want to cry out. The streets were crowded and it felt as if every face I passed was watching me, accusing me, condemning me: the man in the parked car, the homeless woman curled in her sleeping bag, the pizza-delivery boy revving his scooter. I wanted to scream at them that Behrouz was not a terrorist and that I was going to prove it. I slowed down, overcome by a sudden hopelessness. How could I prove anything? I was alone in a foreign city full of angry people who were convinced that my brother wanted to kill them.

A crowd of men pushed past me. They knocked me off the kerb, shouting words I didn't understand, and pulled at my headscarf. I ducked away from their tattooed arms and slopping beer cans and started to run. I heard them coming after me, roaring, laughing, swearing. I rushed into a takeaway and slipped behind a woman with a baby who was buying kebabs. I pressed my cuff to my teeth, ripping at the fabric as I peered between the faded photos of burgers, pizzas and fried chicken stuck to the window. The drunken men staggered past without seeing me. I closed my eyes, waiting for their shouts to fade. When I opened them again, the woman at the counter was staring at me without smiling. A crowd of teenagers burst in, the girls laughing, the boys pushing each other, raising their voices. One of them poked my shoulder. 'Come on, hurry up, we haven't got all night.'

I searched the list on the wall, looking for the cheapest thing. The girls began giggling and whispering. I asked for a small pizza and fumbled for the money, praying I'd have enough to pay for it. The purse fell from my hands, spilling vouchers, coins, cards and scraps of paper across the floor; I crouched down, trying pick them up and stuff them back but the purse wouldn't close. The girls' laughter grew louder. My eyes blurred as I dropped a handful of coins on the counter. Without waiting for the pizza I stumbled out of the shop, tugging at the crumpled card jammed in the zip of my purse.

Hating myself for being so weak, I ran round the corner, plunged into the nearest doorway, and let the tears come. The fear and loneliness took hold, my knees buckled and I slumped on to the step, not caring about the cold or the damp or the dirt. I laid my head on my knees, too wretched to move. A blast of pumping music jolted me out of my misery. I looked up. Two tall, thickset men in black suits came sauntering out of a door in the purple-painted wall across the road, their shaved heads and gold chains glinting in the light from the street lamp. I pulled my scarf across my face and prayed they wouldn't see me.

They came closer. I felt the heat of their stares and kept my eyes on the card in my fist. One of the men hawked and spat. A shiny slug of phlegm landed near my foot. I looked up into their faces. They stared back, then they grinned at each other and walked on. Anger grew and swelled inside me, filling the emptiness.

I wiped my eyes with my sleeve, scrambled to my feet and dusted the dirt from my clothes. I'd show them. I'd show everybody in the whole world that my family wasn't scum to be spat at and accused of evil crimes they hadn't committed. I held the card tightly in my fingers and hurried away to find a phone box.

DAN

'Hey, Danny.' Dad's voice boomed up the stairs.

'What?'

'Phone.'

No one ever called me on the house phone. 'Who is it?'

'She didn't say.'

I didn't need to see Dad's face to know he was grinning and winking at Mum. What were the options? Force myself to take the call or face Dad coming up and ribbing me about giving some girl a hard time. I ran downstairs and took the receiver.

'Yeah?'

A voice whispered something I couldn't make out.

'What?'

There was a gasp on the line. 'I am Aliya Sahar . . . from Meadowview.' The shock was like touching a live wire.

'Where'd you get this number?'

'Your father . . . he gave us a card.'

I glanced over my shoulder. Mum and Dad were gazing at the TV, pretending they weren't listening. I lowered my voice. 'What do you want?'

'I . . . I . . . need . . . your help.'

Panic squeezed my chest. Did she know what I'd seen? I swallowed hard. 'Why me?'

'You were kind.' Her voice cracked. 'You helped me to hide the gun from your father.'

I dragged my fingers down my face, feeling relief give way to a burning rush of guilt. Mum was looking up, ears flapping. 'Give us your number,' I said, quickly. 'I'll call you back.'

'I am using a telephone in a box.'

'It'll be on the wall above the phone . . .'

'Yes, now I have it.' She read out the number. I scribbled it on my hand and hung up. Dead casual, I walked towards the door. Just when I thought I'd made it, Mum said, 'Who was that, love?'

'No one you know.'

I darted into the hall and rushed up the stairs two at a time. Aliya answered on the first ring. 'My brother is in trouble.' Her voice was steadier, as if she'd been practising the words.

'I know. I saw it on the news.'

'The people on the television are telling lies. He did not make that bomb. He is not a terrorist.'

I closed my eyes and saw his bruised, desperate face as they threw him into the van, but I had to pretend I only knew what I'd seen on TV. 'So what was he doing in that lock-up with all those explosives?'

'That is what I must find out. I have to prove he is innocent.'

'How?'

'I . . . I will start with his phone. I think maybe he hid it because there is something in it that is connected to what happened.'

My heart pounded. 'Like what?'

'I don't know.'

'Are you going to show it to the police?'

'No. They do not care about the truth. They believe he is a terrorist and that is all they want to prove.' The flutter was back in her voice. 'I hid the phone and the gun and now I need you to get the phone back for me.'

I gripped the handset. 'Where is it?'

'On a boat on the canal. Near the bridge. I put the bag under the tarpaulin.'

'Why can't you get it?'

'I am not allowed to go near to Meadowview.'

'Who says?'

'The police.'

I wanted to help her but this talk of the police was stopping me thinking straight, making me panic, holding me back.

'Are you there?' she whispered.

'Yeah . . . but I—'

'Please, do this one thing for me.' For a moment all I could hear was her breath, jerking and rasping, then her voice came out in a rush, as if she was afraid I'd hang up. 'They have put us in a hotel called Holly Lodge. It's in a road called Swinton Street near to a big railway station called King's Cross. Bring it early in the morning. I will watch from the window until you come.'

'Look, I . . . I don't know. I . . .'

'Please.' Her voice wobbled. 'I have no one else to ask . . . and . . . and there is something else.'

'What?'

'You touched the gun. You must clean away the marks made by your fingers, in case the police find it.'

'Jesus.' Fingerprints. I'd left them all over the loading bay too.

'What's the name of this boat?'

'The *Margaretta*.'

I hung up, pulled on my hoodie and ran downstairs, head spinning. My fingerprints. Whatever happened, I had to wipe them off Behrouz's gun.

'Hey, Mum, I'm going out for a bit,' I said.

'Where to? It's late.'

'Round this girl's house. I won't be long.'

'Does she have a name?'

My brain was too scrambled to make one up. 'Ali. You

don't know her.'

Dad looked up from the tray on his lap. 'You need a lift, son?'

'Nah, I'll bike it.'

'Got your key?'

'Yep.'

I ran into the kitchen, snatched Mum's rubber gloves and a dishcloth off the draining board and headed for the back door. I cycled towards the estate, head down into the spitting rain, nearly hitting the kerb when the top of Meadowview appeared above the dingy rooftops, lit up by the searchlight from a hovering helicopter. I turned off the main road and pushed my bike through the crowd, craning to see into the car park. It was full of vans, police cars and figures in white paper overalls carrying boxes out of the building. People were out on the balconies, staring down at the TV news vans or gazing up at the helicopter that looked as if it was hanging off the end of its own light beam.

The whole area had been cordoned off and the grow- ing mob of onlookers was jostling the barriers, feeding off each other's fury. Some of them were having a go at Aliya and her mother for harbouring a monster, others were waving copies of the evening paper and talking about the evil lurking in Behrouz Sahar's eyes, while people from the other blocks milled around, trying to outdo each other with stories of dodgy characters hang- ing out on the Meadowview staircases and stuff going on around the car park at night. The babble of voices grew louder and shriller until I thought the waves of outrage were going to swallow me up.

I backed my bike away, barging into an agitated woman, who dropped her newspaper and screamed in my face when the wheels crushed a front page picture of Behrouz headlined 'BOMBER!' I jumped on the bike and made off towards the canal, skidding to a halt when a couple of cops in high-vis jackets stepped forward, blocking the entrance to the towpath. One of them shone his torch in my face then ran it over the bike. 'Where are you off to?'

'Home,' I said. 'I just came out to see what was going on.'

He grunted and let me pass. I sped along the track, following the curve of the water towards the bridge. Even out of sight of the helicopter I could still hear the whirr of its blades and the shouts of the crowd. They were chanting now, demanding the death penalty for terrorists.

Worried I'd missed the *Margaretta*, I stopped by a tree stump and swept the bike light across the moorings. It was there, a flash of a white M on the bow of a rotting rowing boat, almost hidden in the shadow of the barges either side. I checked the path, making doubly sure no one was coming before I pulled on the rubber gloves. Drawing the slimy rope towards the bank, I planted my knees in the mud and plunged my hand through the split in the tarpaulin. I stretched down, feeling for the plastic bag, blinking into the blast of rain that whipped my face. The boat kept swinging away and even with the gloves on I shuddered when my fingers touched a clammy layer of sludge, but I kept digging around till I felt the bag scrunched under the seat. I dragged it out and backed into the undergrowth, holding it at arms length to avoid the stinking water pouring off the plastic and trying to dodge the brambles clawing my face. My feet crunched broken glass and empty cans as I went deeper.

When I was sure no one could see me I reached into the bag and took out the gun. Hating the stubby feel of it, I rubbed every inch of the barrel and handle with the dishcloth, imagining all those greasy, tell-tale spirals disappearing under the pressure. I dropped it back in the bag. It fell with a clunk. I flinched and looked around. There was no one to hear it, no sound at all except the distant roar of the crowd outside Meadowview yelling for Behrouz Sahar's blood.

My mind flashed back to the raw fear I'd seen on his face. Almost before I knew it, I was reaching for the tobacco tin and ramming it into my pocket. Slashing the brambles with my elbows, I pushed my way back to the towpath and shoved the bag through the tarpaulin. I cut through an alleyway further up, and once I was well way from all the cruising cop cars I tossed the muddy gloves and the dishcloth into a skip. Mum would go mad when she found out they were missing. That was nothing compared to what she'd do if she found out what else was going on. Shaking, I let myself into our house and eased the front door shut.

'That you, Danny?' Mum was on the landing in her nightie, looking down over the bannister. 'Don't forget to bolt the door.'

'I won't. Night.' I propped myself against the wall and closed my eyes, waiting for my heart to stop crashing against my ribs. Still trembling, I hurried up to my room and checked for news updates on Behrouz Sahar. According to the BBC, he was still in a coma and the police were looking for his accomplices. A whole load of Afghan businesses had been attacked and the boss of his cab company had told the papers he was a lone extremist who deserved the death penalty for bringing shame on a law-abiding community. Even his army mates were turning against him.

The only person in the whole world still sticking up for him was Aliya.

I got out his phone, turning it in my fingers for a long time. Then I picked through the heads on the universal charger Bernie Watts had given me (a key tool if you work with nicked phones) and put it on to charge. A tiny dot of red flickered into life. I paused for a second, knowing that once I'd seen what was in the memory there'd be no going back. I drew a long, unsteady breath and turned on the phone.

There were eight numbers in Behrouz's contacts, a few texts, and some photos, family stuff mostly: Aliya, his mum and his kid sister in their flat, all four of them on a sightseeing trip round London – smiling and waving outside the railings of Buckingham Palace, feeding the pigeons in Trafalgar Square and one of Behrouz standing proudly beside his minicab with Big Ben in the background. Then a few taken ten days later of Aliya and the kid at some dreary-looking fundraiser in the Meadowview car park: a juggler in a droopy jester's hat, a bunch of grown men lobbing balls at a coconut and an old lady selling tea and buns. The only person who looked like he was enjoying himself was a policeman who was leaning across the tea table with his cap under his arm, helping himself to a bright-green cupcake.

The next lot of pictures were low-angle shots of two men carrying parcels between two vans parked under some trees on a deserted patch of waste ground. My room wasn't that warm but as I looked closer sweat prickled the back of my neck. One of the vans was the same red as the one they'd used for the kidnap, and the taller man, who had a stoop and a cigarette dangling from his lips, was obviously Cement Face. As for the packages he was unloading, I was guessing they were full of drugs. What else were they going to be? But it was the white van and the stocky blond bloke loading it up that had got my heart pumping. The man was Jez Deakin. And from what I could see of the number plate I had a horrible, gut-twisting feeling that the van was my dad's.

I thought I was going to be sick. For a few seconds I

just sat there gasping and looking down at the thick brown mud caked round my trainers, before I managed to get up the courage to scroll on to the most recent photos. They'd been taken the day before the explosion and they were all of Cement Face, leaning up against a brick wall, smoking. Whoever he was, he had a serious nicotine problem. This time he was wearing green overalls tucked into white rubber boots. There were four decent shots of him and a couple of blurred ones that had caught another man in the frame, as if Behrouz had grabbed them as he was driving off.

My hand hovered on the delete button, fighting the urge to erase the lot and forget I'd ever seen them. I didn't do it. I sent them to my own phone and tried enhancing them, looking for any scraps of information I might have missed. When that didn't help, I sent them to my computer and worked through all the images, even the blurry ones, clicking, cropping, zooming until the details were almost too pixellated to make out. Almost. Not quite. I'd been clinging to a last desperate hope that the white van Jez Deakin was loading up might turn out to be someone else's. But there was no getting away from it. That van was definitely Dad's.

ALIYA

WPC Rennell was back at the hotel by seven next morning. This time she wore pink lipstick, a tight red jumper, blue denim jeans and boots with high heels, but she still looked like a policewoman. She tried to be friendly. She even brought drawing paper, crayons and a big wooden jigsaw for Mina to play with, and magazines and DVDs for me and Mor. She asked us to call her Tracy and kept saying she was there to protect us from journalists and troublemakers. This was only half of the truth. She was watching us. Or rather, watching me. She thought I knew something about Behrouz. I could see it in her darting blue eyes and sense it in the way she spoke to me.

I hurried away to get dressed. When I came back to my

mother's room, Tracy was clearing the little plastic table so we could sit down together and eat the limp white toast and boiled eggs the kitchens had sent up on a tray. I edged my chair towards the window, worried that the boy would come and go away again before I could make an excuse to go outside. Tracy caught me looking and jumped up to peer over my shoulder. 'Don't tell me the press are out there.'

'No. I was looking to see if it was raining.' That was a lie. 'I'd like to find a library. I don't want to get behind with my school work.' That was true. But studying wasn't on my list of things to do that day. Our eyes locked. I waited for her to tell me I wasn't allowed to go out. But she smiled a fake toothy smile and said, 'Why not? You're not under arrest. You can go anywhere you like, except Meadowview, of course. That's still out of bounds. But, well . . .' The smile slipped. Underneath it was something that looked like real concern.

'Yes?' I said.

'Be careful, Aliya. London's a big city and the people in it aren't always what they seem. There's some you can trust and some you can't.'

I left the table and went to fetch my headscarf. The boy. Would he come? If he did, was he one of the people I could trust?

DAN

For the second night running I couldn't sleep. Instead I printed out all of Behrouz's photos and sat there looking at them while my mind threw out questions I couldn't answer. Who was Cement Face? Why did he want Behrouz dead? How long had Dad been lying to Mum about going straight? And if Behrouz really wasn't a bomb-maker, why would that Al Shaab terror group say he was? I felt like I was drowning in lies: little white ones, big black ones and the grubby grey ones that grow out of all the things you haven't got the guts to say or do. Just before dawn I had a panicky, guilt-soaked moment when telling Dad what I knew and forcing him to go with me to the police seemed like the only option. As soon as light started filtering through my blinds, I knew I couldn't do it.

I didn't know which was worse. The thought of that girl, Aliya, calling me up, going on about her brother being innocent and hassling me for his phone, or the thought of bumping into Dad and having to act normal, when nothing was ever going to be normal again. There was only one thing to do – pull the covers over my head and stay in bed.

I was lying there, staring at the ceiling, when the front doorbell rang. I heard Dad thumping down the stairs muttering, 'All right, all right.' I strained to hear what was happening, picked up men's voices, strangers, at least two of them, then Dad telling them to come in and closing the door. I froze rigid when he called up the stairs, 'Danny, get yourself down here.'

'Who is it?'

'Police. They want a word.'

Police? My insides shrivelled up. I heard Mum calling, 'What's wrong, Ron? What's happened?' Then her footsteps as she ran down to the kitchen.

I rubbed my knuckles against my forehead, trying to stop the pounding, hoping they'd come about the phones I'd been 'recycling' for Bernie Watts. For a first offence what would I get – a slap on the wrists? A few hours' community service? It'd break Mum's heart, but not so badly it wouldn't mend. But if they'd come for Dad . . .

I shoved Behrouz's phone and the printouts under my pillow, stumbled to the bathroom and splashed my face with cold water, telling myself that all I'd got to do was just walk down there and say nothing. But I was terrified that as soon as I saw the police I'd either screw up or throw up.

I don't know what I expected – Dad in handcuffs, sniffer dogs, armed men searching the house? When I got to the kitchen, there were two uniformed PCs sitting at the table, Dad was stirring the teapot and Mum was reaching down mugs from the cupboard. I hung around in the doorway, not trusting myself to go in. The older cop, hard-faced and weary, was opening his notebook. 'Is that Abbott with two Ts?'

Dad put the lid on the pot. 'And two Bs.' He caught me staring. 'Don't look so worried, Dan. Come in and sit down. This is PC Trent and PC Collins. They want to ask us a couple of questions.'

Trent gave me a friendly nod. He was late-twenties, tawny hair, thick, fair lashes, freckly face and dark circles under his eyes like he'd been up all night. I nodded back. Collins, the older one, didn't bother looking up, just went on staring at his notebook and tapping his pencil on the table. 'I was just explaining to your Dad. We're here about the terrorist who got blown up by his own bomb. He lived at Meadowview. His mother told us you were in their flat the day before yesterday mending a leak.' He laid a photo of Behrouz Sahar on the table, the grainy one I'd seen on TV. 'This is him. Did you see him at any time when you were in or around the building?'

'Yes,' Dad said, frowning. 'He was coming down the

stairs as we were going up.'

Mum gazed at him, gobsmacked. 'You never said.'

Dad shrugged. 'I didn't see the news last night, never realized it was him.'

'Have you got an exact time for this sighting?' Collins said.

Dad looked at me. 'What time do you think we left Brody's – nine-fifteen, nine twenty-five?'

'Probably gone half past.' My voice came out strangled. I pulled out a chair and perched on the edge. Lighten up, Danny. I tried to smile. My mouth wouldn't let me.

'How did he seem?'

'Scared,' Dad said. 'Petrified, I'd say.'

'Any idea why?'

'Not a clue.'

I stared at him. *Really, Dad?*

Collins wagged his pencil at me. 'Danny?'

Yeah, officer, it's because a load of armed thugs were trying to kill him. 'No,' I muttered. 'Me neither.'

Collins turned his pencil back to Dad. 'Could he have thought you were from the police, Mr Abbott?'

That was a laugh.

'Not a chance. I was wearing my work overalls. Danny too.' Dad pulled a clean pair out of the ironing basket, flipping them round so they could see the bright-orange logo front and back.

'Oh, right, you're that Abbott,' Collins said. 'I've seen your partner around a few times.'

Dad laughed. 'More than likely. Jez spends a lot of time down that estate. He's even been known to drink in the Trafalgar Arms.'

Trent grinned. 'It's got a bad reputation but they do a good pint. So, was Sahar carrying anything, Mr Abbott?'

'Not that I noticed.'

'Danny?'

I shook my head.

'Can either of you tell me what he was wearing?' Collins asked.

Dad looked surprised. 'What does that matter?'

'These guys are clever, they keep changing their clothes to fox the CCTV.'

'Oh, I see. Well, as far as I remember it was jeans . . . dark T-shirt, some kind of jacket – brown, I think. With a zip.'

'Shoes?'

'Trainers.'

'Did you happen to notice the make?'

Dad smiled at me. 'That's more Danny's department.'

I shrugged. 'No idea.'

'How long did you stay in the Sahars' flat?'

'Two, maybe two and a half hours,' Dad said. 'We had to replace a mains pipe.'

'Who was there?'

'Just the mother and a little girl at first. An older daughter turned up a few minutes later. I think she'd been shopping.'

'How did they appear to you?'

'The mum was in a bad way, totally out of it, the little one was very quiet, and the older girl, well, she was a nice kid, serious, made us tea. She seemed to be the one holding things together, clearing up, cooking.'

'Any other visitors while you were there?'

'No.'

'Any of them mention the son?'

'No.'

Collins raised his eyebrows at me. I shook my head again and reached for the mug of tea Mum was handing me.

'Did either of you see anything suspicious in the flat?' Trent said.

I stared into the mug.

'Like what?' Dad said.

'Anything incriminating they might have disposed of before we searched the place, like money, flash drives, phones, computers, weapons?'

A blast of heat burnt through my body. What if they searched our house? What if they found Behrouz's phone in my room? Dad was shaking his head. 'No, nothing like that. Course, we didn't go in the bedrooms, but from what I could see, the flat was pretty empty. Pathetic, really, how little they had.'

Collins nodded. 'We've been up all night helping search the building but we drew a total blank.'

Was I imagining a muscle twitching in Dad's cheek?

Trent handed him a card. 'You've been really helpful, Mr Abbott. If you think of anything else, just give me a shout on my mobile – there's all sorts of departments sticking their oar in and we wouldn't want your call getting lost.' He drained his tea, leant back in his chair and sighed. Dad raised the teapot. Trent nodded and held out his mug. 'Go on, then, just a drop. It's going to be a long day.'

'This your speciality, then?' Dad said. 'Terrorists?'

He had a nerve, dragging this out, topping up their tea, asking them questions. Though you had to hand it to him, his concerned-citizen act was good.

'No, we got roped in because Sahar's local,' Collins was saying.

Trent grunted. 'I was supposed to be heading back to Newcastle for my cousin's wedding but Meadowview's on my patch so when they asked for extra hands, I couldn't say no. My mum's not best pleased, neither's my girl-friend, but what can you do?'

'I bet you see all sorts round those tower blocks,' Mum said.

'Tell me about it. But that's the side of community policing I like, getting the families to trust me, doing what I can to stop a bad situation getting worse. You can't do that unless you put in the hours and get to know who's who.'

Mum folded her arms. 'Someone should do something about those warehouses by the canal. I've heard there's kids in there all hours of the day and night, drinking, smoking and Lord knows what else. Can't they put in some CCTV or a few street lights?'

Collins rubbed his thumb and finger together. 'Same old story, Mrs Abbott. No money.'

Trent put his mug down and stood up. 'Thanks for the tea, Mr Abbott. Anything else you think of, just give us a call. Some idiot back at the nick's already been leaking stuff to the press – so, as I said, it's best to get me on my mobile. Here you go, Danny.' He snapped a second card down on the table in front of me.

Before I could stop myself, I blurted out, 'Behrouz Sahar. Are you sure he's guilty?'

Trent nodded. 'Hundred per cent. Al Shaab have already admitted he was one of theirs, and his finger-prints were all over everything in that lock-up. But take it from me, going by the amount of explosive he had in there, they were planning something big. Our focus is on finding the rest of them. He wasn't in this alone, that's for sure.'

They got up and followed Dad into the hall. I ran upstairs and took Behrouz's phone from under my pillow. My fingers hovered for barely a second before I deleted all the shots of Jez Deakin and Dad's van from the memory. Aliya was right. If she was going to stand any chance of proving her brother was innocent, she'd have to start with what was on this phone. But no way could I let her see anything that would connect Behrouz Sahar to my dad. To make myself feel better, I printed her out a set of the other photos, the ones of Cement Face in his green overalls and white rubber boots. It didn't help. Every time I tried to breathe it still felt like a giant claw was squeezing my lungs.

An hour later I was sitting on the little wall outside the Holly Lodge Hotel, flicking through the photos of Cement Face and trying not to look as shifty as I felt. Shutters rumbled and milk bottles clinked as the cafe across the road opened up. A woman hurried in, came out with a steaming mug and sat down at one of the little tables, battling with the wind as she leafed through the paper. She didn't even go inside when it started to rain.

I pulled up my hood and walked up and down. Just a few paces one way and a few paces back, trying to ignore the voice in my head telling me I shouldn't even be there, I should be down the police station telling Trent everything I knew about Behrouz Sahar getting kidnapped. I tried to block it out but the voice went on nag, nag, nagging, driving me nuts. *Shut up! I've brought her the phone, haven't I?*

The front door swung open and when I saw her coming down the steps, the voice gave a sort of groan before it started going on at me again. She was wearing the same baggy grey dress and trousers she'd had on before but she looked smaller, as if the wind might blow her away, and she had dark smudges under her eyes. She didn't smile. Didn't say hello, in fact she didn't even look at me. For a minute I thought she was going to walk straight past me but she slowed down as she got nearer, pulled her scarf over her mouth and murmured, 'Please. Meet me at the back of the hotel.'

I gave it a couple of minutes, then wandered back the way I'd come. Half my brain was telling me to keep on going and forget I'd ever met her. The other half kept seeing her thin, frightened face and telling me I had to stay. Feeling ripped in two, I slipped down the next side road and counted along the buildings until I came to a gate in a high wooden fence. I pushed it open and stepped into a cramped back yard full of dustbins, crates of empty bottles and soggy cardboard boxes. She was waiting under the roof of an old lean-to and every couple of seconds she glanced up at the back of the hotel.

'What's going on?' I said.

'There is a policewoman upstairs with my mother. I don't want her to see us. Did you bring the phone?'

'Yeah. I charged it too and put a bit of credit on it for you.'

She took the phone and looked at me warily. 'Why are you helping me?'

I shrugged. 'Like you said, I had to wipe my prints off the gun. So getting the phone was no big deal.' Unnerved by the way she went on staring at me, I scuffed the loose gravel with my trainer. 'And I saw your brother.'

'When?' Her eyes brightened, hungry for information

that might help Behrouz.

I felt sick that I couldn't just open my mouth and tell her what I'd seen in the loading bay. 'That morning at Meadowview. He was coming down the stairs. He looked petrified.'

She took a couple of seconds to choke back her disappointment. 'I think he knew someone wanted to kill him.'

'You think that's why he had a gun?'

She lowered her head and nodded. 'I will find out who has done this to him and I will prove that he is innocent.'

'What if you can't?'

'They will put him in prison and they will send us back to Afghanistan and then – ' she screwed up her face and the words came out in a whisper – 'they will kill us.'

'Who will?'

'The Taliban.'

'Who?'

'The fighters who say they are men of God but they are not. They are devils.'

I stared at her. Afghanistan and Taliban were words I'd only ever heard on the news, usually over pictures of wild-eyed men in dusty turbans waving rocket launchers around. 'Why'd the Taliban want to kill you?' I said.

'My brother worked as an interpreter for the British army. They want to punish him for that, so they came to our house. Three of them with guns. That's why we had to leave my country.'

This wasn't a game or a movie I could switch off and

forget. These were real people. Real lives. Real deaths. I couldn't walk away. Not this time. The guilt was growing inside me, churning and swelling, and the voice in my head was getting angrier, telling me to get it over with and call the police right then and there. I couldn't do it. Not just because of Dad. Because of Mum. How could I destroy her life? But one look at this girl, shivering in her flimsy dress, and I knew if I didn't do something, I'd be destroying the lives of her whole family. There was only one way out of this. If I worked with her, then maybe I could find some way to prove Behrouz was innocent that didn't involve Dad. Her frightened green eyes were scouring my face, trying to work me out. I rubbed my sweating neck, pointed to the phone, and for the first time since I'd seen the kidnap I almost took a breath without it hurting. 'Have you seen the photos on there?' I said.

I watched her as she laid the phone on an upturned packing case and opened the picture gallery. She stopped at the ones of the Meadowview fundraiser, tensing up, staring hard.

'Seen something?' I asked.

'No . . . I don't know . . . it's just that the day he took these was the day he started to get nervous and worried.'

I glanced down at the bunting and the tea stall and the little kids crowding round the juggler. Of course there was nothing on the screen to show that I'd deleted any photos, no trace of them at all, and no sign of all the grubby grey lies I was telling except for the quiver in my finger as I clicked open the next file and the catch in my voice when I said, 'This lot are all of the same man – do you know him?'

I bent closer while she took her time studying the pictures of Cement Face. Close up she smelt of soap and a dusty sort of spice. 'No,' she said at last. 'I have never seen him before.'

'What about the wall he's leaning against? Seeing as he's wearing overalls and rubber boots, it's probably some kind of factory. Look, you can see the corner of a red sign and a bit of roof.'

'I do not know where it is. I do not know many places in London.' She frowned a little. 'When did Behrouz take the pictures of this man?'

'Tuesday. I already checked.'

'That's the day before the explosion.' Her eyes blinked nervously. 'The day he came back with the gun. Can you tell what time he took these photos?'

'Between 12.34 and 12.42. Looks like he caught Cement Face having a fag in his lunch break.'

'What is a fag?'

'A cigarette.'

'Why do you call this man Cement Face?'

'Look at him.' I smiled but she didn't smile back. 'Here.' I handed her the set of photos I'd printed out. She looked at them, a bit bemused. 'Why did you make these?'

I just about managed a shrug. 'Oh, you know, I thought you might want to show them around, find out who he is.'

'Thank you.' She folded them neatly and put them in her little backpack. Giving me a careful look she said, 'Can you find out who Behrouz called that day?'

She watched intently as I showed her how to pull up the call log.

'All right, it looks like Khan's Cars rang him at 6.30 in the morning, then again at 11.00; then there's nothing till 1.15, when he phoned someone called James Merrick – you know him?'

She nodded eagerly. 'That's Captain Merrick. He helped us to escape from the Taliban. How do I call him?'

I pressed the call button and put it on speaker. It went straight to voicemail.

She leant in and left a message. 'Captain Merrick. I am Aliya Sahar, the sister of Behrouz. I need to speak with you. It is very urgent. Call me, please. I am using Behrouz's old number.' She hung up and scrolled down to the next call in the log. 'This number has no name.' She pressed recall. It rang once before a crisp voice said, 'Houses of Parliament.'

She shot me a panicked look and hurriedly cut the connection.

'Parliament?' Fear pricked my spine. 'Who does he know there?'

'Colonel Clarke. His old boss, the one who is sponsoring us. He is in the government now.'

'Oh, yeah. The old guy whose wife's that actress. I saw him on TV. He seemed pretty upset about Behrouz.'

'The police are crazy. They think Colonel Clarke is the one Behrouz was planning to bomb.' She pressed her hand to her mouth as if the thought had made her feel sick.

'This next call is to someone called Arif,' I said quickly. 'Who's he?'

She swallowed hard. 'Another driver at Khan's. Behrouz likes him. He went to school with his cousin in Kabul.'

She tried the number. A 'number unavailable' message crackled over the speaker. 'Maybe he worked late last night and wants to sleep,' she said. 'Did he make any other calls on Tuesday?'

'No, why?'

'I told you. That's the night he came home with the gun.'

I kept scrolling. 'At 9.22 on Wednesday morning he got a text from Merrick, look, "Called in a couple of favours, got Clarke's home number, no luck with address or mobile. Will call u. Keep ur head down." Then he rang Clarke's number, the call lasted seven minutes, and that's the last one he made on this phone.'

'That fits with what the police told me. They said he talked to the colonel's wife and got angry and upset when she said he was out of the country.'

She glanced up at the rain and tucked a few strands of hair under her scarf.

'What are you going to do now?' I said.

'Go to Khan's. If Arif isn't there, I will talk to the other drivers. Do you know how I can find a place called Stoke Newington?'

'It's not far. What's the address?'

She handed me a card from her purse. I keyed the postcode into my phone. 'You get the 476 bus to the High Street, then it's like a two-minute walk.'

For the briefest second our eyes met. It was like looking in a twisted mirror – both of us desperate to prove Behrouz was innocent, both of us protecting people we loved, and both terrified of what we might find out on the way.

'Thank you,' she said, and walked towards the gate.

'Hey, Aliya!' I called. 'Hang on!

ALIYA

I turned around. The boy was blinking fast and pulling at the spiky tuft of hair at the front of his head.

'I ... I could go with you if you want,' he said.

It was like being struck in the face. Now I understood why he had come, why he was so nervous. I backed away from him, fury shaking every fibre of my body. 'You told the police about the gun!'

'No!'

'They have sent you to spy on me.'

'No!'

'That is why you brought me the phone.'

'No! Course not.'

He didn't look me in my eyes when he said it.

'Then you want to sell stories about me and my family

to the newspapers!'

'No way! Don't be stupid.'

That made me even angrier. 'I am not stupid. Why else would you want to come with me? You don't even know me.'

'I . . .' His face grew red.

'Go on! Tell me the truth!'

'I want to help you.'

'Why?'

'Because . . . because I know how you feel about your family.'

How dare he! How dare he say that! My lip quivered. 'Do you have a brother who is in hospital accused of something he didn't do?'

He bent his head and gave it a small shake.

'Have you got a sister who's so scared that she won't speak, or a mother who has gone crazy with sadness?'

He shook his head again.

Anger slowed my words. 'Then how can you know how I feel about my family?'

He raised his eyes and spoke so quietly I could hardly hear what he was saying, 'I meant . . . I meant if something bad was threatening them, there's nothing I wouldn't do to save them.'

His answer surprised me so much that for a moment I didn't know what to say. 'That is why you want to help me?'

'Yeah.'

'Do you swear to this?'

'Yeah.'

I was still suspicious but the misery on his face made me want to believe him.

'It could be dangerous,' I said quietly.

'What do you mean?'

In my head I heard the hate-filled crowd outside the police station and saw the men in black suits who spat at me. 'People are angry. They think that I and my mother were helping Behrouz to make bombs. Even when they don't know that I am his sister, this is a bad time to be seen with someone who. . .' I pulled at my head scarf '. . . who looks like me.'

He shrugged. 'So ditch the outfit.'

'What does that mean?'

'Get rid of the scarf. Wear something that blends in. I dunno, jeans or something.'

'I do not have jeans.'

'I'll lend you some.'

'You! I cannot wear the clothes of a boy! It would not be decent.'

'Come on. We'll get the bus back to mine.' He was speaking as if I'd agreed. As if we were friends. I stepped back, still unsure. 'Your family will be there.'

'It's OK. My mum and dad will have left for work ages ago.'

An uneasy feeling spread inside my chest, but what choice did I have? I needed help and this skinny English boy with a tuft of hair like the beard of a billy goat was the only person in the whole world who was offering me any. 'All right,' I said. 'I will come with you.' I watched him carefully: all I saw in his face was relief.

We walked through the thin cold rain, side by side in silence. The streets were busier now, full of cars, lorries, bikes, taxis and people who belonged in this city, people who knew where they were going, while I was following a boy I barely knew. A boy I wasn't even sure I could trust. I felt a moment of doubt, an overwhelming urge to run while I still could.

'Quick, that's our bus,' he said.

Before I could resist, he was tugging my sleeve, pulling me along the crowded pavement and on to the bus. With a hiss and a clunk the door folded shut behind me.

The boy held out a plastic wallet. The machine beeped and the driver let him through. I opened my purse, uncertain how much to pay. The boy looked back. 'You can't use cash.' I felt myself go red. He held a bank card to the machine. It shot out a ticket. Still embarrassed I followed him upstairs, clinging to the handrails, toppling first one way then the other, while he took long easy steps down the aisle and flopped on to the long bench seat at the back. The bus braked sharply, throwing me on to a man reading a newspaper. I tried to pull myself up. 'Excuse me, please. I am sorry, I didn't mean . . .' but the picture on the front page sucked the words from my mouth. It was a pile of scorched bricks, charred wood and melted metal. Even before I read the words, 'Bomber's Cache of Hate Back-fires', I knew this was the garage where they'd found Behrouz.

The man glared at me. His lips moved. For moment I thought he was going to spit at me, like those men with the golden chains. The bus jerked forward. I fell backwards into the aisle and stumbled into the corner next to the boy. I grabbed a crumpled newspaper from the floor. There were pages and pages about Behrouz, all of it twisting the truth, saying he'd only worked for the British army so he could spy on the soldiers and wait for the best moment to strike. I pulled my scarf across my face and whispered, 'My father told me that in Britain everyone is innocent until they are proved to be guilty. Not Behrouz. No one is giving him a chance.'

'So, go on,' the boy whispered back. 'Why are you so sure he's innocent?'

'I know him. He's good and kind and he would never hurt anyone.'

'That's not going to sway a jury.'

'All right. It would take many weeks to get hold of the things they found in that garage – the chemicals, the parts to make detonators. He did not have time or money to do that. And until last week he was happy and normal, making plans for our future and smiling and joking, then suddenly he was so frightened that he jumped when anyone walked past our door.'

'So why didn't he go to the police?'

That question had been haunting me from the moment I'd found the gun, and now that the boy had asked it aloud, the dark coldness was filling my mouth.

'I . . . I . . . don't know.' I rubbed the steam from the window and peered down at the passing city through the spatter of raindrops. The answer to everything that had happened to Behrouz was out there, somewhere in that sprawling mass of streets full of dangers I couldn't see, people I didn't know and secrets I didn't understand.

'Come on,' the boy said. 'This is our stop.'

I made my way downstairs, gripping the handrails and avoiding the eyes of the other passengers. We hurried down a main street, cut down a side road, passed a garage, a shop selling phones, another selling brooms and plastic bowls piled up on the pavement, and turned a corner into a square of new houses, built of pale yellow bricks with garages at the side and neat patches of garden at the front.

The boy walked down one of the gravel drives and when he unlocked the door, it was as if I was stepping into another world, one where everything was brighter and clearer than the dirty grey chaos I'd lived in since I came to London. It was how I'd imagined England would be: fresh, colourful, clean and safe, with soft carpets, shining paintwork and air that smelt of pine trees and lemons. I stood at the door of the sitting room gazing at the photos on the shelves – proud, smiling faces, snapped at weddings, birthdays and picnics – and thought of all our precious family photos left behind to be trashed by thieves and looters. I followed the boy up the stairs and along the hall, peeking through the half-open doors at a large pale-blue bedroom with a white frilly cover on the bed, and a smaller room laid out like an office, with a computer and a desk piled high with papers. I felt shy about entering the boy's bedroom, so I stayed by the door and looked at the posters, the laptop and the games console that was so much newer and slimmer than the old one my cousins used to play on. The boy rummaged through his drawers and threw me a pair of jeans, a black T-shirt, a hooded sweatshirt, a pair of thick white socks and a baseball cap. 'You'll need this as well.' He tossed me a belt. 'Change in the bathroom if you want. I'll look out some of Mum's old trainers.'

I crossed the landing to the sparkling white bathroom and sat on the edge of the bathtub, running my fingers across the fluffy towels and the rows of bottles and creams before I took off my scarf, stepped out of my sandals and salwar-kameez and pulled on the boy's socks and jeans. Even with the belt drawn in as tightly as it would go, the jeans hung loosely on my hips. I rolled up the legs, put on the T-shirt, and took some steps around the room. The clothes made me walk differently and feel different. I pushed my hair into the baseball cap and glanced in the mirror, shocked by the stranger who stared back at me. I was pleased. If I didn't recognize her, there was a good chance that no one else would either. I slipped the phone into the deep pockets of the jeans. I'd never owned a phone before, but the girl in the mirror looked as if she'd feel lost without one. I stuffed my old clothes into my backpack and I was standing on the landing when the boy came out of his parents' bedroom holding a pair of trainers. His eyes swept from my face to my feet. My cheeks burned.

'Yeah, that works,' he said. 'You want something to eat before we go?'

I hopped after him, pulling on the trainers, and sat down at the table in the kitchen while he made me a peanut butter sandwich and a mug of sweet, milky tea. I took a small bite of the sandwich. I'd tried peanut butter before, when Behrouz brought a jar of it home from the army base, but I still wasn't sure if I liked the taste or the way it stuck to my teeth and I definitely did not like this square white English bread that felt like sponge. But it was kind of him so I ate it. The kitchen was very neat and everything in it was shiny and new, just like the kitchens I'd seen in movies and magazines.

'You are very lucky to live in a house like this,' I said.

'We nearly lost it when Dad's business was on the skids.'

I wanted to ask him what that meant but he seemed upset and began to clear the table, so I said, 'Your father is a nice man.'

He crashed the plates together so hard I thought they would break.

'I've been thinking about Behrouz not going to the cops,' he said.

'Yes?'

'Maybe whoever did this to him was so powerful your brother didn't think the police could protect him.' He kept his back to me, as if he didn't want to turn around. 'Has he made any enemies since he's been here? You know, anyone dodgy he's rubbed up the wrong way?'

Dark doubts numbed my tongue. I couldn't let them win. 'Maybe this terror group Al Shaab, who claim he is their bomb-maker. Perhaps they did this to him because he refused to make their bombs.'

The boy turned to look at me. His face went still. I thought the mention of Al Shaab had made him angry and he was going to order me out of his house. But he didn't. He fetched out his phone. 'How do you spell Shaab?'

'With two As. It's Arabic for "The People".'

'Is that what you speak, then, Arabic?'

'No, I speak Pashto and Dari, but we learn Arabic at school. It's the language of the Koran.'

He scrolled up and down, his jaw muscles tense. 'There's not that much about them, it just says they're a shadowy terrorist organization that's claimed responsibility for attacks in Britain, Pakistan and Afghanistan. Maybe someone used their name to make it look worse for Behrouz.'

I shook my head. 'No. The man who called the police told them things about other Al Shaab bombings that only the bombers would know.'

He chewed on his nail as if he was thinking this over,

then he handed me a little plastic card. 'Here.'

'What's this?'

'Mum's Oyster card. It's a pass – for buses and Tubes. She hardly ever uses it.'

My eyes burned. I looked away. This boy had done more than give me clothes and food and a travel card. He had pulled me back from despair and given me hope. Though I still didn't understand why he would do all these things for a stranger.

'Thank you,' I whispered.

'Are you all right?' he said.

'Yes.' I quickly slung my backpack over my shoulder and slipped the pass into the pocket of my jeans.

'OK,' he said. 'Let's go.'

DAN

It was weird how different she looked in my clothes – stronger, straighter, more determined. She was still on edge, though. All the way to Stoke Newington her eyes kept darting to my face as if she was still trying to work me out. I just had to hope she wouldn't manage it. Khan's Cars was on the corner of a long string of shops but you could see a mile off which one it was, due to the massive hole in one of its front windows and the angry-looking graffiti sprayed across the other. A bloke on a ladder was busy scrubbing it off, working his way down to the dripping red 'OUT!' scrawled at the bottom. As soon as Aliya saw the state of it she pressed her wrist to her mouth and her eyes slid away, shiny with tears.

We squeezed past the bored-looking men hanging

round the doorway and walked over to the woman at the dispatch desk. She was about Mum's age, smooth dark skin, tiny red-streaked plaits scraped into a bun, and pink plastic earrings that rattled and clacked when she looked up.

'Are you Corella?' Aliya asked.

'That's me. Where do you want to go?' Her voice was deep, with a strong Jamaican accent.

'I don't want a cab,' Aliya said. 'I am the sister of Behrouz Sahar.' She said it quietly but with a touch of defiance. Every head in the room snapped round. Corella's smile faded fast. 'Please,' Aliya said. 'I need to ask you some questions.'

'What about?'

'The jobs Behrouz did this week and the people he picked up.'

A scuffle broke out behind us, one of the drivers elbowing people aside in his hurry to get to the street. Corella shouted after him, 'Hey, Karim, where are you going? I've got a job for you.'

He didn't stop. Her dark eyes flashed back to Aliya. 'You shouldn't be here. You'd better leave. Before Mr Khan gets back.'

'Please,' Aliya said. 'It's important. It will take only a few minutes.'

Corella wasn't happy about it but she unlocked the side door. Keeping a wary eye on the entrance, she beckoned us into the cramped office.

'Behrouz is not a bomb-maker,' Aliya said. 'You know him, you know he would never hurt anybody.'

Corella sighed and shook her head. 'When I saw the news I said to my husband this doesn't make sense, not at all. But you've got to admit it looks bad. All those chemicals and detonators. We had a gang of bikers round here last night, threatening to torch the place and accusing Mr Khan of running an Al Shaab terror cell. The punters are keeping well away, even our regulars are cancelling.'

'Can we have a look at Behrouz's satnav?' I said.

Corella threw me a suspicious look. 'Who are you?'

'My name's Dan. I'm . . . I'm helping Aliya. So, can we see it?'

'Sorry. The police took it away when they came for his cab.'

'Can we speak to Arif then?' Aliya said.

'Arif?' Corella kissed her teeth. 'He's been picked up by Immigration.'

'What do you mean?'

'He got caught in one of those government spot checks.'

Aliya's eyes widened. 'Are they going to deport him?'

'Who knows? He told me his visa was all sorted, just a few more days and the paperwork would have been through.' She glanced across at the other drivers. 'They blame Behrouz. They think they're all going to get harassed now. Half of them daren't even come in to work.'

'But he didn't do anything!'

A green light flashed on the desk. Corella quieted her with a raised finger and leant into the speaker. 'Khan's Cars. How may I help you?' She tapped the computer, her brightly painted nails clicking against the keys. 'Pick-up address? Phone number? Thank you, sir. I'll have a cab with you in five minutes.'

She called to one of the smokers in the doorway. 'You can take this one, Steve.' She tore a slip of paper off the printer and poked it through the grill. A lanky man with a thin grey ponytail dropped his cigarette, ground it out on the step and came over to collect the docket. When he'd gone, I pointed to the computer. 'Have you got all Behrouz's jobs on there?'

'Of course. The police took copies of them going right back to the day he started.' Corella made a snorting noise. 'What are they going to do, interview every punter he ever picked up?'

'Was there anything strange about the jobs he did just before the explosion?' I said.

She pressed her knuckles to her mouth, thinking hard. 'There was one thing.'

'Yeah?' I tried not to look desperate.

'I had an airport run come in, Tuesday morning, pick up at nine from Luton. That's good money. I rang him at six-thirty to offer it to him and he turned it down, said he was in Tottenham and wanted work that would keep him in that area till lunchtime – Finsbury Park, Seven Sisters, anything out that way.'

Aliya was frowning as if she was having trouble taking this in. 'Why was my brother in Tottenham at six-thirty in the morning if he was not working?'

'You tell me,' Corella said.

'Why did he want to be round there at lunchtime?' I asked.

'Didn't say.'

'Did you find him a job up there?'

'Yes.'

'Can you give us that address?'

Corella looked doubtful. 'I don't—'

'And a list of all the other jobs he did this week?' Aliya said.

'Mr Khan wouldn't like it.'

Aliya was getting agitated. 'Please. I have to find out where he went.'

Corella hesitated, glanced at the door, then starting tapping the keyboard with her crazy nails. 'This might take a minute or two.'

The back door banged open and a heavyset man with close-cropped grey hair and a bristly black moustache stomped into the office.

Corella jumped. 'Oh, Mr Khan—'

The man's eyes flew from my face to Aliya's and lingered on her clothes for a couple of seconds before he exploded, yelling at her in some language I didn't understand. Aliya looked petrified, so I said, 'Look, Mr Khan. We don't want to make trouble. We just want to know what jobs Behrouz did this week.'

Khan's lips curled back in a snarl. 'Why? Why do you want to know this?'

'We think he is innocent.'

'I'm not giving you anything. All this trouble happening to me and my drivers because of Behrouz Sahar. Police here, people writing filthy words on my windows. He has brought shame on my community and my business!'

He was a pretty scary guy but I managed to keep calm. 'I told you, Mr Khan, we think he's innocent. If we knew where he went and who he picked up, it might help us find out what really happened to him.'

A vein bulged on his forehead. He moved towards me, jabbing the air in front of my chest. 'You stay away from my office and my drivers. Do not mess with this or there'll be trouble for you!'

Corella touched his arm. 'Come on, Mr Khan. It's just a few addresses. Where's the harm?'

He smacked her hand away, hissing through yellow teeth, 'You keep out of this!'

He stepped back to the door and called, 'Karim!' A young, hard-faced bloke ambled in, the one who'd run off in such a hurry when Aliya said who she was. He moved towards us, flexing his fingers.

'You heard Mr Khan,' Corella said, slipping her plump body between us and Karim. 'He wants you to leave.' Her bracelets clicked as her arms swept us out into the waiting area. Khan lumbered after us, still ranting. We pushed through the staring drivers into the street and broke into a run, cutting through a twisting pathway, down past a churchyard, through to another street, round the back of some scabby flats till we got to a park. I pulled Aliya through the iron gates. There was a cafe in a building that looked like it used to be a big posh house. We ducked under one of the dripping umbrellas outside and flung ourselves down on the chairs.

'I cannot believe that man was my father's friend,' Aliya said gasping for breath. 'He cares only about his business and the "shame" for his community. Nothing for Behrouz. I hate people who think their stupid honour is more important than truth or people's lives.'

I got out my phone and did a search for a number.

'Who are you calling?' Aliya said.

'Khan's.'

'Are you mad?'

Corella's voice rasped through the speaker. 'Khan's Cars, how can I help you?'

'It's Dan.'

There was a split-second pause. Then she said, 'Where are you now, sir?'

'The caff in the park down the road.'

'No problem. I'll arrange for the item to be picked up and brought to you at twelve-thirty.'

'OK. Thanks.'

I thought Aliya would be impressed. Wrong. She glared at me. 'I don't understand. How did you know she would send someone?'

I made a 'phone me' sign with my thumb and little finger. 'She was doing this when she chucked us out.'

'What does it mean?'

'Call me. People do it on telly when they want viewers to ring in and vote for them.'

Going by the blank look she gave me, I guessed she wasn't a big fan of TV talent shows, but the explanation calmed her down a bit.

'Do you want a drink?'

'I don't have much money.'

I shrugged. 'I'm buying. What do you want? Tea, Coke?'

'I will have tea.'

She followed me inside and sat down at one of the tables while I went over to the counter. When I got back she was checking the screen on Behrouz's phone and writing on one of the napkins.

'What are you doing?'

She turned the napkin so I could see it. She'd drawn a kind of grid and filled in all the stuff she knew Behrouz had been doing from the moment he started acting strangely at the Meadowview fundraiser till the moment that lock-up exploded: the times and dates of the phone calls he'd made and received, the texts he'd been sent, the photos he'd taken.

We drank our tea staring at the blanks on the grid, not saying much at all.

Corella had seemed trustworthy enough but I didn't want to take any chances. At twenty past twelve, even though it was raining, I made Aliya leave the cafe and we huddled under a tree to one side of the entrance so we could see who Corella had sent before they saw us. Aliya was nervous, chewing the cuff of the hoodie I'd lent her, the brand-new Hollister one that had cost me a fortune. Did I say anything? No. She could trash everything I owned and we'd still never be even.

We were getting soaked, watching mothers hurrying past with buggies, kids wobbling along on rollerblades and old people walking ratty little dogs in tartan coats. Then a scrawny guy came down the path, tugging the collar of his jacket. He was young, seventeen maybe, ginger hair, spots. He glanced nervously over his shoulder before he walked up the steps of the cafe. We followed behind, skirting the busy seating area, while he bought a can of Coke at the counter and took it over to one of the tables. We still weren't sure he was the right person till he started turning a bright-orange Khan's Cars card in his fingers.

I started forward. Aliya pulled me back. 'I don't trust the look of him,' she whispered.

So we hung around a bit longer, checking to make sure he really had come alone, before we went over to his table and sat down.

'Here.' He kept his eyes on his Coke and pushed a printout into Aliya's hand. 'That's all Baz's jobs for this week. Anyone asks, you didn't get it from me.' He pushed his chair back and stood up. I wanted to keep him talking. 'You're young to be driving a cab, aren't you?' I said. Feeble, but the best I could do.

'I'm not a driver,' he snapped. 'I'm an apprentice mechanic. It's a good job and I don't want to lose it. So keep your mouth shut.'

Aliya was frowning at him, probably thrown by his broad Scottish accent.

'Course. What's your name?'

'What's it to you?'

I shrugged and held my hands up. 'Just being friendly.'

He hesitated, as if strangers being friendly wasn't something he was used to. 'Connor,' he said grudgingly.

'I'm Dan. She's—'

'I know who she is.'

'Are you a friend of Behrouz?' Aliya said.

He scowled in her face. 'Not any more.'

She held up the job list, her eyes cold with fury. 'Then why did you bring me this?'

'Corella made me. I owed her a favour. If you ask me, your brother deserves everything he gets.'

Aliya's head jerked back as if he'd slapped her. 'No!'

Connor dropped his fists on the table and hissed at her, 'I used to think he was all right, but bad stuff's happening to good people because of him.'

'No! This is not true!'

I kicked her foot to shut her up. 'What people?'

'My mate Arif, for starters,' Connor went on, staring Aliya down. 'He's been letting me kip on his floor and he was doing fine, sorting his visa, getting a bit of money together, never been in any trouble till Behrouz turned up.'

Aliya lifted her chin. 'If Arif is in trouble, it is not because of Behrouz.'

'Oh, no?' Connor dropped his voice and hunched forward. 'Tuesday afternoon he turns up looking shifty as hell, drags Arif behind the workshop and they're talking together for ages, yackety bloody yack.'

'What were they talking about?' I said.

'How do I know? They weren't speaking English, but Behrouz kept pointing to something on his phone.'

I glanced at Aliya then back at Connor. 'Was it a photo?'

'Maybe, I couldn't see.'

'Did he say anything that might have been a name?'

Connor frowned. 'I dunno, it was all gibberish to me, but maybe . . . Aerobi, something like that . . . no . . . Sarobi. That's right. Sarobi. Next thing I know, the two of them have disappeared and Arif doesn't come home till three in the morning. Following day he's all agitated, checking his messages every two minutes, and there's no sign of Behrouz. I know something's up but

Arif won't tell me what. That evening we're nipping out to get a takeaway and suddenly there's four blokes in black, flashing IDs in Arif's face and hustling him into their van.'

I sat forward. 'What kind of van?'

'One with "Are You Here Illegally? Go Home or Face Arrest" in letters a mile high down the side. Anyway, he starts shouting, telling them his visa's coming through and this old lady steps over, demanding to know what's going on and they tell her they've had a tip-off that he lied on his application.'

'What has this to do with Behrouz?' Aliya said desperately.

'Are you thick or something? That was the night his bomb factory blew up in his face. I reckon that's what all the whispering was about. Your brother was trying to drag Arif into some bomb-making scheme with him and his terrorist mates from Al Shaab and when Arif refused, Behrouz called Immigration and told them a pack of lies to get rid of him.'

Aliya didn't flinch. 'Arif was Behrouz's friend. He would never do something like that to him.'

Connor jabbed his finger into his chest. 'I was there. I saw it with my own eyes, and no one's heard a word from Arif since. Nothing. Your brother's trouble. Everyone at Khan's knows that.'

'Corella doesn't believe he is guilty.' Aliya's voice was steady but I could tell she was having trouble keeping it that way.

'Corella's a soft touch. She helped me out when I had a problem with a bent MOT. But this is different.'

'Yes! Different because Behrouz is innocent!' She said it so loudly people were turning round.

He glared at her for a couple of seconds, too angry to speak, then he kicked the chair and stormed off.

I couldn't believe she'd lost it like that. 'What did you do that for?' I hissed. 'We need to get him on side.'

'I'm sorry. He made me angry.' She got up to go after him.

'I'll do it,' I said. I caught up with him at the top of the steps. 'Hey, Connor. C'mon.'

He shrugged my hand away. 'You want to teach your girlfriend some manners.'

'She's not my—' I stopped. Let him think what he wanted. 'Look, she was well out of order but she didn't mean it. She's upset.'

'Yeah? Well, she's not the only one. My best mate's gone missing.'

'I know. But you want to find out what's happened to Arif, we want to know what was going on with Behrouz, and they've got to be connected, so why don't we swap numbers and if we hear anything, we can let each other know?'

He eyeballed me for a bit, then he nodded and got out his phone. As soon as he'd sent me his number I ran back to Aliya, pressing keys, saving it to the memory, and knocked into a man heading for the next table. He brushed off my apology but when he sat down I could see he'd spilt his coffee all down his front. I turned my back to him and dropped my voice below the hum of chatter and clinking plates. 'Connor's OK. He was just upset about his mate. And you've got to admit, Arif getting picked up the same night as Behrouz was nearly killed, it's a bit weird.'

She looked down and nodded. 'I know. I should never have said those things.'

'Maybe you should tell him that yourself. I'll send you his number. So what does Sarobi mean?' I said. 'Could it be Cement Face's name?'

She was thumbing through the contacts on Behrouz's phone, only half listening. 'I know only a place called Sarobi. It is a town between Kabul and Jalalabad.'

'Oh, right,' I said, disappointed. 'What are you looking for?'

'The number of Mrs Garcia at the refugee centre. I am going to send it to Connor. Maybe she can ring Immigration for him and find out what happened to Arif.'

'Would she do that?'

'I think so. She helped us with our papers when we first got here.' Her eyes drifted across the crowded room as if a memory had caught her off guard. I waited. Whatever it was, she was keeping it to herself.

'Hey, you OK?' I said.

She rubbed her hands across her face. 'I am scared.'

Me too. Scared to go on, scared to stop, scared of the

truth, scared of the lies, and right then scared stiff she was going start crying. I couldn't deal with that.

'It's OK,' I said. 'We can do this. You and me.' *Who was I kidding?*

I snatched up Behrouz's job sheet and checked the list. 'OK, so the last job he did was this Tottenham one on Tuesday. He picked up a woman called Vera Barnes at eleven-thirty and took her to Tottenham Hale station. According to Corella, he was in the area already and took the job so he could stay round there till lunchtime.'

She wiped her face with her sleeve. 'Yes, and lunchtime was when he took the photos of Cement Face.'

'Exactly. So I reckon he went to Cement Face's work, waited for him to go outside for a fag in his lunch break, grabbed a few shots of him, then drove off in a hurry.'

Aliya unfolded the napkin with her grid on it and added the stuff about Behrouz going back to Khan's, talking to Arif and mentioning Sarobi. Even from where I was sitting, there were still more blanks on it than facts.

'What we need is a motive,' I said.

'What is that?'

'A reason for doing a crime.'

She nodded and wrote MOTIVE in big letters under her grid, underlining it twice and putting a big question mark next to it.

'OK. Let's go to Tottenham and see this Vera Barnes. You never know, he might have said something to her on the way to the station.'

Aliya was very quiet on the bus and the Tube. To be honest, I preferred it that way. It gave me time to think. We'd found out quite a lot in one morning. Some of it, I really didn't like. And the thing with this Al Shaab terror group claiming Behrouz was their bomb-maker kept buzzing round my head like a fly in a can of rotting worms.

ALIYA

'd really believed my English was good and getting better. Today I realized that knowing words would never be enough. It was the things people didn't say, the hints and gestures, like Corella signalling 'phone me' with her fingers, that were going to save Behrouz. The underground station was the same, full of arrows, maps and signs sending people scurrying off in every direction. The boy seemed to understand them all, twisting and turning through white-tiled corridors and rushing down steep juddering escalators on to a crowded platform with a tunnel at the end that gaped like the mouth of a cave. I stared into the circle of black, wondering what other signs he'd been following that I hadn't even known were there.

'When we see Mrs Barnes, I want to ask her the

questions,' I said.

He shrugged. 'OK. What's your cover story?'

'What is that?'

'A fake reason for talking to her. You can't tell her the truth.'

I'd forgotten that I'd have to lie. 'I will think of one,' I said.

The train pulled in with an ear-splitting screech. I flinched away from the clumsy whoosh of the doors. The crowd swept me inside, jamming me so tightly that I couldn't free my hand to reach for the rail. The train gathered speed. I looked round for the boy. He wasn't there. Maybe he hadn't got on. I didn't know where I was or where I should get off. What would I do? A baby was screaming, someone stamped on my foot. I couldn't see faces, just arms and elbows jostling me. I couldn't breathe. I closed my eyes. The train stopped. The doors opened. The people poured out like rice from a sack, carrying me with them.

'Hey, where are you going?' The boy caught my arm and pointed at the map above the seats. 'It's ages yet.'

He stood next to me swaying with the train. I didn't speak. I stared at the web of colours on the map, reading the names, memorizing the stations, as if I was back in Kabul, studying for an exam.

Half an hour later we burst on to the street. I was so hot and sweaty from the train ride that for once I didn't mind the rain. I tipped my head back as I walked and let the cooling drops run down my face. The street streamed with people rushing to buy lunch, some clutching paper cups and bags of sandwiches, others dashing into cafes. I felt a twinge of hunger and gave my stomach a little punch to stop it growling. A bus pulled away from the bus stop and eased into the traffic, revealing a poster across the road showing the London Eye lit up at night in a rainbow of coloured lights.

'Have you been on it many times?' I asked the boy.

'The Eye? No, never.'

I was surprised. 'Why not?'

'We were going to take my nan for her birthday but she broke her ankle so we couldn't go.'

'I can see it from our flat. I would love to take a ride on it.'

'Yeah, it'd be a laugh. Tell you what, when this is over and we've got Behrouz off, I'll take you on it to celebrate.'

I shook my head and smiled. 'No. I will take you to say thank you for helping me.'

The smiles froze on our faces. We both looked away. What if this was never over? What if we couldn't prove Behrouz was innocent? I think we were both glad when my phone bleeped. I pulled it from my pocket. It was Connor. I put it on speaker and held it between us. Connor's voice sounded quieter. Scared.

'Your Mrs Garcia just phoned Immigration for me. You're right. There's something weird going on.'

I felt my grip tighten on the handset. 'What did she say?'

'According to their records, their officers questioned Arif, checked his details were in order and let him go. But that's a lie. Five minutes after they got him in the van, they drove off.'

Thoughts swirled round my brain, turning into handfuls of nothing when I tried to catch them. The boy had his head down, rubbing the back of his neck, but I could see he was trembling.

'Will you tell this to the police?' I asked Connor.

'Who are the feds going to believe? Me or Immigration? And I just got talking to Geoff.'

'Who is Geoff?'

'One of the other dispatchers. He said some foreign bloke rang Khan's on Tuesday afternoon, asking if Behrouz worked there, and when Geoff said yes, he slammed the phone down.'

I got out my grid. 'What time was this?'

'Around two. As soon as Geoff told Behrouz about it he panicked, and that's when he went running off to find Arif. What's it mean?'

The boy said, 'Dunno. But keep your ears open.'

I cut the call, feeling as if I had kicked over a rock and glimpsed a vast stinking sewer underneath. I waited for the boy to say something. He just chewed his bitten fingernails and frowned at a crack in the pavement.

Mrs Barnes's house was small and old, with bent rusty

railings at the front and stalks of grass sprouting through the path. As I lifted the knocker the boy gripped my wrist. 'Whatever she says, don't lose it. OK?'

'You mean I mustn't get angry?'

'Yeah.'

I shook off his hand and rapped the knocker hard. An elderly woman with a face webbed with wrinkles came to the door, patting a curl of white hair into place.

'Oh, I thought it was the police. They said they'd be popping round. I can't imagine what it's about.' Her pale eyes searched mine. 'Anyway, what can I do for you, dear? Are you collecting for something?'

'No. Um, Mrs Barnes, it is about my . . . friend.' I was speaking too fast but now she'd said the police were on their way, I was anxious to get away. 'He drives a minicab. I think he took you to the station on Tuesday.'

I waited for the anger, the hateful words, the door slamming in my face. Mrs Barnes didn't shout or slam the door. She smiled. 'That's right. I went to my sister's in Hertford. I've only just got back.'

'Do you remember him?'

Her eyes crinkled up. 'As a matter of fact, I do. We had a lovely chat, all about his plans to go back to university and finish his engineering degree. I said to him, that's what this world needs. People who can make things.'

The boy gave me a tiny bewildered shrug. 'Do you watch much telly, Mrs Barnes?' he asked.

'Actually mine's broken. Your friend said if he had a

spare minute, he'd come round and have a look at it for me. Wasn't that kind?'

'So you haven't seen the news lately?'

'No, dear. My sister always turns it off. I can't say I blame her. They never report anything nice, do they?'

'And you don't read the newspapers?'

'I prefer the wireless. They have some lovely music programmes on.'

The boy held out the picture of Cement Face. 'Mrs Barnes, have you ever seen this man?'

The old lady slipped on her glasses and inspected the photo.

'No, dear. Why do you ask?'

It was one thing to think up a lie, another to pretend it was true. My mouth was so dry I couldn't get the words to come out, even though I'd stood at the end of the street and practised the story over and over. But it came easily to the boy.

'He got in our friend's cab after he dropped you at the station,' he said. 'Then he ran off without paying. We were in the area, so we said we'd ask around and see if we could track him down.' He even smiled his lopsided smile as he said it.

'That's terrible.' Mrs Barnes looked shocked. 'Was it a lot of money?'

'Yeah, quite a lot, and his boss is making him pay it back out of his wages.'

'I'm very sorry to hear that.'

'Well, thanks anyway. Sorry we troubled you.'

'Don't worry at all. To tell you the truth, it's nice to have a bit of company. I hope you find this man. And say hello to your friend for me. What was his name again? My head's like a sieve these days.'

'Baz,' I said quickly. 'They call him Baz.'

Mrs Barnes smiled and waved as I opened her creaking gate. I tugged my cap over my eyes and walked away very fast. The boy ran to catch me up. 'Total waste of time,' he grumbled.

'No, it wasn't. We know now that at eleven-thirty he was chatting to Mrs Barnes about university and offering to mend her television, and by two-thirty he was so scared that he ran off with Arif to get a gun.'

I walked on, staring at the ground. I could feel the boy's eyes on me. Finally he said, 'What are you thinking about?'

'An old pot I saw once in a book.'

'What?' he glanced up, not sure if I was serious. He saw that I was and said, 'Go on, then. What was so special about this pot?'

'There were just a few small pieces of it left, but some-one had remade the whole thing by filling the spaces between them with white plaster. And when you saw where the pieces fitted, you knew it was not possible for that pot to have been any other shape.'

The boy walked more slowly as if he was turning this over in his head. 'So?'

'It's like the grid I have drawn. If we are clever, we can use the tiny pieces of information we have to work out the whole of what happened to Behrouz.'

'Yeah.' He seemed unnerved. 'Or maybe just enough of it to get him off. Come on. Let's go to the station. Maybe he passed Cement Face's work on the way there.'

'All right.'

He tapped and stretched the map on his phone. 'It's about a half-hour walk.'

The sky was darkening, purple-edged clouds closing in as the rain grew heavier. We plodded through puddles, getting sprayed by passing cars and searching every side road for the wall in the photos. By the time we got to the station I was so wet I was sure I would never feel dry again.

'I'm starving,' the boy said. 'Wait here. I'll get us something to eat.' He slipped into the crowd, squeezing his way to a little kiosk, while I took one of the free newspapers from the crate by the ticket office. I held the paper in my hands, too scared to look at it in case I read bad news about Behrouz. A woman with short black hair and a brown leather jacket was leaning against the opposite wall, watching the crowd. Our eyes met for a second before she waved at a man coming through the barrier and hurried away. My eyes shifted to the boy. I felt a flutter beneath my ribs. He was talking to the other people in the queue, pointing to something on his phone. They were peering at the screen, shaking their heads. He ran back to me, holding out a bar of chocolate wrapped in shiny red paper.

I did not take it. 'What were you showing to those people?' I said.

'The photos of Cement Face. That wall he's leaning against has got to be round here somewhere and I was hoping one of them might recognize it.'

'Yes, but why do you have copies of Behrouz's photos on your phone?'

He flushed a little. 'My screen's bigger, it made it easier to see the details.'

That made sense. He was helping me, being kind. The flutter grew quieter. I felt ungrateful that it didn't disappear. Maybe I was just hungry. He pushed the chocolate bar into my hand and ran off to show the photo around some more, as if standing still would burn his feet.

I nibbled a small piece of the chocolate. It tasted good. Hard on the outside and crispy biscuit in the middle. I took a bigger bite to give myself courage and looked down at the newspaper, hoping for a miracle. Nothing had changed. Behrouz was still unconscious and the police were still waiting to interview him. The little scrap of relief this gave me was snatched away when I turned the page and saw a photo of Behrouz beneath the words 'The Evil That Men Do: Inside the Mind of a Bomber'. Someone in America had written this. A doctor who had never even met my brother. How dare she write these lies about him! I skimmed the other pages, glancing at pictures of food, cars, houses, clothes, anything to wipe the word 'evil' from my head. A name jumped out at me.

A young British soldier was killed on Wednesday afternoon, just a day after arriving in Jordan with an advance party to prepare for the arrival of his regiment.

Captain James Merrick, 29, who survived three missions in Afghanistan, died in what the army described as a tragic incident in the Jordanian desert in the east of the country. The army has begun an investigation into how he died, but army sources say he was killed by his own weapon while taking part in a training exercise.

My mind wouldn't work. The letters were shifting in and out of focus. The places where thoughts should have been were filling with fear and panic. All around me the station seemed to throb. I shrank back against the wall, seeing Merrick's face beneath his helmet, his beefy hands reaching out to throw me into his jeep, his gruff delight when he told us we were coming to England. The boy came running over.

'What's up?'

I held out the newspaper, struggling to speak. 'It's him. Captain Merrick. The one who helped us to escape from the Taliban.'

'What's he done?'

Blood roared in my ears as the reality sank in. I felt myself sway again, so terrified I could barely whisper the words. 'He's dead.'

The boy turned as pale as dough. His eyes dropped to the article.

'What's happening?' I whispered. 'Behrouz nearly killed, Arif dragged off where no one can find him, and Captain Merrick shot dead. Who is doing these things?'

The boy glanced back at the crowd and steered me towards the exit. 'I don't know, but let's get out of here.'

The street was jammed with cars, vans, lorries and trucks. I pulled my hood over my cap, feeling as sick and scared as the moment the Taliban slid their death threat under our door. Only this time Behrouz wasn't going to appear out of nowhere with a crazy plan to save us.

I plodded along behind the boy, shivering and weighed down by grief for Captain Merrick. I had met him only once, but I owed him my life. Nothing seemed real. Even the honking horns and the rattle of the traffic seemed faint and distant, as if they belonged to another world that had spat me out into nothingness and would never let me back. For a long time the boy was silent too. Maybe he'd had enough of my nightmare and he didn't know how to tell me.

'You don't have to go on helping me,' I said.

He swung round. 'We're going to sort this, Aliya. You and me. All right? Whatever it takes.' He said it fiercely but as he turned away I saw his lip tremble.

'Thank you,' I whispered. He walked on, head down, his hands stuffed in his pockets. We were supposed to be looking for the wall in the photo but I was too deep in my thoughts to see anything, too busy trying to find one single thread of sense in the tangled knot of horrors in my head.

'Aliya!' The boy was calling me. I jerked my head up. He was walking faster, breaking into a run, dodging and swerving through the beeping cars, shouting at me to hurry up. He leapt on to the opposite pavement and kept running as if he was chasing someone, not looking back or slowing down. I speeded up but my legs felt wobbly and I couldn't catch him until he stopped at a crossroads and bent double with his hands on his knees.

'Why did you run?' I gasped.

He was red-faced and panting, trying to catch his breath. He pointed down a street of red-brick terraced houses that looked identical to all the others we'd passed. 'Let's try down there.'

'Why?'

'Some girl at the station thought the wall in the photo might be –' his eyes flicked to the big white building behind me – 'down the road near that church, St . . . Olaf's, but she couldn't remember the name of the street.'

The flutter was back beneath my ribs. It could have been unease, it could have been my heart beating too fast from so much running, or it could have been the continuing shock at the death of Captain Merrick. 'All right.'

I followed him to the end of the street and as we turned down another side road the houses gave way to empty ground littered with rubbish. Beyond that rose big metal buildings surrounded by high wire-mesh fences.

'What is this place?' I said.

'Looks like some kind of industrial estate.'

It was as big as a small town, full of criss-crossing roads and factories pumping tendrils of white smoke into the air, vast yards tangled with broken car parts, dusty machines, bags of cement and wooden pallets. The boy seemed unsure where to go. He glanced up and down, his eyes fixed on the passing trucks. Without warning, he started to move again. I followed him, trying not to breathe in the rancid smell that came and went with the breeze.

I heard him gasp. I looked up. A man in green overalls was crossing the road up ahead. For a second I couldn't work out why the boy had tensed. Then I saw the man's white rubber boots, just like the ones Cement Face had been wearing in Behrouz's photos. The man disappeared into the traffic. The boy started to run again. I tried to think as I pounded the pavement behind him, tried to work out what we should do if we actually saw Cement Face. We turned the corner into a section where the buildings were older, tucked behind high brick walls topped with black metal spikes. The boy had guessed right. He was good at guessing. This wall was just like the one in the photograph and so were the signs dotted along the top. There'd only been a corner of one in the photo, red and shiny, but now we could see they had 'Hardel Intercontinental Meats Ltd' printed across them in bright-yellow letters: a factory where they butchered and packed meat. That explained the stench, thick and fatty like something you could cut. There was a wide entrance gate about halfway down, choked with vans coming in and out. As we followed the wall around, the rancid smell grew stronger and the fear pressing down on my heart got heavier.

DAN

I'd nearly ripped my lungs out running after that red van. Maybe it was the shock of discovering Behrouz's mate Merrick was dead. Maybe it was realizing the power and reach of these thugs that Dad had got himself mixed up with. Either way, I'd been in a sick, angry daze and hadn't noticed the name Hardel Intercontinental Meats Ltd down the side of the van till the lights had gone green and it was pulling away. Then it had clicked: '—tal Meats Ltd' - that's what you'd see if half the letters were cut off by a pile of stolen washing machines. So I'd run like hell to find out where it was going and managed to follow a couple more Hardel's vans right up to the gates. I felt like death, but it had been worth it. I'd found the place where Cement Face worked and now I had a chance to find out his name. I pulled Aliya back around the corner.

'I'll go on my own, check the place out. Give me an Afghan man's name, quick, anything.'

'Dost . . . I don't know . . . Sajadi.'

'Give me one of those pictures of Cement Face.'

She got one out of her backpack. I scribbled the address of Hardel Meats along the bottom and walked back along the wall, repeating the name Dost Sajadi in my head. A couple of security guards stood at the gate, checking passes, sharing jokes with the van drivers, waving them through with their clipboards. I held back, trying to see inside, while I waited for a lull in the traffic. Workers in hats, blood-smeared overalls and rubber boots criss-crossed the yard, trundling trolleys past a couple of men who were directing the trucks down to a huge metal hangar right at the back. There were big signs everywhere – 'Zone A', 'Zone B', 'No Turning', 'Smoking Strictly Forbidden'. I studied the guards' faces. There wasn't much in it, but I went for the friendlier-looking of the two, held out the photo and took a long breath.

'Um . . . 'scuse me. I . . . I'm looking for this man. I think he works here.'

He glared at me. 'What makes you think that?'

I pointed to the Hardel's address at the bottom.

'Why d'you want him?'

My voice sounded thin and squeaky as I gave him the story I'd hurriedly cobbled together. 'I found a wallet with this photo and a load of cash in it. If it's his, I figured he'd want it back.'

The guard looked sceptical. 'Let's see the wallet.'

'My mum's handing it in to the cops, but I was hoping if I tracked him down, he might give me a reward.'

He seemed to buy that. Big black lies, little white ones, grubby grey ones – I was getting good at all of them. Just like my dad.

'Leave us your name and number and I'll get him to call you,' he said.

My stomach tightened. He'd as good as told me Cement Face worked there. He handed me his clipboard. I wrote down a made-up name and number.

'Do you know what time he'll be leaving?'

'He does earlies, so he'll finish at four.' He broke off to wave a van through.

'There was ID in the wallet,' I said, doing my best to sound casual. 'Name of Dost Sajadi. That him?'

'Dost? Nah, he's Tewfiq something or other.'

He called to the other guard. 'Hey, Terry, what's Tewfiq's surname?'

The other guard thought about it for a couple of seconds and called out, 'Hamidi.'

'Oh, right,' I said. 'Maybe the wallet's not his, then.'

He wasn't even listening. I headed back to Aliya, feeling pretty pleased with myself. 'He definitely works there. His name's Tewfiq Hamidi. That name mean anything to you?'

'No.'

'Let's wait for him to come out, then we'll follow him. He'll be knocking off around four.'

'Knocking off? That means to kill someone.'

'That's when you knock someone off. Knocking off means leaving for the day. Going home.'

Shivering, she looked at her watch and wrapped her arms around her chest. 'We must wait for forty minutes.'

'Let's get a sandwich and come back.'

She chewed her cuff and stared at the ground. 'I am not hungry.'

She was lying. I could tell.

'It's on me,' I said. 'I got thirty quid for helping Dad at Meadowview.' Thirty quid I wish I'd never earned.

She said solemnly, 'I promise that whatever happens, I will one day pay you back this money.'

I forced a smile. 'OK. I'll hold you to that. Meanwhile, what do you want in your sandwich?'

We got cheese rolls, crisps and cups of tea from the stand in the car park opposite. It wasn't much more than a wooden shed with a drop-down hatch on the side but it was doing a good trade, catering to anyone who fancied a snack and wasn't put off by the stink from the meat-packing plant. The man who served us said that after a while you got used to it. I couldn't see how.

My phone rang while we were eating. I nearly choked on my roll when I saw Dad's name on the screen and I couldn't believe it when he told me that that nosy cow

Eileen Deakin across the road had called him at work to tell him she'd seen me bringing my girlfriend back to the house.

'I don't want you having girls round when there's no one there. It's not right, Dan. Do you hear me? Anything could be going on, and Eileen says she was foreign.'

It was like a sick joke. Jez's mum and my dad telling me what was right and what was wrong. I was so angry I cut the connection and pretended I'd lost the signal.

I chucked the rest of my roll away and we wandered off among the cars, trying to work out exactly where Behrouz had been parked when he took his photos. Not in the car park, that was for sure. We followed the road round to a disused warehouse and spotted the side door of Hardel's bang opposite. There were even a couple of men in wellies standing beside it, lighting up. It was obviously where all the smokers went for a fag. Aliya had gone quiet again, her face screwed up, concentrating, thinking something through. 'To knock off is to stop work,' she said, suddenly.

'Yeah.'

'So what does "those DVDs are knock-off" mean?'

'What?'

'I heard someone say it once in the market.'

'Oh. Right. It means they're stolen.'

'But "he knocked his cup off the table" means he hit it and it fell?'

'Yeah.'

'It would be better to use different words.'

'S'pose.'

It was getting on for four o'clock by then so we walked back towards the main gate and slipped behind a row of cars in the car park, watching the early shift come straggling out, looking none too happy about life. I scanned their faces, worried we'd miss Cement Face in the crowd.

'Over there.' Aliya nudged me and looked away. I held up my phone, zoomed in on the tall stooping figure and caught his face full frame: the lumpy pockmarked skin, the hooded eyes, the mean mouth that had twisted into a smile when he'd said he was going to make Behrouz famous. It felt like the pavement was giving way. For a second I prayed it would swallow me up. It was definitely him. On his own, walking fast, towering over the rest of the workers. His head jerked around. Trying to keep my hand steady, I panned the phone to see what he was looking at. The security guard was calling him over. Cement Face didn't like it, but he went anyway, looking surly. The guard was rifling through the sheets on his clipboard. He tore something off. Jesus. It had to be the fake name and number I'd left. The guard leant forward, telling him something. When he held his flattened hand up level with his chin, I knew he was giving him a description of me.

As I ducked behind a green Mondeo, Cement Face glanced round, scouring the street for a thin boy, medium height, brown hair, wearing jeans and a grey hoodie, before he walked off, stuffing the strip of paper into his pocket. I tore off the hoodie and kicked it under the Mondeo.

Aliya stepped back. 'What are you doing?'

'That guard just told him what I look like. Give us your cap.'

She bent her head and took off the baseball cap. We'd found Cement Face, adrenaline had kicked in, and I should have been concentrating on our next move. Instead I was looking at the curve of her neck and the way her silky hair tumbled free as she lifted her head. I rammed the cap on my head and slipped my arm around her shoulder. She spun round in horror and shook it off. 'What are you doing?' she hissed.

'He thinks I'm on my own, so act like we're together. Cap, no hoodie, girlfriend – it's part of the disguise.'

'Oh.' She set off, walking beside me, stiff and awkward as a zombie.

'Relax,' I whispered. 'Act normal.'

'I can't. For me this is not normal.'

It wasn't normal for me either, but I wasn't going to tell her that. 'You've got to pretend. If he turns round, put your face close to mine so he can't see what either of us looks like.'

We merged into the stream of workers crowding the pavement, hoping Cement Face wasn't about to jump in a car and drive off. He headed for the bus stop and made a call while he waited. I stood with my back to him, keeping well out of his eye line. Aliya, who'd been peering over my shoulder, suddenly jerked her head back and looked up at me. 'He just turned round,' she whispered.

Close up, there was a weird mix of dark and light in her eyes, as if someone had splashed green ink in a glass of water and swirled it around. And they were nervous, like a lost dog's, watching everything, taking it in, trying to survive. I wanted to tell her I was sure we'd find the truth, that Behrouz would be all right and her family wouldn't get sent back to Afghanistan. Only it would have been another lie. I wasn't sure of anything.

We stood like that till the bus came, cold, uncomfortable and embarrassed. When Hamidi went upstairs, we stayed on the lower deck, ready to get off when he did without it looking too obvious. We'd been travelling for nearly forty minutes through parts of London I'd never seen before when he finally thudded down the stairs and pushed past us. The bus stopped. The doors swung open and he jumped off. Aliya made a move towards the exit. I held her back, waiting till the very last moment before I pulled her on to the pavement. By then Tewfiq Hamidi was about fifty metres ahead of us and we stayed right back as he turned down a dingy lane, trailed past a terrace of scruffy little houses that backed on to a railway line, crossed the road and disappeared down the drive-way of a corner plot that was almost hidden behind a thick jungle of shrubs and trees.

We broke into a run, squeezed through a gap in the

rotting fence and crept through the undergrowth just in time to catch him going into a scabby pebble-dash house, standing on its own in the middle of an overgrown garden. It had a peeling, dung-coloured door and filthy windows half covered with some kind of creeper that crawled across the front to a crumbling garage stuck on one side. The whole place looked totally abandoned until you noticed a tiny sliver of light seeping through a rip in the upstairs curtains.

'What do we do now?' Aliya whispered.

'We wait,' I said.

ALIYA

The overgrown garden looked ghostly in the misty rain but the damp earth smelt good after the rancid stink of the meat factory. Without taking my eyes off the house, I sank down with my back against a tree trunk, hugging myself for warmth and imagining what the old Aliya would be doing now, the one who always wore a salwar-kameez and a scarf on her head. The one who would never dream of running across London, searching for a man with brutal eyes, or standing close to a boy she'd known for a day and looking up into his face. But that Aliya didn't have a brother lying in hospital accused of being a terrorist.

Was Behrouz drifting in a haze of pain, listening for my voice? Wondering why I wasn't there? Or was he dreaming of life in Kabul when we were younger: my mother singing while she cooked, filling the house with warm delicious smells, my father reading aloud from the newspapers, sharing gossip from the hospital, tuning the radio to catch the news from the BBC, helping us with our homework.

A light snapped on in the hall. I started forward. The boy tensed too. Seconds later the front door opened, Cement Face came out, pulling on an old brown jacket. The burning in my chest made it painful to breathe. He waved his keys at the garage. The dented door jerked slowly upwards. I glanced at the boy. He had his phone out, taking photos. The car inside was low, black and shiny. It purred softly when Cement Face started it up. He nosed it forward, left it running and went back into the house. Minutes later he came out with another man, who was wearing a long black coat that flapped around his knees and carrying a hold-all which he threw in the back as he got into the passenger seat. As the car roared past I caught a glimpse of his face – leathery cheeks, fleshy nose and a hairless, knobbly head.

'I got the number plate,' the boy whispered. 'Any more cars turn up, get theirs too. I didn't get much of a look at the other guy. Did you recognize him?'

'No ... I don't think so.'

'Come on, let's see if we can get inside.'

I was shocked. 'We can't. We're not thieves.'

'How else are we going to find out what's going on?'

'What if they catch us and call the police?'

'Believe me, the last thing Hamidi's going to do is call the cops.'

'How do you know?'

'You don't get to drive a forty-grand BMW on a meat-packer's salary, not unless you've got some really dodgy sidelines going on.'

I glanced up at the chink of light in the curtains. 'What if someone is still in there?'

'Only one way to find out.'

He scrambled forward, pushing the branches aside. I stayed back, watching him walk up to the front door and ring the bell. I closed my eyes and counted. I'd got to twenty when he rang it again, holding his finger down. The shrill sound screeched through the silence. Nobody came.

'Come on,' he called, and disappeared down the side of the house. I crouched low as I shot past the front window and slashed my way through the waist-high brambles growing around the sides and back of the house. It made me think of a story Mor used to tell about a sleeping princess locked inside a castle surrounded by thorns. I didn't want to think about the way Mor used to be, and I didn't want to ask myself what it was that drove this boy, who had already fought his way to the little terrace at the back of the house and was peering through one of the windows with his hand cupped against the glass.

'Do you see anything?'

'An empty kitchen.'

He rattled the window frame, then stepped backwards, gazing up at the other windows and circling round to the side of the house.

'What are you looking for?'

'A way in.' He pointed up at a small window in the wall above the garage. 'That looks like our best bet.'

He dragged a rotting garden chair over to the back wall of the garage and used it to scramble on to the flat roof. I stood in the fading light, keeping an anxious lookout as he worked his penknife between the window and the frame. He levered it open a little and slipped his hand inside. A mixture of fear and excitement made me gasp as a catch clicked and the window swung open. I climbed up after him on to the roof, dropping on to my belly as I slithered across the wet buckled asphalt to scan the driveway.

'It's all right,' I whispered. 'No one is coming.'

The boy lowered himself through the window and disappeared for a couple of seconds before his face appeared again, gaunt and pale in the half-light.

'It's OK. You can step on to the toilet under the window.'

The terror, panic and disbelief I felt as I swung my legs through that narrow space was swept aside by the thought of Behrouz. If this is what it took to save him, then I would do it. I wriggled through the window feet first and dropped into a narrow bathroom. It smelt bad. There were finger-marks all over the sink, the tiles and the pink painted walls, and a pool of greasy water in the basin. We tiptoed on to the landing, adrenaline flooding my veins and sharpening my senses as we pushed open doors and looked into the bedrooms. There were three of them. All with bright-flowered paper on the walls, mattresses laid out on stained carpets and messy heaps of clothes scattered everywhere. The boy searched under the mattresses while I went through the clothes. We didn't find much, just a few coins, Hamidi's driving licence and the passport of someone called Wafik Faryadi.

'Come on,' the boy whispered. 'We can't hang around.'

We slunk down the stairs like prowling animals ready to flee at the first sign of cars or voices. The sink in the kitchen was full of dirty plates caked with slimy shreds of chicken, congealed curry sauce and chunks of pizza. I opened the cupboards one by one, not sure what I was looking for. I even checked inside the oven, smearing my hands with thick brown grease. The tall white fridge was empty too, except for some bottles of beer which rattled when I tried to close the door. I had to slam it twice before it clicked shut. The boy swept his hand across the top, scattering dusty menus and vouchers for takeaway food on to the floor. I quickly gathered them up and shoved them back. By now my heart was beating faster than a wedding drum. I took a breath and peeked into the room at the back. It was empty except for a dirty old couch and a wooden chair tipped sideways on the carpet. The boy nudged open the door of the front room, let out a low whistle and flung it wide. 'Look at this.'

The first thing I saw was a television so big it covered the whole space above the fireplace. In front of it was a couch covered in shiny leather and two matching armchairs with built-in footrests. The boy squatted down and flipped open the laptop on the coffee table. 'This is nearly two thousand quid's worth,' he said, 'and that TV must have cost a fortune.'

'If they have money to buy this television and this laptop, why do they live like dirty animals in a house that's falling to pieces?'

'This way no one knows they're loaded.'

'Loaded? That means "rich"?'

'Yeah.'

There were papers on the table, held down by a chipped glass ashtray overflowing with cigarette butts. With trembling fingers I set it aside and went through the papers: receipts for the TV and laptop, a letter from the landlord, payslips from Hardel Meats, and two coffee-stained envelopes. The letters inside them were typed on thick white paper and full of words I didn't understand. I handed them to the boy. 'What are these?'

He skimmed the writing. 'This one's a summons telling Hamidi he's got to go to court for assaulting some bloke called Greg Parkin.'

'What is "assaulting"?'

'Beating up. Attacking.'

Something creaked behind me. Fear spun me round. It was only the door swinging loose on its hinges. The boy read the second letter and frowned. 'He got lucky. Parkin dropped the charges.'

He handed them back to me. 'OK. Try the edges of the carpet. If you find any sections that aren't nailed down, we'll take a look under the floorboards. I'll check the ones upstairs.' He got to the door and looked back. 'If you hear anyone coming, run up to the bathroom.'

I refolded the summons and as I put it back I noticed a scrawl of pencil on one of the envelopes. It was Greg Parkin's name and address, written by someone uneducated who could barely form their letters. For a second I hesitated, then I tore it off, slipped it into my pocket and tucked everything back under the ashtray. The swirly red and orange carpet was so dirty it felt sticky to touch, and when I'd gone right the way round it without finding any loose nails, I went into the back room to search in there. As I knelt down my fingers brushed a dark mark on the carpet beside the fallen chair. It was wet.

'Hey, Aliya. Up here!' The boy sounded excited.

I ran to the staircase, freezing when I heard car tyres sweep the gravel outside. In a panic I saw the fridge door had swung open. I dashed down the hall and slammed it hard. A couple of leaflets fluttered off the top. I stuffed them into my pocket and hurtled up the stairs to the bathroom.

'Quick,' I hissed. 'They're back!'

The boy had removed one of the plastic tiles from the ceiling and he was standing on the toilet, shoving thick packets of money into the hole.

'Go on,' he said. He balanced the tile on his shaking fingers and hurriedly slid it into place. I squeezed past him, scrambled through the window and flattened myself on the wet roof. Beneath me the garage doors rumbled open. The boy pulled himself up after me and eased the window shut.

'They brought back a takeaway,' he whispered.

He didn't need to tell me – the rich scent of curry was making me woozy with hunger. He rolled over next to me and we lay side by side listening to the men shouting at each other as they got out of the car, arguing in English and Pashto about who owed who money for the food. I picked out at least four different voices before the front door banged shut. In my mind I did a frantic check of every room, every object and every door, trying to reassure myself that we'd left them all as we'd found them. A light snapped on in the bathroom. I stopped breathing. Some-one started to do his business. He made a lot of noise. The boy grinned. My cheeks burned hot. The man stomped out, leaving the light on, and went back downstairs to join the argument in the hall.

'What did you do to your hand?' the boy murmured.

I held it up to the glow from the window and felt a shiver of horror. It was blood, but it wasn't mine. 'It must have been on the carpet in the room at the back.'

I thought of the fallen chair beside the patch of damp and shuddered to think whose blood had been spilt on that carpet. Thunder rumbled across the sky and heavy spots of rain began to fall. We shuffled over to the wall, to get what shelter we could.

'Did you see that money? There must have been at least fifty grand in there.'

He was proud of his discovery, waiting for praise. The words stuck in my throat. How did he find these things – the bundles of money, the place where Hamidi worked? Why did little pockets of silence spring up whenever we talked about Behrouz?

'How did you know where to look?' I said.

'Didn't you see the dirty finger-marks round the edges of the tile? Dead give-away.'

I should have thought of that. I owed this boy so much and I felt ashamed that I had let my doubts creep back.

'Listen.' He jerked his thumb at the house. 'That music. It's the football. With any luck they'll be eating curry glued to the telly till half-time.' He crawled across to the side of the garage and looked over the edge. 'There's a pipe here, coming off the gutter. You OK to climb down it and sneak through the trees to the road?'

I nodded. He swung himself on to the drainpipe and jumped on to the gravel below. I followed behind, grabbing the gutter. As I scrabbled for a foothold between the crumbling bricks, headlights split the darkness and a car turned out of the lane into the driveway. The boy flattened himself against the side of the garage. I clung on to the gutter and leant out a little so I could peer through the leaves of the vine. The front door opened, splashing light on to a battered pale-blue hatchback. I strained to see the licence plate, flinching back as the driver's door opened and a man got out. The guttering creaked and shifted. I could feel it giving way, about to snap and bring me crashing down. As if from nowhere, the boy caught my dangling feet and guided them on to his shoulders, taking my weight. I closed my eyes and leant into the wall. We stayed frozen like that until the man had gone inside.

The moment the door banged shut, the boy crouched down so I could jump on to the ground. He caught my arm, dragged me through the trees and helped me to wriggle through the hole in the fence into the lane. 'That was close,' he panted. 'Did you get a look at them?'

'Not really.' I took out my phone as I ran.

'What are you doing?'

'Putting in the number of that car.'

We moved quickly, keeping our heads down, listening out for cars and footsteps. Even when we reached the bus stop, I was still trembling, partly with fear, partly with excitement. I whispered to the boy, 'We know Cement Face's name is Tewfiq Hamidi, we know where he lives and where he works, and that he is violent and probably a thief. This is good. I think he is the man who Behrouz was afraid of and now I need to find out why.'

The boy nodded but seemed troubled. 'How are we going to do that?'

It was my turn to feel proud of a discovery. 'I have

found the address of Greg Parkin. Let's go there tomorrow morning. Maybe he can tell us more about Hamidi.'

We were so wet and so muddy that other passengers on the buses and trains edged away from us. I didn't care. Inside I felt strong. I wasn't running from anyone. I wasn't cowering in a doorway being spat at. I was looking for the truth. I looked up at the boy. And I wasn't alone any more. I had a friend I could trust.

He promised to meet me outside King's Cross station at eight the following morning and offered to walk back with me to Swinton Street. He seemed surprised when I said no, but I needed a few minutes on my own before I returned to being the Aliya who looked after her mother and sister and didn't lie or wear jeans or break into houses.

It was nearly eight o'clock when I walked through the doors of the hotel. I crept into my room and pushed my phone under the mattress. Desperate to get clean and warm, I dropped my backpack and wet clothes in a heap and I went into the little bathroom to take a shower. It felt good to wash away the traces of Hamidi's filthy house, and as I scrubbed my fingernails I wondered for one heart-stopping moment if the blood on my hand could have been Behrouz's. I came out towelling my hair, shocked to see the empty backpack on the bed, my crumpled salwar-kameez hanging over the back of a chair, and WPC Rennell standing by the bed holding my jeans. She flashed me a big smile. 'Hello, Aliya. I thought I'd get these wet things laundered for you.'

I forced myself not to look at the mattress where I'd hidden the phone and fixed my eyes on the jeans dangling from her hands.

'Gosh, wherever have you been? They're all muddy.'

'Please, don't worry,' I said. 'I can wash them in the bath and dry them on the radiator.'

'It's no problem. There's a few things of Mina's that need doing as well. If I take them down now, they'll have them ready by the morning.' She shook them out and went on chattering. I watched her fingers slide in and out of the pockets. 'We don't want anything clogging up the hotel's washing machines, do we?' She gave a little laugh to ease the lie. It felt unreal. She was searching my things, just like I'd searched Hamidi's, and we were both pretending she was helping with my laundry. Still smiling, she pulled out my room key and the leaflets I'd stuffed in my pocket as I was leaving that house. I froze as I saw the damp scrap of envelope with Greg Parkin's address scribbled on it clinging to the back of one of them. She peeled it off.

'What's this?' she asked, scanning the writing. 'Something important?'

I held out my hand. She frowned as she handed it over and a silent whoop of relief rose in my throat. It was written in Pashto.

'It's a . . . shopping list,' I said, and dropped it in the bin. 'I need to wear those jeans tomorrow. Are you sure they will be dry?'

'Don't worry. I'll make sure you get them back first

thing. I was just the same when I was your age, always running home, doing a quick change and scrubbing off my make-up before my dad caught me.' She sat down on the bed, right on top of the phone, leaning back as if we were friends enjoying a chat. 'You were gone so long I was worried. Did you find a library?'

I was tired of her games. 'I'm hungry. Do you know where I can get something to eat?'

'There's kebabs and rice in your mum's room, but they'll be a bit cold by now. I could order in something else.'

'The kebabs are fine. I would like to get dressed now.'

'OK . . . I'll take these things down for you.'

'Next time, please don't worry about our washing. I will do it myself.'

I bolted the door behind her and tested it before I retrieved the paper from the bin.

As soon as I was back in my salwar-kameez I hurried to my mother's room. I found her just as I had left her that morning, sitting in the high-backed chair by the window, watching one of the news channels. Without moving her eyes from the screen, she murmured, 'Where were you, Aliya?'

I walked over to her and rearranged the shawl that had slipped from her shoulders, surprising us both when words I didn't expect dropped from my lips.

'I was looking for the truth, Mor.'

She turned her grief-stricken face to mine and for a

second a spark of pride appeared in her red-rimmed eyes. She lifted her hand and stroked my face the way she used to, and said, 'Pray God you find it.'

DAN

The house was empty when I got home and I managed to shower off the mud and change into clean clothes before Mum got back from her Zumba class. Cheeks flushed, ponytail swinging, she slipped off her jacket and I followed her into the kitchen.

'It's just you and me tonight, so I picked up a pizza on the way home.' She laughed and patted her thighs. 'Put back some of those calories I just burnt off.' She opened the box, filling the kitchen with the warm doughy smell that always meant a night in with Mum, because Dad didn't like pizza. But tonight, all I could think about was how miserable she'd be if it was just her and me permanently.

'Get some plates out. We'll have it in front of the TV.'

'Where's Dad?'

'Pub with Jez. Why?'

'Just wondered.'

I reached for the plates and closed my eyes for a minute, not sure how to ask her what I wanted to know. 'You know when his business was in trouble . . .'

She was heading for the door with the open pizza box. She stopped and looked back, surprised and frowning slightly. 'It's doing fine now, love. Don't you worry about that.'

'Yes, but does he ever talk to you about how he turned things around?'

'You're in a funny mood tonight.'

'Does he, Mum?'

'Well, no, not really. I mean, I know getting those big council contracts helped a lot, and I don't like to admit it, but Jez does his bit bringing in new work and doing the books. It was just a blip – that's the way it is when you run a small business.'

I followed her into the living room. She handed me the TV remote. 'Here,' she said. 'You choose. Anything you want as long as it's not football.'

I flicked through the channels, itching to check out the news, but that really would have got her worried. She held up a slice of pizza and bit off the corner. 'Eileen told your Dad you had someone round this morning,' she said, trying her best to sound offhand and not succeeding. 'A girl.'

'She's just a friend, Mum.'

'The one who phoned the other night?'

'Yeah.' I could feel my heart thumping.

'Eileen said she's foreign.'

'It's not a disease.'

'Don't be silly. Your Dad wants you to bring her round. We'd like to meet her.'

My heart almost stuttered to a stop at the thought of Dad meeting Aliya, looking her over, judging her, finding out who she was. 'It's not like that. She's not my girlfriend or anything. I'm just . . . helping her out.'

'What with?'

'Filling out forms and stuff. Her family haven't been here long.'

She gave me a funny little smile and ruffled my hair, as if she was about to say something sloppy.

'Get off!' I dodged away and turned up the sound. 'There's a new cop show starting – do you want to try it?'

Dad usually had a lie-in on Saturdays but I was up and on my way out well before seven, and not just to avoid him. Sleep had stopped being an option the night I saw Behrouz Sahar get kidnapped, and now the only time I could breathe properly was when I was doing something to help prove he was innocent. I'd seen him twice in my life for a total of maybe ten minutes, but he was all I could think about. Well, him and his sister. As I ran past Eileen Deakin's house I felt like chucking a brick through her front window. Interfering old bag. I got to King's Cross so early I had to hang around outside, watching bleary-eyed tourists dragging their suitcases into the station, but Aliya was early too, running across the concourse waving, with her backpack bouncing on her back, and by seven forty-five we were on our way to Wandsworth to find Greg Parkin.

The guy who opened the door was late twenties, six foot, packed with muscle, wearing track pants, a sweat-soaked T-shirt and a towel round his neck like he'd just got back from a run. He took a swig from a carton of juice and wiped his mouth with the back of his hand. 'Yes?'

'Um . . . are you Greg Parkin?' I said.

He glanced up and down the street, looking wary. 'Who are you?'

'My name's Dan and she's Aliya. It's about Tewfiq Hamidi.'

He slitted his eyes. 'What about him?'

'He . . . got in a fight with . . . my brother,' Aliya said.

'Why're you telling me?'

'We heard it's not the first time Hamidi's attacked someone,' I said, treading carefully. 'And, well, if it's OK with you, we wouldn't mind knowing why you dropped the charges.'

He tightened his jaw, about to tell us to get lost when a voice called out, 'Who is it, Greg?'

The woman who came down the hall was wearing a

short white dressing-gown. She was slim and pretty, with brown hair, honey-coloured skin and huge dark eyes, like a model or something. Parkin went on glaring at me. 'Couple of kids, asking about Hamidi.'

'Hamidi?' She glanced at me, looked questioningly at Aliya and said something in a language I guessed was Pashto. Aliya nodded and smiled and they chatted for a minute or two. I don't know what they said but the woman put her hand on the man's arm and said, 'It's all right, Greg. Let them in.' She nodded at me. 'I'm Zahra, Greg's wife.'

He hesitated for a minute, then stood back reluctantly to let us pass. We followed the woman into a warm, bright, open-plan room that was half kitchen, half lounge. Still chatting, she and Aliya sat down on the sofa, leaving Parkin and me a couple of armchairs. He sat there looking at me as if I was roadkill. After a bit he flicked his eyes at Aliya and said, 'What happened to her brother?'

Zahra stopped talking and turned to listen as I spun him the story we'd come up with about Hamidi driving into a petrol station, overtaking Behrouz in the queue and throwing a punch at him when he complained. The harder Parkin stared, the harder I tried to make the story sound authentic. I was so busy dropping in real details about Hamidi's black BMW and how the petrol station had been near his work at Hardel Meats that I couldn't work out why Aliya had suddenly stiffened and gone pale. I could have kicked myself when I realized I'd said her brother was called Behrouz, not Jawid, like we'd planned. But I ploughed on, talking faster, trying not to let Parkin see I was flustered.

Zahra glanced at him and raised an eyebrow. I couldn't tell if that was good or bad. He folded his arms and said, 'How did you get my name and address?'

Aliya chipped in then, like we'd planned: 'My brother talked to a lawyer who looked up Hamidi's police files.'

Who knew if that was even possible? Greg just worked his jaw and said, 'So why didn't this brother of yours come and see me himself?'

Aliya looked up, her eyes brimming with tears and told him the truth. 'He's too sick,' she said.

'Yes,' I added quickly. 'He's been off work since Hamidi hit him, getting headaches and dizzy spells, so we thought we'd, you know . . . help him out.'

I'm not sure Greg was convinced, but Aliya's tears had definitely won Zahra over.

'That man is a menace,' she said. She took a tissue from the pocket of her dressing-gown and as she handed it to Aliya I grabbed the chance to start asking a few questions of my own. I gave Parkin a nervous smile. 'So how come he had a go at you, then?'

He crumpled the juice carton, strode over to the kitchen area and dumped it in the bin. 'Because he's a nutter.'

It didn't look like he was going to say any more so Aliya turned to Zahra. 'What happened?'

She sighed. 'It was all because of me. I was waiting to pick Greg up from the station when Hamidi came burning round the corner in his BMW and smashed into the side of my car. So I got out and as soon as he realized I was Afghan he started yelling at me, trying to make out it was my fault and telling me a decent Afghan girl should be at home, not flaunting herself on the streets. You know what these people are like. I wasn't having it, though. I told him he'd been driving like a maniac. He went ballistic and came out with all that "how dare a woman talk to him like that?" stuff. Then Greg arrived. When he told Hamidi to back off, the guy grabbed a crowbar out of his car and attacked him, like really laid into him. I don't know what would have happened if the police hadn't turned up.'

Greg grunted and rubbed his jaw, as if he was reliving the pain.

'So why did you drop the charges?' I asked. I'd obviously hit a nerve, because he turned away like he hadn't heard me and started unloading the dishwasher, leaving his wife to answer.

'I went round to tell my parents about it, and an uncle of mine who was over from Kabul told me not to go ahead with the case because it was too risky.'

'Why?'

She gave a little shrug. 'He knew all about Hamidi, said he'd got dangerous connections who were known for intimidating people who got in their way.'

I glanced at Aliya; at last we were getting somewhere.

Zahra stood up. 'Do you kids want some breakfast? Greg just picked up some croissants.'

'Thanks,' I said, though I could tell by the look Greg threw her that he hadn't been planning on sharing them with us.

We moved over to the kitchen area and sat at the breakfast bar while he fiddled with this big fancy coffee machine and Zahra laid out plates, butter and jam, and ripped open a bag of warm croissants. It turned out she'd been born in London and her Pashto was a bit rubbish, so she asked Aliya if she'd like to come round some time to help her practise. The friendliness would have been great if she hadn't kept probing her about her family, where they were from, why they were here, stuff like that, and Aliya had to keep dancing round the details, trying not to give too much away.

'So did your uncle say anything else about Hamidi?' I said, as she handed me a croissant.

She pulled a disgusted face. 'Apparently he calls himself Commander Hamidi, but everyone else calls him Mad Dog because of his crazy temper.'

'Was he in the army, then?'

'You must be joking. He ran a private militia that did all the dirty work for some big warlord back in 1980s.'

I glanced at Aliya. 'What sort of dirty work?'

'Basically they guarded the fields where this warlord grew his opium poppies and ran a checkpoint where they robbed anyone who passed through, kidnapped them too sometimes. Then when the Taliban took over, this warlord was smart. Instead of fighting them, he cut them in on his drugs racket. They say he made millions. He'd probably still be at it if the Brits and Americans hadn't started cleaning up the Afghan drugs trade and put him at the top of their most-wanted list.'

'Did they catch him?'

'Oh, yes. And they had a big show trial.'

Aliya shifted in her seat and said quietly, 'The warlord that Hamidi worked for, do you know his name?'

Zahra frowned and snapped her fingers softly. 'Hang on . . . It'll come to me.'

'What happened to Hamidi?' I said.

'You won't believe this – somehow he managed to avoid prosecution and claim asylum in the UK. He said the Taliban were after him!' She gave a little snort. 'Which they probably were, for double-crossing them over some drug deal. And now he's here, I bet you any money he's importing heroin from his old connections in Afghanistan.'

I stopped chewing, suddenly not hungry any more. The thought of the wads of cash in Hamidi's bathroom, the little packets of white powder stashed in those appliances at Meadowview, and the footage they'd shown on the news of crazy-eyed Taliban fighters made me want to throw up. Did Dad have any idea what he'd got himself mixed up in?

Greg stuck a jug of milk under the electric steamer and raised his voice over the din. 'Can you believe it? Immigration letting that joker in. He's either got friends in high places or he gave someone a bloody enormous backhander.' He handed the steaming jug to Zahra, who spooned the frothing milk into the coffees.

'Greg still wanted to go ahead with the prosecution, but a couple of days after the attack we started getting harassed – threatening phone calls, car windscreens smashed, that kind of stuff – and I got scared. Then I found out I was pregnant and we decided we just didn't need the hassle, so we withdrew the charges.'

Greg pulled up a stool. 'I tell you, it stuck in my gullet, but what can you do?'

Zahra smiled at him and squeezed his arm as she went to fetch her iPad from the counter. 'I'll find you the name of that warlord, Aliya. My uncle sent me some of the trial reports from the Afghan papers. Honestly, I need to sort out my inbox.'

She took a sip of her coffee and peered at the screen. Out of nowhere her perfect face turned ugly. Her eyes darted over to Aliya then back again. As if in slow motion, I saw her coffee splash on to the shiny black floor tiles followed by her cup. The smash of breaking china coincided with her yell of fury: 'Get out!'

Startled, Greg jumped up. 'Hey, babe, what's wrong?'

She was so angry she didn't even hear him. 'I don't know what you want or why you came here, but you can get out now!'

Greg looked at us, half confused, half apologetic, and put his hand on her shoulder. 'What's the matter?'

She thrust her iPad into our faces. Her home page had a feed of news stories and she'd clicked on one of the photos. It showed a family lounging on a rug by a river, above the caption, 'Bomber's family picnic in the sun'. She jabbed at the girl in the photo. 'Aliya Sahar. That's you, isn't it? You're the sister of that bomb-maker!'

Greg sprang to his feet. Aliya stood up, her eyes fixed on the photo, her chest heaving. 'Yes, I am Aliya Sahar. But please, you must believe me. Behrouz is innocent. We—'

Zahra backed away as if we were contaminated, screaming at us to get out. Greg was yelling too. We didn't hang around. We were out that door and down the steps, running across the road on to the High Street.

Aliya was shaking and stumbling, dry sobs ripping through her chest. I pulled her into a doorway. 'Come on. Don't let it get to you.'

'It's not only their anger that has upset me. It's the photo of my family. Someone must have stolen it from our house in Kabul and sold it to the newspapers. Why can't the press leave us alone?'

'Who cares what they write or what they think?'

'I do.' She sniffed. 'How can I look for the truth if every-one knows who I am?'

She was wiping away her tears and scanning the

street. 'I must hurry before the whole world sees that photo. I need to use a computer.

'Over there,' I said. 'The library.'

ALIYA

When I first arrived in England, a big old library built of stone the colour of honey, full of rows and rows of books waiting to be read, would have filled my heart with joy, but now the beauty of the building and the sight of all those books meant nothing to me. All I could think about were the questions humming, fizzing and overheating in my brain. While the boy was at the desk getting a ticket, I slunk over to the computer desk with my cap pulled right down and my hand over my face, flinching every time someone looked up and wishing I could make myself invisible. As we logged on a youngish man in a grey puffa jacket sat down at a table nearby. The sight of the newspaper in his hand made my body tremble. The photo of our family picnic was probably on the front page. I caught his eye. He looked away. I tensed, ready to stand my ground if he started to shout.

'OK, what are we looking for?' the boy whispered.

'The connection between Hamidi and Behrouz.'

We'd only had four very old computers in my school in Kabul, shared between thirty girls, so I didn't get to use one very much and I could feel the boy's frustration as I tapped carefully at the keys. But I shrugged away his offers of help and after a few minutes I found what I was looking for: a photo of ten swarthy, weather-beaten fighters perched on a rocky mountainside, their weapons slung from their shoulders.

'Who are they?' the boy said.

'Hamidi and his gang at their roadblock. Look, he is there at the end.'

Hamidi looked younger and wilder in the photo but he had the same hooded eyes, hard features and rough, pock-marked skin. The boy leant towards the screen, his eyes sparking excitement as he turned to look at me. 'The road-block he commanded was at Sarobi. That's the place Connor heard Behrouz mention to Arif.'

My hand gripped the mouse and I gasped. 'That does not matter. This is what matters.'

'What?'

'This man! The warlord Hamidi worked for. His name was Farukh Zarghun. That is him.' I circled the cursor around the face of a man with a mass of curly black hair and a thick beard who was sitting in the middle of the group, holding a huge rifle above his head. There was something chilling about his staring eyes and the way he was sneering, as if he truly believed he was invincible. No wonder he was arrogant. The website said he'd made millions and millions of dollars growing opium poppies, setting up heroin labs all along the Pakistan border and running a distribution network that reached out to sellers on the streets of almost every city in the world.

The boy looked very worried and said slowly, 'What's he got to do with Behrouz?'

'A year ago my brother was one of the interpreters at Zarghun's trial.'

A hiss of 'Yes!' burst from his mouth and his fingers clenched into a fist. Our eyes met and held. For a moment I thought he might tell me why he cared so much but he just blushed and lowered his voice. 'Did he talk about it?'

'Of course. He worked on three or four trials for the British, but this one was a very big case that went on for weeks and we were proud that Behrouz had been chosen for this job. Every night when he came back, he'd tell us which important people he had seen in the court and what the judge had said. Sometimes our neighbours came round to drink coffee and listen to his stories.'

'What happened to Zarghun?'

'The judge said he must be hanged. But he had clever lawyers who got the punishment changed to his whole life in prison. People were angry about that and they held demonstrations outside the court. But after a few months he died anyway, and many people said that was justice.'

'Died? How?'

'He was stabbed by another prisoner. Behrouz heard a rumour that the authorities paid the man to kill him, because Zarghun's people were still loyal to him and he was running his drugs business from inside the prison.'

We sat for a moment gazing at the face of the dead man, Farukh Zarghun. I knew in my heart that I had found an important piece of the puzzle, but far from explaining anything it had only deepened the mystery. The boy pulled his tuft of hair and said thoughtfully, 'Maybe Hamidi set Behrouz up as a terrorist to punish him for helping at the trial.'

I wanted the answer to be that simple but it just didn't make sense. 'Behrouz translated for Zarghun and his lawyers as well as for the prosecutors. He did not take sides, and anyway if Hamidi wanted to hurt him, why didn't he just beat him up, like he did with Greg Parkin?'

The boy nodded. My mind was spinning, trying to make shapes out of shadows, but nothing fitted. Nothing made sense. The library was filling up, old people mainly, wandering in out of the rain to read the papers. The computer next to ours became free. The man in the grey puffa jacket folded away his newspaper and came over to use it. I hid my face from him and asked the boy if we could print the web pages about Hamidi and Zarghun before we left.

'Sure.' He tapped the keys and went over to the desk to pay for the copies.

While the boy was at the desk, I gave in to a yearning. I couldn't help it. I searched the internet for the photo of our picnic. For a moment it made me feel strong to see Baba's face smiling in the sunshine, with a sticky piece of baklava glistening in his fingers, Mor looking young and happy, cradling Mina in her arms, and Behrouz leaning back, laughing at one of his own silly jokes. More memories flickered through my head. Baba reading my school report, nodding approval. Mina learning to walk, proud and wobbly. Behrouz coming home from his first day at university. Baba's rusty old car wheezing and rocking on its springs. Women playing tabla drums at my cousin's wedding, my aunts dancing to the beat of the music. My heart pounding faster as I crawled along the beams to the bakery, the drop into nothingness, the Talib at our window. Merrick running towards us, reaching for Mina. Coming to England. So much hope and relief, all destroyed by Behrouz's fear and the photos of Hamidi on his phone. It all came back to that. The photos of Hamidi. Why would Hamidi want to kill Behrouz for taking his photo? Hamidi was here legally, everyone at his work knew who he was, and if he was going around attacking strangers with crowbars and getting dragged off by the police, he obviously wasn't at all worried about keeping a low profile.

I reached for my phone to go through the photos again.

The battery was low. Too low to use. The boy had left his phone on the desk. I glanced up. He was at the back of the queue, shifting impatiently from foot to foot while a group of mothers jiggled wailing toddlers and handed in piles of picture books. I slid my fingers on to the screen, searching for his photo gallery. I skimmed through the thumbnails, curious about his life, and saw shots of his father holding hands with a pretty blonde woman with pink lipstick who must be his mother. They were laughing and happy. I felt a pang of grief for the parents I had lost, angry that my father's death had destroyed them both.

Through a shimmer of tears I tapped on photos of a group of boys pulling faces, the same boys in a park, shy and awkward with some girls with high heels, tight trousers and pouting lips. An older woman with glasses, smiling down at a frosted cake alight with candles. Feeling guilty, I flicked on quickly to his copies of the photos Behrouz had taken and slid them across the screen, working backwards. The blurred pictures of Hamidi with another man outside Hardel Meats, the clearer shots of Hamidi on his own, puffing on a cigarette, scowling at the sky. I slid to the next photo. My heart grew hot.

It was a shot of Hamidi I'd never seen. He was with a shorter, fair-haired man on a scrubby stretch of waste ground, and it looked as if they were transferring parcels from a red van to a white one. I spooled through two, three, four more pictures of the same scene. They'd been taken from far away in the grainy grey light of early morning or evening, which made it difficult to see much detail except for a smudge of yellow down the side of the red van. It wasn't much but it was enough to blow away the last wisps of doubt that this was a Hardel Meats van. Each of the parcels they were carrying was the size and shape of a brick. Given Hamidi's history and all the money we'd found in his house, I was sure they contained drugs. I checked the date. These photos had been taken the day before the ones outside the meat factory. Questions shrieked in my head. Why had the boy deleted these pictures from my phone and kept copies of them for himself? Why didn't he want me to see them? I watched him in silence as he turned away from the printer and walked towards me. He laid the printouts on the table.

'Here you go,' he said. 'Two sets. One each.'

I held up his phone. 'What are these pictures?'

He blinked at the screen. 'Haven't you seen them?' His words didn't fit with the misery on his face or the pain in his eyes.

'No. You sent copies to your phone and you removed the original ones from Behrouz's.'

He shrugged. He was always shrugging. 'They must have got deleted by accident ...'

'You are lying.'

He looked down at the floor 'I'm not ... I ... I thought those pictures were still on Behrouz's phone with the others.'

I stared at his bent head and thought back to the way

– 200 –

he'd found the meat factory, how he'd chopped and changed between running so fast that I could hardly keep up and stopping and looking round like a dog sniffing prey until we found ourselves outside Hardel's.

'This is how you found the wall in the other photos, isn't it? You saw vans like the one in this picture and you followed them till they led us to the factory.'

He didn't answer, and it was as if a little piece of me was withering away, the piece that had trusted him, the piece that had taken strength from his friendship. The piece that had liked him. 'Why didn't you tell me? Why didn't you say, "I saw a picture of Hamidi in a van like that one, so let's follow it"?'

His lips were trembling as if he was about to burst out crying or shouting, I couldn't tell which. 'OK!' he hissed. 'I saw the red van, and, yeah, I followed it and we found the meat factory and Hamidi. You'd never have done that without me. So what's the big deal?'

I stood up and whispered fiercely, 'The deal is big because you lied to me and you hid things. Important things. Look at these parcels they are putting in the white van. I think Behrouz took these photos to prove that Hamidi is selling drugs, maybe bringing them here from Afghanistan. Maybe he went to the Hardel factory to get a better picture of Hamidi and maybe . . . I don't know . . . to see if more of their vans were carrying drugs, and Hamidi saw him. This picture could be the reason that Hamidi tried to kill him, the motive – and you kept it from me! So now I give you one chance. This minute. Tell me why you hid these pictures.'

He wanted to tell me. I could see it in his eyes. Shame. Conflict. Weariness. His teeth biting down on his lips as if he was trying to hold back the truth. When the moment came, he said only, 'I want to help you, Aliya. I want to prove Behrouz is innocent. You have to believe that.'

'Why? Why do you care about me or my brother? We are strangers to you.' My voice rose. 'Why are you so sure he is innocent? Or are you lying about that too?'

Heads were turning. The librarian half rose from her chair, frowning hard with her finger on her lips.

'It's you who rang me, remember?' he hissed. 'It's you who asked me to help you.'

'And now I am telling you that I don't want the help of a liar. Who are you working for – the police? Do they think I am a bomber? That I will lead you to the terrorists of Al Shaab?'

'Aliya, I swear—'

'I don't want your swearing, and I don't want your help!'

I snatched the printouts and ran from that place, propelled by an anger so fierce it blotted out the confusion and fear and sadness. At the door I looked back. The boy didn't look up. He just went on sitting there, staring at the pictures on his phone.

PART THREE

ALIYA

I got lost going back to King's Cross. Not lost like a stranger in this city, lost like someone who is learning to read the Tube map and can find their way back even though they've taken the train going north instead of south by mistake. Anger was holding back the misery and making me icy and calm. I turned off my phone and flicked through a crumpled magazine left on the seat, glad of anything to take my mind off the boy and his lies, even if it was just pages and pages of stupid gossip about singers and actors.

All the women in the photographs were smiling and thin as wheat stalks, but the articles were mean and said they looked fat and unhappy. They were even unkind about Colonel Clarke and his wife, India Lambert, hinting that they might get a divorce because she preferred shooting films and travelling the world for her charity to spending time with her husband. They said it was no wonder that a beautiful woman like her had got bored with an ugly old man like him. I was sure it wasn't true. That's what newspapers and magazines did, they told lies. They destroyed lives. The colonel might be old and a little bit ugly, but he was good and kind, and it was sly to write such shaming things about his wife. She was shooting a movie about an English queen called Anne Boleyn at a real castle, and there was a picture of her on the set smiling up at a tall handsome man. But the caption said this man was her assistant, so of course she spent time with him. I flung the magazine on the floor, sick to my bones of lies and liars.

When I got back to the hotel, a policewoman who said her name was Sandra was sitting on the bed doing a jigsaw of a farmyard with Mina. Mina looked up. I felt a rush of love for her and kissed her and tugged her plaits. She didn't smile back. I wondered sometimes if she'd forgotten how.

My mother sat hunched in the chair by the window, her hair straggling limp and loose on her shoulders. I went to her and kissed her hollow cheek. 'Shall I make you some tea, Mor?'

Her eyes moved from the television and rested on my face. 'Tell them my son is a good boy. Tell them.'

'I know, Mor.' As I reached for her hand her tears came,

falling on to her stiff fingers.

Sandra tutted. 'She's been like that all day. Saying the same thing over and over again. Hasn't eaten a thing.'

What did this woman expect? My mother had lost her husband, her country and now her son. I felt ashamed of all the angry thoughts I'd had about her being weak. My mother wasn't weak. She was broken.

I fetched a comb from the chest of drawers, lifted a hank of my mother's lifeless hair and began to tease out the matted strands, pulling gently at the knots. Her eyes strayed back to the television as if she expected them to announce that Behrouz was innocent. When her hair was smooth, I twisted it into a knot and pinned it. Her lovely hair, which had once been as thick as a horse's tail and so black it shone blue in the sunlight, now sat on her neck like a little ball of grey thread.

I made tea for us all, using the plastic kettle, and tried to get her to drink just a few sips. 'You have to keep your strength, Mor.'

She pushed the cup away like a child and looked at me angrily. 'Tell them he is a good boy. Tell them!' Her voice was harsh and scary, not like Mor's voice at all.

Mina ran over and wrapped her arms tightly around my legs. I picked her up and rubbed her back like I used to when she was a baby, and when she was calmer I sat with her, pushing cow-shaped pieces of jigsaw into cow-shaped holes while Sandra ordered in a takeaway that none of us would have the heart to eat. As I worked on the jigsaw I kept one eye on the news updates rolling along the bottom of the television screen: Police still waiting to interview suspected terrorist Behrouz Sahar . . . Doctors say his condition remains unchanged . . . MPs call for tighter checks on asylum seekers.

I finished the cow, found all the pieces of a fat, red-faced farmer, fitted a horse's legs to its body and went back to my own room, thinking about the boy and asking myself over and over again how his lies fitted into the puzzle of Behrouz.

I'd never felt so alone. I switched on the television, just to hear human voices. The strange calm that had gripped me since I left the library had melted away and while a cartoon comedy played on the screen I curled up on the bed and buried my head in the crook of my arm, unable to hold back the waves of misery and confusion. I had nothing to cling to except anger at the boy, and I lay there stoking it with memories of his shrugs and his smiles and his endless, endless lies. An announcement of breaking news cut through the canned laughter on the television. I lifted my head.

'Terror group Al Shaab have posted a video of Behrouz Sahar, filmed an hour before Wednesday's explosion, in which he confesses to planning a bomb attack on the home of Colonel Mike Clarke.'

A face I barely recognized stared from the screen. The eyes were Behrouz's but they were dazed and haunted, the nose was his too but scratched and bruised, and his lips were curled and twisted. There was writing behind him. Big red letters daubed on a white sheet, spelling out the words 'Al Shaab' in Arabic. The monster in my mind went crazy. Behrouz's lips parted, showing broken teeth, and a voice came out, stiff and dry as a robot.

'My name is Behrouz Sahar. When you see this video, I will be dead. A willing martyr. I planted the bomb to punish the foreigners who invaded my country. They said they wanted to give us freedom. Instead they destroyed our homes, our families, our farms, our innocent women and children. Some of my people collaborated with these invaders, others took their revenge in Afghanistan, but I came to the UK to punish those at the very top, the leaders who destroyed my country. You see, I have a plan. A plan to seek out Colonel Mike Clarke so that justice can be done. By destroying those who led the invasion of my country, I will ensure that the name of Al Shaab will live on to strike terror into the hearts of all who hear it.'

A sound wailed through the walls. It was my mother screaming in the next room. I ran to her. She was shrivelling up, shrinking away from the television screen, her eyes and mouth three dark circles of horror.

Even as I tried to comfort her they played the tape again and she rocked forward on her chair, tearing at her clothes and hair, screaming over and over, 'Who has done this to my son?'

I switched off the television and signalled to the

policewoman to take Mina away. She shouldn't have to see my mother like this. But even in Mor's frenzy of shock and horror she did not doubt her son, even for a moment. Her conviction gave me strength. Someone had done this to Behrouz. Beaten him and forced him to say those terrible, terrible things.

I made my mother take a tablet and lie down on the bed and all the time I kept seeing the look in Behrouz's eyes, the strange twist of his face, the way he'd blinked away from the camera when he said, 'I have a plan.' Was he telling me not to doubt him? Reminding me that, whatever happened, he was still my crazy big brother who had used an old washing line to save us from the Taliban? Or was there another message hidden in the words he was reading out? Some meaning in his hate-filled rant that I'd missed.

That night I slept fitfully and dreamt of the Taliban. The men who came down from the mountains before I was born, with whips and guns and eyes smeared black with *surma*, vowing to drive out the warlords who had plunged Afghanistan into chaos. My father had never trusted them but even he thought they would rid our country of a greater evil. But you can't make a devil dance to your own tune and by the time the Taliban revealed themselves to be even bigger devils than the warlords, it was too late. I woke up blinking into the darkness and thought of the boy. I had sensed the lies in him from the moment he'd come to the hotel, but I'd ignored my suspicions because I'd thought he would help me to save Behrouz. But the boy had turned out to be a devil too. A devil with secrets that I needed to find out before it was too late.

I texted him and called him. If I didn't hear from him by morning, I swore I'd go to his house and shame him into telling me the truth. I told myself I didn't care if he'd been working for the police. All I cared about was why he'd hidden that photo of Hamidi and lied about following that meat van to the packing plant. But still I felt an ache inside and it was the thought that he'd betrayed me that hurt. I lay awake with my phone on my pillow. He didn't call.

In the morning I left my mother and Mina staring at the tray of breakfast and ran out of the hotel. High above me a silver aeroplane skimmed the sky, its engines roaring as it flew towards the airport. Less than a month ago it had been me sitting up there, peering through the clouds, giddy with hope and excitement as I caught my first glimpses of London.

DAN

As Aliya stormed out of the library it was like my whole world was disintegrating, dropping away, leaving me with nothing but blackness, emptiness and guilt. What if I never saw her again? I tried to blank out the image of her face when she'd called me a liar and picture the way she'd look if I told her I'd cracked this on my own and Behrouz was free. It was the only thing keeping me from falling apart.

I snatched up the printout of Hamidi and his thugs at Sarobi with that big warlord, Zarghun, sneering down like he owned the lot of them. His beard was longer, his tunic was whiter, even his rifle was bigger than theirs, glinting new and shiny in the sunlight. Not surprising, I suppose, considering the millions he'd been raking in. But there was something weird about the way he was holding that rifle that set my brain buzzing. I peered closer, focusing on the fingers of his right hand. He only had three of them. The index and middle fingers had been cut off just below the first knuckle. My eyes stared at his stumps, held there by something echoing in my brain like a half-heard tune I couldn't remember.

I couldn't face going home, so I stayed on at the library reading stuff about Behrouz Sahar – the work he'd done for the army in Afghanistan, the medal he'd got for bravery – and trying to think of one good reason why he hadn't gone to the police with his photos of Hamidi and Jez Deakin the minute he discovered they were dealing drugs.

Voices broke through my thoughts. People were gathering round one of the computers, jostling to get a better look. The librarian stomped over to tell them to be quiet. Once she saw the screen, she just stood there, with her hand clamped over her mouth, not shushing anyone. I moved round to see what was going on. And there he was. Behrouz Sahar, with a black bandana round his head, his face wiped clean of blood but still puffy and swollen, confessing through a mouthful of broken teeth that he was a terrorist.

A rumble of fury spread around the library, worse than the night outside Meadowview. For a second I saw what they saw: a face twisted with hatred, a crazy blank-eyed bomber hell-bent on destroying everything he could, including himself. What would they do if I jumped on the desk and told them he was innocent? That his eyes were glazed and his face was twisted because he'd been beaten and kidnapped by a load of drug-dealing thugs, who'd probably threatened his mum and kid sisters to make him record that confession? Lynch me, probably. It wasn't what they wanted to hear.

I ran back to the computer I'd been using and searched for the clip on YouTube – 10,000 hits and counting. Dizzy and panicked, I grabbed my stuff, ran out of the library, and walked the streets for a long time, feeling as if I was stumbling along a crumbling cliff edge in a blindfold and it was only a matter of time before I went crashing over the edge.

By the time I got back to North London, I'd calmed down a bit, and I stood at the end of my street trying not to think about anything, just staring at the parked cars, the houses, the clipped hedges, the grey sky. Our house looked the same as always, shiny paintwork, flowers in tubs, a faint glow of light down the hall, Dad's van parked on the drive. Coming round the corner and seeing it sitting there, knowing he was home, used to make me feel safe. Not any more. I slipped round the back, hoping I could sneak straight up to my room without seeing anyone. My heart sank when I walked in on Mum and Dad at the kitchen table going through holiday brochures. Mum glanced up. 'Where have you been?'

I shrugged. Dad winked at her. 'Mooning after that girlfriend Eileen saw him with – Ali, wasn't it?'

It was a joke, a wind-up, and normally I'd have brushed it off, but hearing her name in his mouth caught me off guard. I looked away and stared angrily at the floor, willing him to shut up. He didn't take the hint.

'When are we going to meet her, then?'

Mum reached for the oven gloves. 'Don't tease him, Ron.'

'I'm serious, Debs. I want to see this mystery girl.'

I shot him a look and saw his surprise as he caught my contempt. Mum took a plate of sausage and chips out of the oven and put it down on the table. 'Sorry, love. It's got a bit dried up.'

'It's his own fault.' Dad was glaring at me, annoyed now. 'Next time you're going to be back late, you show your mum a bit of respect and give her a call.'

I sat down. I wasn't hungry, it was just the easiest way to avoid a row. Mum topped up Dad's mug, trying to smooth things over. 'We've found a lovely hotel in a resort called Bodrum. Here, have a look.' She pushed a glossy leaflet across the table, all sandy beaches, candle-lit restaurants and sun loungers round the pool.

I tossed it back. 'What's that going to cost?'

Dad's face darkened. 'Never you mind what it costs. I work hard for my money and I decide how I'm going to spend it.'

I jabbed at my food, breathing slowly, trying to calm down. Mum pushed the ketchup bottle towards me.

'Linda from work went last year, she said her kids loved it, and the hotel's got a spa with one of those steam rooms – what do they call them, Ron?'

'Hammams.' Dad thumped his gut. 'I'm up for that, sweat a bit of this off.'

'I'm not going,' I said.

He carried on as if he hadn't heard me. 'There's wind-surfing and diving and if you play your cards right, I might sign you up for a bit of sailing.'

'I said, I'm not going.'

Mum frowned at me like I was a toddler having a tantrum. 'Don't be silly, you've always wanted to have a go at sailing.'

'Not any more. So just stop going on about it!' I don't know why I was taking it out on her, but I couldn't stop myself.

Dad pointed his finger at me and snarled, 'I've just about had it with you. If I say you're going, you're going.'

Mum squeezed my arm. 'Come on, Dan, your Dad wants to give us a treat, what's wrong with that?'

Something snapped inside me. I threw down my knife and fork, splattering chips and chunks of sausage across their brochures. 'Flash holidays, flash washing machines, keeping up with Linda at work. Is that all you care about?'

Dad jumped to his feet. 'Don't you dare talk to your mother like that! I don't know what's got into you lately. You clear up this mess and apologize to her, right now, or—'

I stood up and stared him in the face. 'Or what, Dad? You going to send some of your mates round to sort me out?' I backed towards the door. 'Or maybe Jez could do it. He likes getting his hands dirty.'

He was shocked, I could see that, but there was something else, a flicker of uncertainty in his eyes that kicked the punch out of his voice when he shouted, 'You come back here!'

Mum's voice rose above his, 'It's all right, Ron. Leave him, he's upset.'

I ran upstairs, tripping on the top stair in my hurry to get away. As I lay there rubbing my ankle a bit of me wanted Dad to come storming after me, demanding to know what was going on, and then I'd tell him what I'd seen and what I knew. And maybe it would turn out I'd got it all wrong and he and Jez weren't up to their necks in Hamidi's rackets. He didn't come. I hobbled into my room and slammed the door.

Fired up by anger and desperation, I spent the next few hours trawling the internet for information about Hamidi. Every time I came across the photo of him on the Afghan mountainside with Zarghun and his band of thugs, I'd feel a stab of annoyance that I couldn't work out why that warlord's mangled fingers were getting to me.

'Danny!' I swung round. Mum was standing at my door. 'No wonder you've been looking so peaky. It's two in the morning.'

'You're s'posed to knock!'

'Sorry, love, I thought you'd dropped off with the light on. What are you doing?'

I closed the lid of my laptop. 'Nothing.'

She came over, rested her hands on my shoulders and said gently, 'Are you in trouble, Danny?'

'No, Mum.'

'If you ever had a problem, anything at all, you know you could tell me.' Her voice jammed, as if she was forcing herself to think something unthinkable. 'I wouldn't care what you'd done, I'd always stand by you. Your dad too. He thinks the world of you.'

For a minute I was tempted to tell her everything so she could make the bad stuff go away, like when I was a kid. But I couldn't tell her anything, because this time it was me trying to keep the bad stuff away from her. I shrugged her hands away. 'I'm fine, Mum.'

'You're not. You're exhausted. Go to sleep.'

She kissed the top of my head and the smell of her soap lingered for ages after she'd gone. I slipped under the duvet fully dressed and fell into a weird half-sleep full of dreams of Dad being dragged off by the police, Mum smashing down the door of the loading bay, and Aliya blinded by tears, running and stumbling to escape Zarghun's massive stumpy claw.

My eyes snapped open. My head was emptying of all the crap and debris of the last few days, leaving just one terrifying, impossible thought. I switched on the light and grabbed my phone, my pulse thrashing faster and faster as I skimmed through Behrouz's photos. There he was, Hamidi outside Hardel's, smoking with his bald mate. I slid on to the next picture, the one where Behrouz had cut off their heads. The bald man's right hand was in shot, holding his cigarette in a really awkward way, with his little finger stuck out like some old lady drinking tea. Like a flash of lightning on a dark night, I realized what had been gnawing at me – his index and middle fingers were missing! Behrouz hadn't made a mistake when he'd taken that shot. He'd been going for a close-up of those knuckles.

Two photos of Hamidi with two different men who both happened to be missing the middle and index fingers of their right hands. What were the odds?

I flicked back to the only shot of Bald Guy's face in focus. Now I bothered thinking about it, I was sure he was the passenger we'd seen in Hamidi's car the night we followed him home, which upped my pulse rate another couple of notches as I compared his picture to the picture of Zarghun. Bald Guy had yellowish skin and heavy-lidded eyes, whereas Zarghun was weather-beaten and squinting at the sun. With all that hair and beard, it was impossible to guess what he'd look like if he'd been living in England for a while and shaved his head. Even so, those matching fingers kept my pulse pumping and my hopes sky high. I ran through the possibilities:

Number one: this was just a weird coincidence, Bald Guy wasn't even Afghan and he'd lost his fingers cutting up meat at Hardel's.

Number two: Bald Guy was an Afghan, but that didn't mean anything because losing those exact same fingers on that exact same hand was something that happened all the time if you handled guns or butchered meat.

Number three. Bald Guy was Farukh Zarghun.

I got both photos up on my laptop, resized the faces to make the best match I could, and laid the printouts side by side. There was software for this kind of thing. I'd seen it in films. But I'd have to make do with a ruler and a pencil. I measured the distances between the corners of Zarghun's eyes and all of his ugly features that weren't covered by his hair and beard, including his bushy eyebrows, broken nose and fleshy lips. I did the same with Bald Guy and carefully compared the proportions. I'm not the greatest at maths, and it would have helped if the photos had been taken from similar angles and the ones of Bald Guy had been sharper. Even so, the match was pretty good. Too good. I was positive it was the same man. Which meant that convicted drug lord Farukh Zarghun wasn't dead at all. He was working in a meat-packing factory, living in a crappy house in North London with a brand new BMW in the garage and shed-loads of cash stashed in his bathroom ceiling. That's why Hamidi had wanted Behrouz dead. To protect Zarghun.

*

I went over to the window and watched the early-morning sky turning pink over the rooftops, imagining how petrified Behrouz must have felt when he'd locked eyes with Zarghun and realized he'd been recognized by a man who was supposed to be dead. I still couldn't work out why he hadn't gone straight to the police and demanded protection, but I wasn't going to make the same mistake. I was going straight to the cops. I was on a high. I'd found exactly what I'd been looking for – evidence that could prove Behrouz was innocent that didn't involve Dad. I ran on to the landing. I stopped, went back into my room and deleted the photo of Hamidi and Jez Deakin loading up Dad's van from both my laptop and my phone. That picture had done enough damage. I felt a little lift of relief as it disappeared from the screens. Still, it knocked me back a bit to find Jez Deakin sitting at our kitchen table poring over an Excel spreadsheet on his laptop and eating a bacon sandwich. Whoever had put him in hospital had packed a pretty good punch. One eye and half his face was dark purple, tinged with yellow, and his neck and hands were covered in cuts and bruises. Served him right, his injuries were nothing compared to the state Behrouz Sahar was in. I grabbed a carton of juice out of the fridge and took a big slug.

'All right, Danny?'

Act normal, Dan. Not easy when all I wanted to do was even up the bruises on his smirking face. 'Yeah. You don't look so good, though.'

'Don't you worry about me. I'm fine. At least I would be if I didn't have this lot to sort.' He smacked his hand on a thick pile of invoices and tipped his head at Dad. 'I keep telling him, if he doesn't behave, I'm going make him go back to doing his own books.'

Dad looked at me and laughed, as if our argument last night hadn't happened. 'No, thanks. I still have nightmares about that ruddy VAT man.' He pointed a fork into the spattering frying pan. 'Bacon?'

'No, thanks.' I headed down the hall.

He called after me, 'Where are you going?'

I slammed the door. *To the police, Dad. If it goes the way I'm hoping, there's an outside chance Aliya Sahar won't ever need to know that you and your mate Jez are thieving, drug-dealing lowlifes, or that it's my fault her brother is lying in hospital fighting for his life.*

The air was fresh and crisp as I walked out of the house. I checked my phone – a text and a couple of missed calls from Aliya. I ignored them, too much of a coward to speak to her till I could tell her that Behrouz was a free man. It wouldn't be long now. I walked down to the precinct and sat on one the benches while I dialled Trent's number. He answered after a couple of rings.

'PC Trent.'

'Um . . . This is Dan Abbott. I don't know if you remember me. You came round our house to interview me and my dad about seeing Behrouz Sahar at Meadowview.'

'Oh . . . yes. Danny. What's up?'

'I need to see you. I've got information that'll prove Sahar is innocent.'

He paused before he spoke. 'Is this a wind-up? Because if it is, there are stiff penalties for wasting police time, specially on a case as serious as this.'

'No. I promise this is for real.'

'Hang on, you're breaking up. I'll go outside.'

His voice was lower when he started talking again. 'Look, Danny, there are all sorts of rumours going round the estate, so whatever it is you've heard . . .'

'I've got proof. But I want this off the record. Like we never met.'

'Proof of what?'

'That he was set up. But I want my name kept out of it.'

His voice was sharp. 'Have you told this to anyone else?'

'No.'

'All right. Keep it that way till we've talked. But if you want this off the record, you'd better not come to the station. Look . . . um . . . there's a service road behind the snooker hall and the new chippy in the High Street. Do you know where I mean?'

'I'll find it.'

'The turning's after the DIY shop. I'll meet you there in thirty.'

I turned off my phone. I didn't want Aliya calling while I was spilling my guts to Trent. The service road he'd mentioned wasn't far. Funny how you think you know a place, then suddenly you discover bits of it you never even knew existed. Same with people, I s'pose. I must have walked past that turning a thousand times without noticing the potholed cinder track that led past the back of the shops to a world of rackety sheds, flapping tarpaulins and dumping grounds piled high with tyres. I hung around by the back of the chippy, breathing in the smell of fish and cheap fat. My hands were shaking, my stomach was churning and, despite the cold, my T-shirt was sticky with sweat.

ALIYA

'd got a seat by the window and I stared out, wishing the anger would leave me so I could concentrate on what I would say to the boy. I would stay calm and cold like Inspector McGill, the detective who had interrogated me at the police station, and if he tried to go on lying, I would rip his lies to pieces word by word. The bus turned into the High Street. It was crowded. People texting, pushing buggies, swinging briefcases, crossing the road. Suddenly, as if my anger had conjured him out of the air, I saw the boy, striding down the road. He didn't look upset. He looked purposeful and distracted. I shot from my seat and reached for the bell. A burly man in a grubby sweater stood in the way.

'I have to get off,' I said. The man grunted and shifted a

little. I toppled forward, jamming my finger on the button just as the bus roared past the stop. I kept on pressing it and shouted to the driver, 'Please! I need to get off!'

He didn't stop. I ignored the glares of the other passengers and craned over their heads, looking for the boy. He'd disappeared. Gone. It seemed to take for ever before the bus stopped again. I jumped off and ran back along the shuttered shop fronts, stopping to peer inside the few that were open and scanning the slowly moving traffic to see if he'd got into a car. Ahead of me a pale-blue hatchback was flashing its indicator, waiting to turn right. I caught the last three numbers of the licence plate and darted forward to read the rest. Dizzy and sick, I stepped back and checked the note on my phone. The numbers matched. It was the car I'd seen when I was dangling off Hamidi's drainpipe. I pulled my cap low and ran to catch it up, slowing right down as I drew level with the driver. He had freckles on his skin, short hair the colour of sand, and he was drumming his fingers on the wheel, checking the mirror every couple of seconds. I knew his face. I must have glimpsed him going into Hamidi's. Only it had been dark. Too dark to see his freckles and his hair-style. The car turned into an alleyway. I followed a few metres behind, with my back hugging the wall. The boy was there, halfway down, leaning against an old wooden shed. I opened my mouth to shout a warning. I shut it quickly. The car was drawing up beside him. He was raising his hand as if he knew the driver, looking furtively up and down, opening the door. Getting in. My eyes blurred. Now I knew for sure that the boy had been spying on me. Reporting back. Not to the police. To a man who worked for Hamidi.

DAN

Trent had brought along couple of coffees in a cardboard container. He shoved one into my hand. He was in scruffy jeans, needed a shave and the dark circles under his eyes reached halfway down his cheeks.

'I wasn't sure it was you. Where's your cop car?' I said.

'I was on my way home when you called. Been up all night.' He plucked at his crumpled shirt. 'All I need now is a hot shower, a fry-up and forty-eight hours sleep.'

'Sorry, I didn't realize—'

'Don't worry about it. All part of the service.' He flashed me a tired smile. 'So, what's this about, Danny? Sahar's guilty. He's confessed. Haven't you seen the video?'

'No. He's innocent. Someone forced him to tape that confession.'

'How d'you make that out?'

'Like I said, if I tell you, I want it off the record. If you swear not to tell anyone you got it from me, or make me go to court, I can give you everything you'll need to prove what really happened. Do we have a deal?'

'I don't make deals, Danny. But if you give me information that helps us crack this, I'll do everything I can to protect your identity as a source.'

'OK.' I guessed that was about as good as I was going to get. I closed my eyes. If I was going to keep Dad out of this, I still had to watch every word I said. 'I was at Meadowview the night of the explosion. I saw Behrouz being chucked in the back of a van by four blokes. They had him at gunpoint.' Just saying it out loud was like bursting a throbbing boil.

Trent nearly choked on his coffee. 'When?'

'Around two in the morning.'

He shifted round and gave me a long hard look, like he was testing me. 'There's nothing on the Meadowview CCTV. We've been over the tapes a hundred times.'

'It was out of sight.'

'Where?'

'In the loading bay.'

I started to describe what I'd seen and I could hear myself gabbling. It was all the festering guilt pouring out. 'They must have grabbed him on his way home. Check the CCTV. You'll see two men and what looks like a hunched-up old woman with a shawl over her head coming across the car park. I've hardly slept since. I keep seeing the gun and the look on his face . . . he was petrified, like he knew they were going to kill him.'

Trent rubbed a hand over his chin. 'That doesn't mean he's innocent. Those people with guns were probably from Al Shaab, trying to stop him bottling out.'

'No. Only one of them was Afghan, the other three were English. One had a Union Jack tattooed on his neck.'

He took a long sip of his coffee and wiped a fleck of milky froth off his lip. 'Why didn't you come forward with this before?'

I looked down. It had felt good telling the truth. Now I had to stop.

'I . . . I didn't want my parents knowing I'd been out that late . . .'

'Why not?'

'I'd been grounded and I . . . I was meeting people they don't approve of . . .'

It sounded exactly like what it was. A feeble lie. He wasn't impressed.

'Sahar's facing life in jail, Danny. You should have told me this the day I came round.'

'You think I don't know that? It's been tearing me up.' My lip trembled and my voice rose out of control. 'I've been trying to find some other way to prove he's inno-cent. And now I have. These people wanted him dead, and making out he was a terrorist was a cover-up.'

He frowned at me like I might be crazy and said slowly, 'Why would anyone want to kill a nineteen-year-old Afghan cab driver who's only been here a couple of weeks?'

'To silence him.' I thought of what Zarghun's people had done to Merrick and Arif as well as Behrouz and my voice sank to a shaky croak: 'He . . . he saw someone who's supposed to be dead.'

Trent blew out a long breath, as if he could see this was going to take a while. 'OK, take it easy. Have your coffee.' He took a sachet out of his pocket, ripped it open and tipped it into my cup.

I held up my hand. 'That's enough.' He went on pouring.

'State you're in, you need the sugar. It'll calm you down. Go on, drink it.'

I took a couple of glugs. It tasted good. Sweet and creamy with a hint of bitterness. He was right. I felt calmer straight away.

'Better?'

'Yeah. Thanks.'

He looked straight at me. 'So come on, then, who did Behrouz Sahar see?'

'This guy called Zarghun—'

'Who?'

'Farukh Zarghun. He's an Afghan warlord.' I got out the printouts. 'That's him in Afghanistan and that's him in

England. He's shaved off his hair and his beard but you can tell it's the same man by his missing fingers. Run these through a computer if you don't believe me – all the features match. I measured them. He got life in prison for running drugs and officially he got stabbed to death in a Kabul jail, but that's a lie. He must have bribed his way out and now he's over here, working in a meat-packing factory. That man next to him is this psycho Tewfiq Hamidi, who was his top commander in Afghanistan. He's the one I saw in the loading bay kidnapping Behrouz Sahar.'

'Go on,' he said, quietly.

For a minute I just sat there staring at the dots of rain on the windscreen and trying to catch the thoughts trickling through my brain. 'Behrouz was one of the interpreters at Zarghun's trial. That's how he recognized him. Zarghun saw him taking his photo and got Hamidi to kidnap and kill him so he wouldn't tell anyone.'

'That's a hell of a leap, Danny. Are you sure it was this . . . what's his name, Hamidi . . . you saw kidnapping Behrouz?'

'Positive. The van they drove him off in . . . it was a Hardel Meats van. That's where Zarghun and Hamidi work, at their packing plant in North London. But I think they're using the meat deliveries to move drugs around.'

He squeezed his chin again, like he was thinking hard. 'Why make out Behrouz is a terrorist? Why not just run him over or chuck him off a building?'

'To skew the investigation.'

'What do you mean?'

I was getting tired but I ploughed on. 'Behrouz told two of his mates about Zarghun, this army captain James Merrick and another cab driver called Arif. The next day Merrick died, in a freak "accident", Arif got taken off in a phony immigration bust and hasn't been seen since, and Behrouz got blown up in that lock-up.' My voice seemed to be detaching itself from my mouth and my face was starting to feel numb. 'That's what Zarghun's people do. They're clever. They get rid of people who get in their way and make it look like their deaths aren't murder or connected in anyway. They couldn't do that on their own. They've got to be paying off people in high places to help them out.' My hands started to shake.

'All right, Danny. You're doing fine. Take a deep breath and finish your coffee.'

I took another slug from the cup and felt the last of the guilt swill away like gunk from a blocked drain. It was going to be all right. I never knew that relief could make you feel so different, so light. It was as if I was floating. 'You've got to start by arresting Zarghun. Check his passport. It'll be fake. Once you prove who he is, you've got his motive for silencing Behrouz. Then check the Hardel Meats vans for Behrouz's DNA. The one they used for the kidnap had a number plate starting GLR.'

'All right. But there's a couple of things I need to know. First of all. How the hell did you find all this out?'

'Behrouz's sister found his old phone with the photos of Zarghun and Hamidi on it, and we used them and his call log to piece it together.'

Trent sat up. 'This phone. Where is it now?'

'She's got it.'

'And she can back you up on all this?'

I dropped my eyes. 'She doesn't know about me seeing the kidnap and, if it's all right with you, I don't want her to find out . . . she . . . she'd hate me for not coming forward before.'

'All right.'

I looked up at him again and heard my voice crack, 'Will it be enough to get Behrouz off?'

'If it pans out.'

I smiled for the first time in days.

'Did you mention what you saw in the loading bay to anyone else?'

'No.'

'You sure about that, Danny? None of your mates or a girlfriend, trying to impress her?'

'I haven't got a girlfriend,' I said, my voice sounding echoey and even further away.

'And there's nothing else you want to tell me?'

'No.'

'I'll need you to make a statement—'

My eyelids drooped. 'We had a deal. You said you'd keep this off the record.'

'I will, but I need exact times, dates, addresses.

Nothing formal. Don't worry. I'll keep you well away from the nick. There's a safe house we use for talking to informants. You've done the right thing coming to me. It's going to be OK.'

A wave of warmth washed over me, deep and soft like I was drifting on a slowly sinking cloud. His voice was muffled, soothing. I heard him say, 'That's it, Danny. You have a nice little kip.'

ALIYA

The blue hatchback was backing up, turning round. I squeezed behind a row of stinking waste bins, staying low until it had passed. It didn't make sense. It was the boy who had led me to Hamidi. Why had he done that if he was working for him? I ran back to the bus stop, furious with the boy and furious with the small stubborn part of me that still wanted to trust him.

When I got back to the hotel, Sandra and Tracy were both there and my mother was sitting on the edge of the bed with a shawl around her head, holding her handbag on her knees, ready to go out.

'Where have you been?' Tracy said, crossly.

'For a walk. I needed air.'

She didn't believe me. I didn't care.

'I've had a call from Inspector McGill.' Every muscle in my body tensed. 'He says I can take you and your mother to visit your brother. Sandra will stay with Mina.'

'Oh.' My eyes watered. I wiped them dry. 'Did Behrouz wake up?'

'Yes.'

I sank on to the bed, expecting a rush of joy. What I felt was the hollow trembling exhaustion of waking from a nightmare. I told myself Behrouz was conscious and now he could destroy all the doubts and demons in my head and tell the police who had done this to him. I looked up. Tracy was chewing her lip. I turned from her to Sandra. Something was wrong.

'What is it?'

'He's got no idea who he is or what's happened to him.' Tracy said. 'They're hoping some familiar voices might help to jog his memory.'

I knew the big white hospital building well. I saw it every day on the television and every night in my dreams. But something inside me still ripped a little as WPC Rennell's dented red car swept us through the gates. We passed a row of ambulances striped with chequered bands of blue and yellow and drew level with two news vans topped with satellite dishes, parked to one side of the entrance. I pulled my cap low over my eyes. A group of reporters stood watching the passing cars, laughing, chatting and drinking from paper cups. Some of them had set up folding chairs along the wall. Others were walking around with headphones clamped to their heads and one of them, a woman reporter with long glossy hair, was holding a microphone to her red-painted mouth and talking into a camera. They were here because of Behrouz. If they'd known who we were, they'd have chased our car like street dogs hungry for meat. I wanted to run over and yell into that camera that Behrouz was not a bomb-maker, whatever lies their experts told about him. Instead I shrank away from the window and kept my eyes on my hands.

To avoid the reporters, we had to go in the back way and creep through the basement and up the stairs like thieves. I put my arm around my mother. Her head had sunk into her shoulders as if she'd suddenly grown very old, and she kept her scarf pulled tightly across her face. Two policemen were guarding the door to Intensive Care, checking everyone who went in. Tracy went up to them and said something quietly. They hardly glanced at her. Their hard, curious eyes were fixed on me and my mother, taking in every detail, so they could go home and tell their wives what we looked like or sell what they'd seen to the newspapers. One of them took my backpack and rooted through my things with his big hairy hand. I felt the press of Behrouz's phone against my thigh and held my breath until the policeman thrust the backpack at my chest and waved me on.

WPC Rennell pushed open the door and led us into a reception area where a nurse made us clean our hands with a sharp-smelling gel. She talked very softly and only looked at us when she thought we weren't looking at her. She pointed down the corridor to a door with two policemen sitting outside holding guns across their laps.

I knew my brother was badly injured, but nothing had prepared me for the twitching bundle of tubes and bandages that lay on the bed. I heard myself murmur, 'No, no, no.' The policewoman sitting beside him looked up and let her magazine slip to the floor. My mother reached out to touch Behrouz's agitated fingers and let out a howl. His burnt, bandaged hand was cuffed to the bed. My tears grew hot with rage. I couldn't stop them pouring down my cheeks. The policewoman got up and moved to the window. Mor straightened a little, dropped her bag to the floor and, with more purpose in her face than I'd seen for months, she sat down and began to rock backwards and forwards, murmuring Behrouz's name and crooning a song she used to sing to us when we were little, 'Sleep, sleep, sleep, my child, as still as a stone in the water.' His fluttering eyelids opened. The blankness in them was a blow to my heart. He didn't know her and he didn't know the song. His gaze wandered from her face to mine. He didn't know me either. A nurse came in to look at the monitors. 'When will he remember?' I said.

'We don't know, but his vital signs are much stronger.' Her voice was crisp and professional, as if she wanted to prove she would do her best for him, even if he was a killer. She removed the empty bag from his drip, snapped open a fresh one and attached it to the tubes.

The next few hours passed in a hushed blur punctuated by the murmur of my mother's voice, the clicks and beeps of the equipment, the swish of the door as nurses came and went, and the muted voices of the policemen in the corridor. With every minute I felt more useless and frustrated. By late afternoon I couldn't stand it any longer. There was nothing I could do here. I couldn't sing to Behrouz or change his drip or check his monitors. I could hardly even bear to look at his burnt, restless body. But I could prove he was innocent. I backed towards the door, turned on my heel in my borrowed trainers and ran out of there.

If I were Behrouz, I would have had a plan all worked out in my head. I wasn't Behrouz and all I had was a burning urge to find out why everything that had happened led back to Tewfiq Hamidi.

It was very late by the time I found my way to Hamidi's house and when I got there it was in darkness. Dilapidated and menacing in the pale moonlight, dark stems of creeping vine stretching like tapering fingers across its frontage. I took out my phone to check it was switched to silent. There was no need. The battery had died. Fear trickled cold through my veins as I slipped it into my backpack. Breathing hard, I inched along the side wall and peered into the garden. Nothing moved. With a silent prayer I launched myself across the brambles, dropping to a crouch when I saw a sliver of light filtering through the curtains of the back room. I stayed low, head down, pushing my cuff to my mouth until I found enough courage to creep towards the window. I put my eye to the tear in the curtains and peered through the web of threads. A bare bulb threw a dim light across a heap of cables and silver boxes lying on the floor. I was straining so hard to see what was in them that it took me a moment to realize there was a figure curled on the couch. It was the boy, fast asleep, with his knees pulled up to his chest. The first thing I felt was envy. I hadn't slept properly for so long it hurt to see him curled up like that, lost to my pain. Then the fury kicked in, rolling over me so I wanted to bang on the glass and scream at him. As I dug my nails into my palms the door of the room swung open. A fat man in a dirty white vest and track pants strolled in. Bleary-eyed and scratching himself as if he'd just woken up, he squatted down and began to pack away the cables. When he'd finished, he ambled over to the couch and bent over the boy. Gripping the window ledge, I stepped on to a broken brick and stretched up, angling my head to see what he was doing. He slapped the boy's face, shook him roughly by the shoulders and let him fall. The boy's head bounced against the arm of the couch and lolled sideways. Slits of white appeared between his twitching eyelids and a trickle of spit dropped from his gaping mouth.

Shock loosened my grip on the damp windowsill. I toppled off the brick, my foot skidding on the gritty surface of the terrace. Numb with terror, I dropped to my haunches, crawled along the cracked concrete and flattened myself against the back of the garage. The curtains flew apart, throwing light into the darkness. Another light came on in the kitchen. Stiff bolts creaked. I scuttled around the side of the garage, freezing as tyres crunched the drive, headlights swept the trees and the bonnet of a pale-coloured car slid to a stop at the end of the wall. The headlights snapped off. Someone walked to the front door. The doorbell rang, loud, impatient bursts. I raised myself up, poised to run for the gate as soon as the driver had gone inside, dropping down again when the door opened and a voice yelled, 'There's someone out there! Check the front.'

Seconds later the back door crashed open behind me. I heard someone run out, trip and swear loudly. I cringed into the brickwork as the car's headlights came back on ahead of me. I couldn't go forward to the drive. I couldn't go back to the garden. I took the only option left and crawled towards the car. My stomach caved in as I recognized the pale-blue hatchback. I lay in the strip of shadow between the tyres and the garage door, craning through the knotted stems of the vine to see the driver run to the gateway and stand on the pavement, flashing a torch up and down the darkened street. While his back was turned, I pulled open the passenger door and slipped inside. The back seat had been folded down to make a large flat surface, half of it heaped with boxes and cans of beer and the other half covered in plastic sheeting that crackled as I scrambled under the seat and squeezed into the cramped footwell. I pushed my head into my knees, listening to the men stomp around outside shouting to each other.

More cars were arriving. More voices. I lifted my head, tipping the seat up just enough to see into the wing mirror. After a few minutes I saw the freckled man coming out of the house bathed in the light from the hall, carrying the boy on his shoulder like a carcass of meat. My heart seemed to stop. Was he dead? I ducked down. The boot creaked open and the folded seat thumped hard against my neck as he threw the boy inside. A phone rang. The man cursed and got in the driver's side to answer it.

'Yeah. No . . . worse than that. He was in the bloody loading bay. Saw everything . . . and he found Sahar's phone in the flat.' I knew that voice. The throatiness of it, the way he stretched some sounds and blunted others. 'Yeah, he and the sister went through the photos . . .' He was talking about me. I bit down on my lip to stop myself passing out. '. . . I don't know . . . fourteen, fifteen maybe . . . I know . . . not yet, but don't worry, we're on it. She won't get far . . .' I trembled in the darkness, tasting blood on my tongue. 'Yeah, he's in the boot . . . Nah, leave it to me, I've got it sorted. We're going have a party . . . too many drinks, too many drugs and, apart from a line in the local paper and some do-gooder moaning about teenagers today, no one's going to bat an eyelid.' He laughed. 'Yeah . . . just another stupid kid who made a mistake and ended up dead.'

A deadly coldness poured through my aching body. I hadn't understood everything he'd said, but enough to know they were going to kill the boy, then come after me. Terror spewed a memory from the back of my brain. The police station. That's where I'd heard the freckled man's voice. He was the policeman who'd brought me tea and sandwiches. He'd looked different in uniform but it was definitely him. Thoughts splintered into tiny pieces and reformed into ugly, unimaginable shapes. A policeman? Working with Hamidi? Drugging the boy?

I knew now why Behrouz had got himself a gun instead of trusting the police.

'No, I'm keeping it local,' he was saying. 'That way I'm on it as soon as they find the body. Yeah, I'll get a couple of the lads from the block to swear blind they saw him getting off his head. Nah ... too risky. I'm going to use the three brothers ... I know, the boss was all for it ... All right, mate. Call you later.'

Who was his boss? Who were these brothers who killed people? What did it mean to bat an eyelid?

I willed him to go back to the house and give me a chance to run. When he started the engine, I struggled to hold on to my sanity. This man was going to find me and kill me before I could discover what any of this had to do with Behrouz. I heard the passenger door open. The car bounced as someone heavy got in. Another man said, 'What shall I do with his phone?'

'Text his mother. Tell her he's staying over at a mate's.'

'What mate?'

'I dunno, do I? Make up a name, then give it to me.'

I caught the smell of cigarettes, heard the men murmuring, then a click and a blast of music that shook the seat I was squashed against and pulsed through my cramped body. The car swung out of the drive, rattling the beer cans. The boy groaned. He wasn't dead. Not yet. And I couldn't let him die. Not before he'd told me everything he knew. The car stopped and started in the traffic, moving slowly for ten, fifteen minutes, then it got up speed, jolting my crushed bones for what seemed like a thousand dark, stifling, unbearable hours, made worse by the terror of what would happen when we stopped. I could barely breathe as the car turned off the smooth road and slowed down, bumping on to rough ground as it came to a halt. The music stopped. The men jumped out. The back door opened. I balled myself tighter and felt the seat lift a little from my back as they dragged the boy out.

The freckled man said, 'It's all right. I've got him. You grab the beers. There's some vodka in the boxes. Couple of bottles should do it.'

The boxes moved. Glass clinked. I listened to their footsteps fade and waited ten more excruciating minutes before I pushed back the folded seat and wriggled up to peer through the window. Clouds covered the moon but the night wasn't pitch black like the night in Kabul and I didn't know whether to be relieved or disturbed to see I was on a stretch of waste ground by the canal and that

Meadowview was one of three light-sprinkled slabs in the distance. I scrambled into the front of the car, throwing aside cigarette cartons and sweet wrappers, searching for anything that might be useful. I got out on wobbly legs, struggling to stand, and gazed down the towpath. The boy was somewhere out there in the darkness with the freckled man, the passenger from the car and the three brothers. Five killers. All I had to save him with was a cigarette lighter I'd found shoved down the back of the driver's seat.

DAN

I knew that noise. It was the click and fizz of a beer can spurting open. There it was again. Weird. Voices too, and footsteps, the hiss of an aerosol, the smell of paint and . . . what was that? Crisps. Yeah, that was it. Salt and vinegar, and something else. Something foul and rotting, like ditchwater. I was on my side, in darkness, stiff and heavy. I couldn't move. Not my hands or my feet or my head or my eyelids. Had I been run over? Or beaten up? Why was I so cold and numb? Why was the world rocking and creaking? The emptiness in my head was terrifying. Black and sticky, smothering any memories of how I'd got there. I concentrated on my eyes, straining to force them open. The left one felt like it had been glued shut. The right one drooped and dragged, then fluttered a little, letting in a dim slit of light. Figures flitted past, chucking litter around, smashing bottles, opening beer cans, spraying a fat blue tag on the wall, trashing a low-ceilinged dimly lit room while my numb, useless legs were slipping sideways, dragging my top half with them. My mind churned, searching for a shred of reality that would make sense of any of it. 'Help me!' The howl stayed inside my skull, my tongue and lips too bloated to move. Suddenly I was crashing to the floor. My arms couldn't move, couldn't reach out to stop my head hitting some-thing sharp or protect me from the weight smashing across my legs and clamping my foot in iron jaws. Footsteps. Someone kicking my ribs. A voice swearing in my ear. A sharp prick in my arm. A moment of helpless fear. Then the blanket of sticky blackness, wiping it all away.

ALIYA

I hobbled along a ditch at the edge of the towpath, frantically rubbing my legs to get the blood flowing. Gritting my teeth against the pain, I made for a shed on the far side of the allotments that was bleeding light through the cracks around its door. In my head I pictured the freckled man killing the boy in that cramped space and burying his body in one of the vegetable patches, where nobody would ever question a heap of newly turned earth. I tripped and stumbled among piles of rotting plants, easing on to my belly as I neared the shed. There were voices coming from inside and movements causing the light to flicker. Shielded by a clump of bushes, I wriggled closer, searching for a weapon. I grasped a piece of wood. I was sweating but my skin was cold and my mouth was as dry as ashes. A scream pierced the silence. Panic squeezed my heart. The door of the shed flew open. I rose up, dropping back when a girl in shorts and a white skimpy top burst into the night, her long hair streaming out behind her. A boy ran out after her, carrying a torch. Then he kissed her. She giggled and kissed him back and they ran off into the darkness, hand in hand.

I dropped the wood, it was useless – soft and rotten – and hurried back towards the canal, angry that I had lost so much time. I moved quickly, keeping behind the hedges and fences that ran between the allotments and the canal.

Voices drifted along the water. I dropped behind a rusty water-butt and waited to see who would come. Two figures appeared on the towpath. It was them, the freckled man and his passenger, walking fast. Without the boy. Had they left him for the three brothers to deal with? I watched them hurry to their car and had to stop myself gasping when the freckled man stopped for a moment with his hand on the open door and looked back, sweeping the gloom with his eyes. And then, as if he was pleased with his night's work, he got in and drove away. I let the red tail-lights disappear before I dared to draw a breath.

The boats on this stretch of the canal were little more than wrecks, abandoned, empty and creaking softly in the wind. I moved carefully, terrified that the men would come back or the three brothers would leap from the shadows and grab me, but I felt a little better when the gravel gave way to soft mud that muffled the sound of my footsteps. I crouched down and sparked the lighter with shaking fingers, knowing in my heart that every second, every fragment of a second, counted now. The frail light caught two sets of shoe marks. Large footprints twice the size of mine, pointing both ways. As I moved the lighter the ripples on the water caught the reflection of the tiny flame. I stared at the shifting surface and imagined the boy at the bottom of the canal, weighted down in slime. I sprang back from the edge, shaking the image from my mind. I told myself they wouldn't carry him all this way just to throw him in. Surely they'd have done it nearer to where they'd parked their car. The canal was just as deep back there. Just as deserted.

I walked on, checking the footprints for perhaps a hundred metres, and then I saw it: a swirl of wet earth, a muddle of footsteps and drag marks leading to the edge of the towpath and stopping beside the wreck of a wide, windowless cargo barge. It was as long as a bus with a deck at each end. I held the lighter high, picking out the clutter on the roof – buckets of coal, coils of cable, a small upturned boat made of some kind of plastic, and on the far deck a rusty little crane, leaning out over the water like a beaky bird. I lowered the lighter. The guttering flame caught letters painted on the side, half hidden behind drapes of rotten rope. *The Three Brothers*. I nearly cried out with relief. They weren't men. *The Three Brothers* was a barge.

I pulled on the rope and jumped, landing on the deck

with a thud that rocked the huge hull and sent a clutch of bottles rolling across the metal floor, glugging out their contents. The smell was acrid. Like medicine. I picked up one of the bottles and read the label. VODKA. I tried the door handle. It was jammed. I pulled again, heaving with all my strength until it swung open. I stumbled down the wooden steps, nearly falling when the end of the handrail swung loose from the wall.

'Dan?'

There was no answer. My skin felt too flimsy to hold the swell of fear but I edged backwards and forced myself to pull the door shut before I flicked on the lighter. All I could see was a lake of oily water, littered with beer cans and broken bottles, stretching out to another set of steps and a door at the far end. Flashing the lighter across the brightly coloured tags on the walls, I stepped down into the water, gasping as the icy wet lapped over my knees and soaked through my jeans.

'Dan,' I whispered again. The dying flame touched a shudder of water bubbling through a hole in the side of the boat and causing the debris to bob and dance. All of it, except for one pale mound in the middle, which broke the surface like a small island. My world slowed. As if in a dark dream, I waded forward. Something sharp smashed my shin, ripping my jeans and flesh. I toppled sideways, struggling to keep the lighter clear of the water. I moved on, shuffling between the lumps of twisted metal lurking beneath the surface, until I was close enough to sweep the light across the mound. It was a dome of flesh; the boy's cheek and the bump of his nose, his head twisted sideways, his mouth a grey slit beneath the surface. I flung myself towards him, grasped the floating tangle of his hair and lifted his head.

'Get up!' My voice broke apart. 'Quickly! Get up!'

His eyes were closed. A trickle of water dribbled from his lips. I yanked his head higher. A choking retch shook his body. His eyes opened.

'Dan!'

He stared past me, his eyes blank. Even as I looked the water was rising. The lighter flame dwindled and went out with a hiss. The darkness was shocking. Total. As if I'd been blinded. I stuck the lighter in my pocket, pushed my hands under his armpits and tried to drag him back towards the door. His top half swayed, his arms flopped loosely, then his body jerked to a stop, held fast by something under the water. I tore off my soaking hoodie, bundled it into a pillow and pushed it under his neck, raising his mouth a couple of inches above the water before I plunged my hand back down and groped along his legs. He seemed to be lying sideways across a pile of concrete blocks, with one foot trapped in the coils of a heavy iron chain. I felt around it. The chain was too heavy to lift, each link the size of my fist and tangled up in a heavy hunk of metal, maybe part of an engine. I couldn't lift it. Not on my own. But there was no time to run for help. It was just me and the boy, and with every second the water was getting higher. Make a plan, Aliya! Think! What would Behrouz do now? A lever. He'd lever the chain up.

I staggered back, thumbing the wheel of the lighter again and again until it sparked a tiny spark that burnt my thumb but gave me my bearings. I launched myself towards the door I'd come in through, bashing my shins again as I found the steps and fumbled for the broken handrail. I twisted it free from the rotten panelling and turned back, guided by the fading image of the interior etched in my head.

'It's OK, Dan. It's OK,' I whispered.

I dropped to my knees, crawling and splashing in the dark and wet until I found the chain. I slid the tip of the handrail between the coils, working it as deeply as I could, then I pressed down with all my strength. The links creaked. I tore at the boy's leg. I couldn't free his foot. I tried again, jamming the rail between the coils but pressing on the end of it with my knee this time, releasing both hands to pull at his leg. The chain lifted very slightly but I wasn't strong enough to yank his foot out. I could feel the rail bending, about to snap.

'Pull,' I begged. 'Please, Dan. Pull your foot.'

I heard him groan. The sound wasn't human. As I heaved on his leg a tiny spasm twitched through his muscles.

'Again, Dan. Pull. I'll count to three. One, two, three!'

I wrenched hard. He let out another animal groan and,

with a muffled clank of falling chain, his foot jerked free. I jammed the rail into my belt, tied the arms of my hoodie under his armpits and used it to lug his slack, slippery weight over the scrap. I had no bearings now. I just knew the door at the far end was nearer and I kept on hauling him, praying that we were moving in the right direction. He was a dead weight and he kept sliding under the water as I slapped frantically at the clammy walls. I let out a cry when I found the steps to the far door. I strained to get him up halfway, held the knotted hoodie with one hand, wrenched the bolt back with the other and kicked and kicked until the door burst open. Thin red darkness poured through the gap, diluting the dank blackness inside. Gasping and panting, I grappled him up the last two steps and collapsed beside him on the metal deck. He was barely breathing. He didn't respond when I shook him and his damp skin felt like frozen rubber. Had I saved him from drowning, just to let him die of cold?

My eyes slid to the distant outline of Meadowview. I didn't care that the police had forbidden me to go there. If I could just get him to our flat, at least I could warm him and dry him. But I knew I could never drag him that far and I felt my last reserves of hope and strength draining away. My leg throbbed with pain, my knuckles were raw and bloody, and the whole world seemed to be tipping and spinning. I let my head drop back against the wall and closed my eyes, numb with exhaustion and defeat.

'No!' I forced my eyes open. 'You can't give up. Not

now.' My voice sounded so frail and cracked I didn't even think it was mine. Still dazed and nauseous, I pulled myself up, telling myself there had to be a way. I gazed round frantically and saw it as a hump at first, a black blob rising above the junk on the roof of the barge. Slowly, it took on the shape of the little upturned boat and, when I looked back and saw the lowering outline of Meadowview framed between the metal struts of the crane, the fragments of an idea began to come together through the fug in my head. Could I get the boy into the boat? Could I drag him down the canal like a child with a toy?

Holding tightly to the boat's dangling rope, I tottered along the walkway and pushed the plastic hull as hard as I could. The sinking barge was so low in the water the boat didn't have far to fall before it hit the surface with a rocking splash. I slithered on to the deck, lashed the rope to the base of the crane and ran my fingers up the struts, feeling the mechanism for cogs and winches. The boy groaned. I stopped and turned. In the distance headlights fanned and narrowed as a car pulled on to the waste ground. I felt a surge of joy. People. I could run to them, they would help me. Relief turned to panic. Who would come to this deserted place so late at night? More boys with their girlfriends? Or was it the freckled man, checking to see that the boy was dead? I couldn't take that chance.

Although the crane was stiff and rusted, I strained with all my might and managed to swing the boom around so the head hung directly above the boy. Heaving hard on the handle, I lowered the dangling hook and jammed it under his belt. I grasped the handle with both hands and heaved again. The cogs grumbled and my muscles burned, sending sharp stabbing pains through my stomach and arms as I winched him up from the deck, his limp body twisting in the air and water dripping off him like a drowned corpse. I swung the boom back again and turned the handle to lower him into the boat. He crumpled into the bottom, face down, limbs bent awkwardly. I pulled the boat closer and dropped my feet over the side, tipping it sharply and nearly plunging us both into the water. Struggling to keep balanced, I knelt down and grappled the iron hook from his belt. Footsteps sounded on the towpath, coming closer. I threw myself down beside him and we lay in the darkness, silent as shadows. The distant scrape of gravel gave way to the closer squelch of mud. The footsteps halted. A thin torch beam flashed through the darkness. I felt for the bent rail I'd stuck through my belt and gripped it tightly in my hand.

'Look at that. Going down fast. What a tragedy.' The freckled man's voice was sneering.

'Do you want me to check inside?' the other man asked.

'No, I'll do it. Give us the torch.'

I closed my eyes, listening to the clank of his feet on the far deck and the scrape of the opening door. A moment of quiet then the door creaked shut.

'What did I tell you? He's totally submerged.'

Their fading footsteps did nothing to calm my fear. It

would take them at least fifteen minutes to get back to their car and I didn't dare move until I was sure they weren't coming back. I was cold and weary but the silence and the gentle sway of the boat were so soothing that after a while I drifted into a numb, exhausted sleep. Strange dreams came; I was falling spreadeagled from a rooftop and Behrouz was reaching from a window, grasping the tips of my outstretched fingers, calling out, 'Hold on, sis,' as strong winds tried to suck me away. A sharp gust broke his grip and the last thing I saw as I was whisked into nothingness was the look of defeat on his face.

I sat up, blinking into the dark. The black bulk of the barge seemed further away. I tugged on the rope. It felt slack. Horrified, I pulled harder and brought the whole dripping length of it into the boat. My hurried knot had come free. We were in the middle of the canal, drifting with the pull of the water.

DAN

'Wake up!' Trent was hissing at me, slapping my face, only his voice was blurring, echoing, melting into a softer sound. 'Wake up!'

Not a bloke. Not Trent. Who, then? My head was throbbing. I was shivering, feeling sick, heavy and confused. It was a girl, someone I knew . . . Aliya. They'd got her too, Trent and the other man. The one who kicked me when I fell. 'Leave her alone.' My voice was slurred, like my tongue had come loose.

'Dan. Please. I don't know about boats. I've never been in one before.'

Boats? What was she on about? I tried to sit up. Lights swilled round my head and liquid lead flooded my veins, weighing me down. It was terrifying not being able to move. She was pulling my shoulders. Turning me over. When I finally got my eyes open, I was staring up at a patch of dark, swaying sky. A boat. We were on one. Me and Aliya. That explained the moving sky but not much else. Like how we'd got there. Or why she was leaning over the side, nearly tipping us over.

I chewed my cheek to get the saliva going and managed to wheeze out 'What . . . you . . . doing?'

'There's a branch in the water. I'm trying to catch it with the rope.'

'Why?'

'There are no oars.'

I tried to focus. No oars. That was bad . . . But all I wanted to do was curl up and give in to the drowsiness. She prodded my arm. 'Stay awake! The water comes nearly to the top. We are too heavy. You have to tell me how to steer.'

The terror in her voice cut through the wooziness and I struggled towards the bit of my brain that was still working. 'Swim . . . can you . . . swim?'

'No. Can you?'

Not in the state I was in. My brain might be struggling back into action but my body still felt boneless and detached. All I could move was my head and if the boat sank, I'd sink with it. Like a lump of concrete. I pushed that thought away. She reached out again, lunging with the rope. The boat lurched with her. 'Nooo! . . . mid . . . middle. Sit . . . middle.'

She shifted back from the edge and kept flinging the rope. The boat was threshing about and I was cursing Trent and whatever it was he'd doped me with and praying we weren't going to capsize.

'Got it!' Water splattered all over me as she hauled the dripping branch into the boat.

In a dazed, groggy way I'd been hoping for something big and paddle-shaped, not a spindly stem with a few twigs on the end.

'What do I do?'

'Stick it . . . in . . . water . . . push . . . back.'

I could tell from the way the sky was spinning that we were turning in a slow, wobbly circle.

'No . . . one . . . side . . . other . . . side.'

The lurching and swaying wasn't exactly reassuring, but she dug in with steadier strokes, got into a bit of a rhythm and after a while the sky started moving in a straighter line. I had no idea where we were or what was happening, so the judder of the bow bumping against something hard was a relief till she reached up too quickly and nearly tipped us over.

Slowly and painfully I twisted my head. We were near the bridge. In the eerie blue glow from the strip lights under its tiled arch I could see she was holding on to the side of an old houseboat, grabbing the dangling tyres they were using as bumpers and pulling us along, hand over hand, towards an empty strip of the canal side. She looped the rope over a mooring post. As she pulled herself on to the bank her foot kicked out and the boat shot away from the edge.

'Get . . . me . . . out,' I groaned, imagining the loop slipping free, leaving me floating helplessly in the dark until I got drowned or swept out to sea.

She crouched down and whispered, 'Wait there.'

'Nooo!' I called after her. 'Don't leave me!' She didn't look back and when it came to the waiting part, I didn't have much choice. I lay there totally helpless, trying to ward off the panic by concentrating on my muscles, working to get some feeling back into the bits that mattered. After a while, agonizing pins and needles started jabbing my hands and feet and the space from my knees to my neck began to feel like melting rubber, which was an improvement on total numbness. But no way was I ever going to be able to get out of that boat on my own. I was more than worried. Where was she?

A lifetime later I heard footsteps echoing off the walls of the bridge and another noise, a faint metallic grinding. Don't let it be Trent. Please don't let it be Trent. I caught a smell, like a pack of rats had curled up and died, only whatever this was it was still alive, because the stench was coming nearer. I craned my head and saw an old wino staggering towards me. With his long white hair, straggly beard and skeletal face, he looked like Gandalf's corpse, and his mangy white dog didn't look much healthier. With any luck he'd be too drunk to see me. He lurched closer. Next thing I know, the stink's so bad I think

I'm going to choke, his ratty beard's brushing my face and there's a huge pair of filthy hands grabbing me under my arms, smashing my head against the side of the boat, scraping it up the concrete edge of the canal and smacking me down on the towpath. If it hadn't been for the foul stink from his trainers and his dog drooling in my eye, I'd probably have passed out again.

'There you go, missy,' he said, as if he was the postman delivering a parcel.

The creaking got louder. Aliya's voice came out of the gloom and her feet appeared behind a supermarket trolley. 'Please help him on to this,' she said.

The wino grunted and got hold of me again, hugging me to his stinking coat so tightly my battered ribs screamed with pain. Before I could find the breath to yell, he'd flung me face down over the handle of the trolley, with my head and arms slumped over the wire seat you stick kids in. When I turned my head, Aliya was slipping something into his hand.

'I will bring back your trolley,' she said. 'I promise.'

'Mind you do, missy,' he said. Through the metal mesh I saw him stagger off, dangling her silver watch in his grubby fingers and watching it glitter in the light.

ALIYA

I walked backwards, pulling the trolley by the front end with the boy flopped forward over the handle at the back, dragging his feet behind him. The path was muddy, the little wheels squeaked and wobbled and I was so exhausted it took us nearly half an hour to heave and shuffle the fifty metres to Meadowview. The stink of urine, the filthy words on the walls and the broken glass in the stairwell brought back all the confusion and sinking hope of the night we'd arrived. I gazed at the steep flight of concrete stairs. I hadn't even thought how I'd get the boy up to the ninth floor. He murmured. 'Wassappening?' I gave the lift button a half-hearted jab, astonished when the mechanism whirred and clanked and the doors juddered open, flooding us with harsh green light. The police must have had it mended so they wouldn't have to trudge up and down nine flights of stairs. The police. I swung round, frightened that the freckled man would be standing there, waiting to snatch us both. I shunted the trolley into the lift and quickly pressed the button.

The boy said blearily, 'You can't . . . come here . . . you're banned.'

This time it was me who shrugged. 'Where else can we go?'

The lift shuddered to a halt. I took a moment to look at him. He was bruised, wet, bloodied and shivering. He lifted his head a little and murmured, 'I hate this place.'

'Me too,' I said.

The police had mended the lights on the landing as well. They blinked on as we stepped out of the lift, throwing pools of dull yellow light across the scarred concrete floor, picking out the cracks and bumps that shook the trolley and made the wheels clatter. For the first time ever I was glad the other flats on this floor were empty.

Our front door was a splintered mess. The police had nailed a criss-cross of planks across what was left of it and covered it in yellow tape, with the words CRIME SCENE DO NOT CROSS printed on it in thick black letters. It made me angry.

It wasn't a crime scene. This dingy, dirty, rundown flat that no one else wanted to live in was the nearest thing my family had to a home. I used the rail from the barge to slash away the tape. Then I jammed the tip of it under the edges of the boards, wrenching hard to lever out the nails. It was a good feeling when the last nail sprang free and the final board swung loose. I left the trolley in the hall and helped the boy into the living room. He shambled forward, leaning against me like an old man. When I tried to manoeuvre him around the gaping hole where the police had ripped up the floorboards, he tripped and turned. Our eyes met and held for the beat of a heart. I pushed him away and let him fall on to the couch.

'How did you . . . find me?' His voice was slow and rasping, like rocks being dragged over rocks.

'I went to Hamidi's house.'

He groaned and rubbed his head, as if that still didn't make any sense. 'My mum . . . she'll be going mental. I got to . . . phone her.'

'It's all right. They texted her. They said you were staying with a friend.'

I fetched him the blanket from my bed and switched on the electric fire. The single bar didn't give off much heat, but we sat on the floor, just me and the boy, comforted by the orange glow and the smell of hot dust, hardly daring to believe we were alive. He gave me a slack, lopsided smile. Anger flowed in and filled the spaces left by panic. How dare he smile at me! This boy was not my friend. He was my betrayer. But I would wait until he was better before I confronted him.

I jumped up and went to the kitchen to search for food. The police had taken all the tins and packets and left nothing except a bowl of leftover rice and *banjaan* in the fridge. The meal I'd made for Behrouz. The meal he'd never come home to eat. That was four days ago, in another lifetime. I tipped it into a saucepan and left it to warm while I went to find Behrouz's charger and plug in my phone. I ached to be clean. I went to the bathroom and turned on the hot tap. The burners lit with a whump, then went out. I had no coins for the gas meter. So I washed in cold water, rinsed out my clothes and hung them in front of the oven to dry.

Then I opened my backpack and took out Behrouz's gun. I had retrieved it from the depths of the *Margaretta* on my way to get help from that old tramp. For a moment I held it in my hand. A deadly reminder of how far my life in England had departed from my dreams. I slipped it into my backpack and ate half the *banjaan* standing up. The boy had fallen asleep without eating his, and for the next few hours he slept and I stood by the window wrapped in a blanket, gazing out at the lights glittering bright across this city that had once promised my family refuge. I did not look at the strip of darkness where the barge called *The Three Brothers* was sinking slowly to the bottom of the canal.

DAN

My mind was floating. Disconnected. I was shivering and sweating. Freezing, burning up, then turning numb, and after a while I must have fallen asleep, because I was opening my eyes, and there was grey light coming through the windows and someone was standing over me, tapping my cheek. Tap, tap, tap, like they were flicking switches, turning my senses back on. I started hearing the traffic outside, feeling the slimy wetness of my clothes, smelling a foul stink that made me want to throw up and remembering the horror of thinking I was going to die. I looked down. My wet clothes were black with slime. I had on one trainer. The other foot was bare, swollen up and crusted with blood. When I tried to move, it felt as if my joints had been injected with ground glass. Slowly the outline of a girl came into focus. Aliya. She was holding out a cup of something steaming.

'Green tea. It's all there is.' She dumped it on the floor next to an untouched bowl of some aubergine stuff she must have given me last night and stood there rubbing her arms.

'Can we turn the fire back on?' My throat was raw and the words came out slowly.

'The meter just ran out.'

She looked terrible. I bet I looked worse. At least she'd had a chance to clean herself up a bit.

'Thanks for saving my life,' I said. I s'pose I'd expected her to blush or smile. Instead her face turned hard and an angry muscle tweaked her cheek.

'We are still not safe. They will kill us both if they can. And I don't want your thanks. I want to know why you met that man with the freckled face. What were you telling him?'

I struggled to sit up and had to breathe in small gasps because of the searing pain in my ribs. Still, it gave me a few seconds to think how best to tell her. 'His name's Mark Trent.'

'Go on.'

'He's a policeman.'

'I know that,' she said crossly. 'I saw him at the police station when they questioned me. He also works for Hamidi.'

'I didn't know that till yesterday. I swear.'

The look she gave me withered my insides. 'Don't you lie to me. You were working for Hamidi too!'

'What?' I was seriously shocked. 'Course I wasn't.'

'I heard them talk. You saw something you shouldn't, so he ordered Mark Trent to kill you.'

'No . . . I mean, yes, but it's not what you think. I wasn't working for Hamidi. No way.'

'So why did you meet with Trent?'

'To tell him Behrouz was innocent.'

She looked away as if the sight of me made her sick. 'Why would he believe you? You said yourself we have no proof.'

'We have now. I found some. Well, not proof exactly, but I know who wanted him dead. And I know why.'

'What reason?' Her eyes flicked back to mine, still accusing.

'That man smoking outside Hardel's with Hamidi. It was Farukh Zarghun.'

This wasn't how it was supposed to be. I should have been telling her this in the same breath as I told her Behrouz was free, all charges dropped, while the newspapers grovelled and printed headlines saying they'd got it wrong.

She scowled and shook her head as if I'd totally lost it. 'I know you are a liar but I did not think you were stupid. Farukh Zarghun is dead. He died in prison. You read it yourself on those websites.'

'He's got two missing fingers. It's definitely him. And when I told Trent about it, he started pouring all this sugar in my drink. Only it was doped.'

She was glaring at me, getting angrier every time I opened my mouth. 'Zarghun? In the UK? How did he rise from his grave? How did he get out of prison?'

'I don't know, but I'm telling you he did. He's moved his drug operation to London and he's got Hamidi, Trent and . . . and . . . loads of other people working for him.'

She sat back on her heels, her pale-green eyes never moving from my face, but there was confusion in them as well as contempt. 'If this is true, do you know how many powerful people must have helped him to do this?' Her voice was slowly losing its edge, as if she was thinking it through. 'Not just Afghans, Americans and British too.'

'Yeah, all getting their cut of the drug money, and if Trent's involved, you can bet your life half his bosses are in on it too.' She was really listening now, so I kept talking. 'Look. I've worked it out. Behrouz took those shots of Hamidi, recognized Zarghun, and panicked when he realized they were after him. He worked out there were bent cops in on it, so the only person he trusted to help him was Colonel Clarke. That's why he asked Merrick to get him the colonel's home number.'

She was frowning but taking in every word. 'That would explain why he was so upset when he heard that Colonel Clarke was away.'

'He wasn't upset, he was scared stiff.'

'So he got a gun to protect himself until Clarke came back.'

'Exactly. So we go to Clarke and we tell him everything. He's the only person with the power to cut through the corruption and get us protection.'

She'd stopped glaring at me and started squeezing her hands in excitement. 'That's what Behrouz was telling me in the video. He said, "I have a plan . . . to seek out Colonel Mike Clarke so that justice can be done." He wanted me to ignore all the horrible words they made him say about killing people and get Clarke to help me uncover the truth.' Her hands grew still. 'But none of this proves that Zarghun put Behrouz in that garage with those chemicals.'

'Clarke will believe us, I promise.'

'How can you know that?'

I had to tell her, but I couldn't look at her. 'Because . . . there's something else.'

'What?'

'A witness. Someone who saw Hamidi kidnap Behrouz at gunpoint a couple of hours before the explosion.'

Her eyes filled with tears. 'Who? Who is this witness?'

My stomach lurched, but it wasn't the lingering stench of canal water or stale vomit that was making me gag. It was the rotten taste of the word that I was forcing through my lips.

'Me.'

ALIYA

Everything seemed to change, the smudged light through the windows grew clearer and the ache in my heart lifted away. This truth he was telling me, and I knew from the agony on his face that this time it really was the truth, was like a lifeline dragging me out of a dark, stinking cave into warm, sweet sunshine. Now I could prove to the police that Behrouz was innocent, that he'd been kidnapped and set up to die like a bomber. The feeling of release lasted less than a second before it was smothered by a rush of hatred so intense I wanted to strike the boy with my fists. I let out a scream that bounced off the walls. 'Why didn't you get help? You could have saved him!'

The boy bowed his head and blurted out a muddled

story of stolen washing machines, drugs hidden at Meadowview, a lost phone and Behrouz getting beaten with a gun. Then he raised his tear-stained face, looked straight into my eyes and told me how he had lied about everything, how he had allowed Behrouz to be kidnapped, injured and arrested in order to protect his father. A man who was a liar just like his son, and also a thief and a seller of drugs. A man I had liked and made tea for and who had smiled at me when he came to our flat.

So many liars: the boy, his father, my own instincts – they had all lied to me. Nothing was real. Even the floor felt as if it might suddenly give way beneath my feet and drop me into emptiness. When I finally forced myself to look at the boy, he was still hunched over, watching me, as if he wanted me to punish him, scream hatred in his face or throw him out of the flat. Maybe it would have made us both feel better. But a cold calm was slowly smothering my anger like damp leaves on a fire. The fury still smouldered, but giving way to it now wouldn't help Behrouz. First I needed to piece things together, fill in the final blanks in the story and decide what to do. My words, when they came, were clipped and stiff.

'Did your father know about the kidnap?'

He closed his eyes. 'I . . . I don't know . . . I don't think so.'

'Why did you delete those photos from my phone?'

'The white van in it was my dad's and the man helping Hamidi to load it up was Dad's partner, Jez Deakin.' He paused. 'I'm sorry.' He crumpled forward as if he knew how pathetic those words sounded to my ears. 'I thought I could make it right. I thought I could find a way to prove Behrouz was innocent that would keep my dad out of it. It'd kill my mum if he went to prison. I . . . I'll go now.' He pulled himself up, gripping the arm of the sofa.

'You can't leave,' I said. 'You are my proof, my witness, and you owe me. Is that what they say?'

'I s'pose.' He was watching me carefully, still waiting for my anger to erupt.

'You smell bad,' I said. 'Wash yourself and put on these.' I threw him a bundle of clothes I'd found in Behrouz's room. 'When you are dressed, we are going to find the colonel and you are going to tell him everything that you have told to me.'

I held on to my tears until the boy had hobbled out of the room and then I let them fall. As I cried myself out I felt as if a wire was unwinding from my heart, letting my blood flow freely. The need to trust him had been confusing me, holding me back, and now that I knew the truth, I felt wretched and lonely but in control.

Calmer now, I called the colonel's house, using the number Captain Merrick had sent to Behrouz. I walked up and down as it rang. A woman answered, a maid or a housekeeper.

'Hello. Please can I speak to Colonel Clarke?' I said.

'The colonel and his wife are away. Can I take a message?'

'Do you know where I can find him?'

'Who is this?'

I opened my mouth to say my name. I shut it again. 'It's urgent, I . . . I really need to talk to him.'

Her voice grew sterner. 'Where did you get this number?'

'I need his help.'

'If you want to contact the colonel, I suggest you write to him at the House of Commons or contact his constituency office.' She hung up.

Now I knew exactly how my brother had felt: blocked, frustrated, lonely and scared. I longed to hear the colonel's firm, powerful voice assuring me he would get Behrouz released and stop the press from printing their hateful lies about my family. But even the colonel had problems with the press. I remembered the shame I'd felt when I read the mean gossip about his wife in that magazine, how they'd tried to turn the photo of her and her assistant into something bad when all she'd been doing was working on her new movie. A thought crept into my head, a tiny wisp, like smoke. I stared through the window and tried to catch the name of the place where she was filming. I ran down the hall and beat on the bathroom door.

'Hever Castle,' I shouted. 'Where is it?'

I heard a splash and a gurgle as if the boy was lifting his head from under the water. In a flash of panic I saw his cold tilted face and the dark canal water lapping against his cheek.

'What?' he mumbled.

'Hever Castle.'

'Never heard of it. Why?'

'The colonel's wife, India Lambert, is filming there. We can't get to the colonel. But we can get to her.' I ran back to my phone, shaking as I keyed in the name.

The boy shuffled in, wrapped in the blanket. He was shivering and swaying and there was blood dripping from the wound on his ankle. 'Found it?' he asked.

I handed him the phone and watched his fingers poke the screen. 'It's thirty miles from London. We'd have to take two trains and a load of buses.' He gave me back the phone, sweaty, pale and wiping his forehead. 'I . . . I still feel really weird. I don't think I can make it that far.'

'You have to,' I said coldly. 'You have to tell her what you saw. Hurry. Put on the clothes I gave you.'

He nodded but his face was grey, his eyes were dull and when he turned away he had to reach for the wall to stop himself falling. I didn't care that he was weak and sick but I did care if he collapsed before we got to see the colonel's wife. I needed someone to drive us. Someone we could trust. Maybe someone from Khan's. But everyone there thought Behrouz was guilty. Everyone except Corella and maybe that apprentice mechanic, Connor, who had seemed to be coming round to the idea that he wasn't. I picked up the phone and dialled Connor's number. It rang for a long time before he answered.

'Yeah?' His voice was soggy with sleep.

'This is Aliya Sahar.'

There was a pause and a grunt. 'It's the middle of the night.'

'No. It's six-thirty in the morning.' I cut through his groaning. 'I know who tried to kill Behrouz.'

That seemed to wake him up. His voice sharpened. 'Who?'

'An Afghan drug gang. They kidnapped him just before the explosion.'

'Jesus. What about Arif?'

'Arif?' In all the confusion I'd hardly thought about Behrouz's missing friend, but now the answer to Connor's question seemed obvious. I said softly, 'I think Behrouz told him about this gang and they took him to keep him quiet.'

He swore. 'Are you going to go to the cops?'

'It's too dangerous. There are policemen helping the gang. We have to tell Colonel Clarke.'

'Who's he?'

'Behrouz's old boss from the army. He's important, he works in the government now, and he's the only person Behrouz trusted. His wife is India Lambert.'

'What, that actress?'

'Yes. You have to drive us to Kent, where she is filming.'

'Me?'

'Yes. Come straight away. I will text you my address.'

'You're crazy. I haven't got a car and I've got to go to work.'

'Take a car from Khan's, one that you are mending. Then call them and tell them you are sick.'

'No way. I'll lose my job.'

'Please, Connor.' My voice cracked. 'This gang are after us. They are trying to kill us.' I could hear his ragged breath as he wavered. 'You said Arif was your friend. Don't you want to save him?'

'Course I do.'

'Then the colonel is the only one who can help you. Please hurry.'

I cut the call. The boy stole a questioning look at me. 'Do you think Arif's still alive?'

I shook my head, feeling bad that I had given Connor false hope. I fetched a tea-towel from the kitchen and began to tear it into strips. The boy winced when I lifted his foot. I didn't look at him while I bandaged his wound and he didn't look at me.

DAN

Considering how I felt, which was pretty close to death – blurred vision, a demolition crew smashing through my skull with jack hammers and a throbbing burn in my guts – I was amazed I had the strength to stand up, let alone get dressed. It was guilt keeping me going. The jeans, shirt and trainers she'd thrown at me were the kind of cheap chain-store stuff I wouldn't normally be seen dead in. Ironic, really. The way things were going, being seen dead looked like a strong possibility. But for once in my life I couldn't have cared less what I was wearing or what kind of danger I was in. I just wanted to make things right.

Connor turned up around ten-thirty, looking pretty wrecked too. Puffy eyes, spots all over his face, and the car he'd borrowed was a heap of junk. Apart from the rusty bodywork, the seats were splitting apart, the windows had been blacked out with some kind of tinted stick-on plastic and the side one at the back had been broken and patched up with cardboard and tape.

'Whose car is this?' Aliya asked, not bothering to hide her disappointment that he hadn't turned up in one of Khan's fast new minicabs.

'Karim's. He's Mr Khan's nephew and he'll kill me if he finds out I've taken it.' He saw the look on her face and grinned. 'Don't worry. It's a good little motor. It's got him out of plenty of trouble.'

He got worried when he saw me sweating and sway-ing. 'You're not going to puke all over the seats are you?'

'No,' I said, but I was swallowing down lurches of vomit before we'd even gone a mile down the road. Too sick to talk, I left it to Aliya to give him directions and tell him what we'd found out. She went through every detail, checking her facts against a new grid she must have drawn up in the night. When she got to the kidnap and told him why I'd lied about it, Connor caught my eye in the mirror. He didn't say anything. He just looked at me like he was wondering if he'd have done the same. Then she asked him straight out if the gun was Arif's.

Connor tightened his fingers around the steering wheel. 'That's none of your business.'

'It is my business if he gave it Behrouz.'

He slid her a sideways glance. 'Did the police find it?'

'No. I hid it before they came.'

He grunted. As if he was surprised and a bit impressed.

'It was Arif's, wasn't it?' She pointed to her grid. 'He and Behrouz must have gone to get it when they left Khan's together on Tuesday afternoon.'

He slowed for a sudden curve in the road. 'Arif's not into shooters.'

'So where did he get it?'

Connor dragged a grimy hand across his face. 'If you must know, it was off a punter.'

She wasn't going to let him off that easily. 'What punter?'

'He said it was some crazy who got in his cab one night, off his head on God knows what.'

'Why would this crazy man give Arif a gun?'

'He didn't. He was puking so badly when he got out of the cab he left his bag on the seat. And when Arif drove back to his house to hand it back, the whole place was swarming with cops. So he took the bag apart and found a gun stuffed in the lining.'

'Why didn't he get rid of it?'

'He was worried about his visa. He didn't want the punter turning up and giving him grief if he handed it in to the cops, and he didn't want the cops doing him for having a firearm if he hung on to it.'

'So what did he do?' she asked.

'Me and him drove out to Epping Forest and buried it.

But don't you dare tell that to this colonel or his wife.' He glared at me over his shoulder. 'You too, Abbott. I'm doing this so we can find Arif, not stitch him up.'

'Sure,' I said.

Aliya was agitated, chewing her cuff. 'Look . . .' she said, as if she was about to admit her fears about Arif. But she stopped herself and as she looked away her eye caught mine. Grubby grey lies. We were both telling them now.

Connor rammed his foot on the accelerator. The car shot forward so fast it threw us back in our seats. I didn't want to know what sort of trouble it had got Khan's nephew out of but from the smirk on Connor's face you could tell he was the one who'd souped up the engine. I wished he hadn't. I didn't know what to do. If I closed my eyes, I saw weird lights flashing through darkness, faces looming down at me then melting away, but if I opened them, the world whizzing past the windows made my stomach heave and my head swim. Still, it was better than trying to drag myself on to trains and buses and after nearly two hours of torture I finally saw the first signs to Hever Castle. By then we'd hit real countryside, the sort Mum used to get Dad to drive us to when she wanted to give my nan a treat. Cream teas, rolling hills, narrow winding roads and me in a strop in the back playing games on my phone. Wondering if that was ever going to happen again tipped me into places I didn't want to go.

The lane where Connor parked the car had woods down one side and a high, moss-covered stone wall along the other. We walked back towards the main road, following a line of yellow arrows nailed to the trees that said FILMING. I was weaving a bit, lagging behind, and by the time I got to the entrance a harassed man in headphones was shooing Aliya, Connor and a half-dozen other people away, shouting, 'No fans on set, can't you read?'

Aliya didn't move. 'We have to see Miss Lambert. It's important.'

'You got a visitor's pass?'

'No.'

'Then you must be joking. Go on, clear off, we've got props coming through any minute.' He scanned the road, raising his clipboard as a truck rumbled towards us. A uniformed security guard came out and herded us further back. 'You heard him. Move away from the gates, please!'

Aliya ducked under his outstretched arm and we followed her as she made for Clipboard Man. 'Please. Could you give her a note?'

'I'm not a ruddy postman.'

'Her husband, Colonel Clarke he . . . he knows my family.' Tears misted her eyes. She wiped them away. 'Please, it is urgent . . . a matter of death and life.'

He darted her a suspicious look, but anyone could see she was serious.

'Oh, give it here, but get away from the gate.'

Aliya had a pen on her but for paper she had to make do with a grease-spotted food wrapper I snatched out of the gutter. Using Connor's back to rest on, she wrote:

Dear Miss Lambert,
I am the sister of Behrouz Sahar. I am at the gate. I have proof that my brother is innocent and I must talk to Colonel Clarke. I am in danger. Please help me. If you cannot talk to me now, please phone me very soon.

She scribbled her number, signed her name and handed it to Clipboard Man. As soon as he'd checked the truck over he stomped away across the field, shouting orders to a bunch of workmen in overalls and grabbing a bottle of water from a stand under the trees. I half expected him to chuck the note in the rubbish but he made his way to a row of trailers and knocked on the door of a luxury model, twice the size of all the others, standing on its own at the end. The door opened. The three of us sucked in our breath as he talked to someone inside, willing him to walk back and let us in. But the door of the trailer banged shut and he hurried off towards the castle, pressing on the mouthpiece of his headset. The uniformed guard walked towards us, walkie-talkie crackling.

'He says it's a no. Go on, hop it.'

We shuffled past the rest of the crowd.

'Now what?' I asked.

Aliya shook her head, totally dejected. 'That was my last hope.'

Connor strolled off towards the lane where we'd parked, kicking a stone around, trying not look as if he was checking things out. He circled back. 'We could have a go at climbing over the wall and knocking on the door of her trailer.'

I couldn't see myself making it over a wall that high, but Aliya was totally up for it, telling me I didn't have a choice.

We were heading down the lane looking for the best place to climb when her phone buzzed. Her eyes widened as the screen flashed up 'number unknown'. She flicked on the speaker. Connor and I crowded round as a man's voice said her name. 'Aliya?'

'Yes.'

'I'm Miss Lambert's personal assistant. She says she'll see you but she's only got a few minutes, so I'll come and pick you up, it'll save the hassle of getting you a pass. There's a bus stop on the main road, past the pub. Wait there and I'll bring you round to the cast entrance. I'll be in a silver Range Rover.'

Before she could say anything he hung up and she started to run back to the main road. I hobbled after her on legs that felt like mush. She was nearing the bus stop when the silver Range Rover came swinging round the corner. I put on a spurt and tripped on a crack in the path. Connor grabbed my arm, helped me up and dragged me to the car. Dizzy and breathless, I peered inside. The dark-haired, square-jawed driver was leaning over, looking up at us through the open window – designer stubble, white teeth and an expensive white shirt rolled up to his elbows, showing off tanned, muscular arms.

'This boy is Connor and this one is Dan,' Aliya was saying. 'They have important things to tell Miss Lambert too.'

The man hesitated, his eyes on me. Something flickered in his face. I couldn't tell if he was annoyed or just surprised that she hadn't come alone.

He said, 'OK. But I'll need your full names in case security stops us at the gate.'

I leant against the side of the car, trying to catch my breath. 'Daniel Abbott.'

Connor ducked his head so the man could see his face and muttered, 'Connor Mackay.'

'I'm Steve Hutchins, call me Hutch. Hop in the back and make sure you stay down when we go past security.' We slid along the seat, breathing in the powerful smell of his aftershave.

'You from Kabul, Aliya?' he said.

'Yes.'

'I did a couple of tours in Afghanistan with the colonel.' He was reaching for his phone and calling a number.

'Hey, Ind— Miss Lambert. Aliya's got a couple of friends with her . . . two boys . . . Daniel Abbott . . . yes . . . yes . . . that's right . . . and . . . Connor Mackay. They've been helping her find out about her brother. They seem like decent kids, so I thought it'd be all right to bring them along . . . yeah . . . no . . . No problem.'

He headed for a side entrance, barking, 'Heads down,' drove through very fast and sped down a muddy track that led behind the trailers.

'Go easy when you see Miss Lambert. She's been working since dawn and she needs to catch some rest before they start shooting again this afternoon.'

He swung the car around and pulled up in front of her trailer. The field we were in was packed with trucks and tents, and beyond the catering van on the other side you could just make out the castle's turrets sticking through the trees. It was like a circus – people running in all directions, guys leading horses around, actors wandering past in old-fashioned costumes, some of them with curlers in, even the men, and one bloke had a sword in one hand and a cigarette in the other. Hutch barely knocked on the trailer door before he pushed it open and stood back to let Aliya pass.

OK, I thought. This is it.

ALIYA

The trailer was like the cave of Aladdin. Bright fabrics and glittering jewels scattered everywhere, a dress of green velvet threaded with pearls hanging from a folding screen, a purple cloak thrown across a chair, the air heavy with the smells of coffee, shampoo, perfume, make-up and something else that could have been the faintest hint of burning. India Lambert was sitting in front of a huge mirror with light bulbs all around it, talking on her mobile and wiping make-up from her face with a little round pad. Her pink silk dressing-gown rustled as she cut the call and swung around in her chair. She looked beautiful even though her hair was wrapped in a towel and her face was shiny with cream.

'Aliya! Come in.' Her voice was warm and welcoming,

as if she knew me.

Hutch closed the door behind the boys and said, with a stiff smile, 'Sorry, lads. After all that's been going on, I wouldn't be doing my job if I didn't pat you down.' They glanced at each other and raised their arms. This was why India Lambert had an ex-soldier for an assistant. He was her bodyguard too. I watched his big, probing hands slide expertly down their shirts and trousers. My breath was coming fast. I stepped back and dug my hands into my pockets. Hutch looked up, as if he'd heard the pounding of my heart. 'Don't worry, Aliya. If Miss Lambert wants you searched, she'll do it herself.'

India Lambert threw me a quick smile. 'I don't think we need worry about that, do you, Aliya?'

'N-n-no, Miss Lambert.' I couldn't stop looking at her. She had a slender face, huge dark eyes that slanted upwards like a cat's, high cheekbones, a slim, delicate nose and a mouth that was pink and full. She was so perfect she seemed to glow. *Please let her believe me. Please let her say she'll help me.*

She turned to the boys. 'Which one of you is Dan?'

'Me,' he said.

'And you must be . . . Connor.'

Connor stared at the floor and nodded.

'Good, I always like to get people's names right.' In one graceful movement she swept a pile of towels off the padded bench under the window and dropped them on a stool. 'Sorry about the mess. Have a seat.'

We squeezed in behind a table piled with magazines, hats and gloves, and as we shifted along the bench I caught our reflections in the mirror, embarrassed at how scruffy and out of place we looked. Especially Connor, who sat with his head down, biting his fingernails.

India leant back on her swivel chair while Hutch propped himself against the wall beside her, texting on his phone. He was a giant in that cramped space and she didn't seem at all embarrassed to be sitting in her dressing-gown so close to a man who was not her husband. She folded her hands in her lap. 'All right, Aliya, what is it you want to tell the colonel?'

'Behrouz is innocent.'

She sighed and said gently, 'He admitted his guilt on tape.'

'He was kidnapped. The kidnappers forced him to say those things. If you look at the tape, halfway through he says, "I have a plan," which is a message to me. He's telling me something is wrong and that I must do what he did and try and go to the colonel.'

'But he said he was planning to kill the colonel.'

'No!' I was getting frustrated, afraid my English wasn't clear. 'They made him say that.'

India shook her head as if this was my fantasy and said gently, 'Nothing would give me or my husband greater pleasure than to find out that you're right. But just because you want something to be true, it doesn't make it the case.'

'We know who kidnapped him. We've got photos.'

I thrust my phone at her and pointed to the face of Zarghun. 'This man is Farukh Zarghun. He's a drug lord and a war criminal and he's supposed to be dead.'

As I explained how Behrouz had recognized him and how Zarghun's people had kidnapped him and tried to make it look as if he'd killed himself by mistake with his own bomb, I saw a look on her face, something that might have been disbelief or shock or something I couldn't work out.

'I saw the kidnap, Miss Lambert,' the boy said. 'I swear. They got him outside the flats where he lives and dragged him into the loading bay at the back. He kept saying, "Please don't hurt my family," then they hit him with a gun, threw him in the van and drove off.'

That was why he was here, to be a witness, but I couldn't bear to look at him while he told her what he'd seen. Miss Lambert shook her head slowly and when she turned back to me, the tears welling in her eyes caught the light of the mirror lamps. 'I knew Behrouz, Aliya. Not well, but I met him a couple of times in Afghanistan. He was a lovely boy and it's terrible, truly terrible, that he chose to go down this awful path. But the obvious explanation for what Dan saw is that he was working for this man Zarghun and got beaten up for stealing some of his drugs. It doesn't mean that he wasn't also making bombs for Al Shaab.'

Hutch nodded and folded his arms. 'Sounds like a typical gangland warning to me. They probably drove him round the block, roughed him up a bit and dumped him back where they'd found him.'

'No!' the boy said. 'It wasn't like that. Look, Behrouz only told two other people about Zarghun. Captain Merrick, who he knew from Afghanistan, and his friend Arif from Khan's Cars, and Zarghun got someone to get rid of both them.'

India Lambert glanced up at Hutch. The look that passed between them shocked me. It was a look of total trust and understanding. When he put his hand on her shoulder, I knew the gossip in that magazine was true. Hutch was much more to her than a bodyguard or an assistant. I felt sad for the colonel and embarrassed that she was shaming a good, kind man in this way. But it was not my business. Her eyes turned back to the boy, and Hutch said, 'Just out of interest. How could Zarghun's people have had any idea who Behrouz told?'

The boy frowned at the floor, then at me. It was a good question. One we should have asked before. As I turned it over in my head a worm of something unsettling stirred inside me. Hutch shrugged and started texting again, as if he was getting bored with us.

'We don't know exactly how he found out,' the boy said quietly. 'But I promise you he's got people working for him everywhere – bent cops, immigration officers, even soldiers. It's too much of a coincidence that on the day Behrouz nearly died, Captain Merrick was killed in an army training exercise and Arif went missing. Tell them what happened, Connor.'

Connor went red when the boy said his name. He refused to even look at India Lambert and when he spoke he mumbled. 'Me and Arif went out to get a takeaway and he got picked up by an immigration spot check. They say they checked him out and let him go, but they didn't. I saw them drive off with him and he hasn't been seen since.'

India Lambert dropped her head and rubbed her temples. 'This is crazy. You want me to believe that an Afghan criminal could frame Behrouz, pay someone inside the army to shoot a serving officer and get British immigration to snatch Arif Rahman off the streets? Things like that just don't happen, not outside the movies.'

The boy's head lifted, his glazed eyes struggling to focus. I saw his lips twitch as if he was about to say something. He didn't, though, he just glanced at Connor.

'Please,' I said, 'even if you don't believe us about Arif and Merrick, it's still true that Zarghun wants to kill us. He's got people from the police out looking for us. That's why we came here and why we have to see the colonel.'

India Lambert pulled the towel off her head and shook out her damp hair. 'Look, I don't know what to make of any of this but if there really are policemen and soldiers involved in major corruption, the colonel will certainly want to know about it. He'll probably be in meetings right now but I'll text him.'

I gazed at her, feeling as if a sack of stones had been lifted from my shoulders. 'Thank you, Miss Lambert,' I whispered.

She smiled her beautiful smile and picked up her phone. 'If I say it's urgent, he shouldn't take long to call back.'

'Where is he?' the boy said, sharply.

India Lambert tossed back her hair. 'Where is who?'

'The colonel.'

'Scotland. He'll be back this afternoon.'

She must have seen the panic in our faces, because she said, quickly, 'Don't worry, you can go back to our London house and wait for him there.' She slipped behind the screen. 'We've got plenty of DVDs, and I'm sure the housekeeper will rustle you up some lunch. Hutch will drive you, won't you, Hutch?'

Hutch shrugged. 'No problem.'

'No need,' Connor said. 'We've got—'

The boy swung round, jabbing his elbow hard into Connor's ribs. Connor let out a grunt of pain. The boy ignored him and said to Hutch, 'Any chance of something to eat?'

Why was he being so disrespectful? Hutch didn't seem to mind. He looked up from his phone and pushed himself off the wall. 'What do you fancy? Catering does great Danish this time of the morning.'

Connor was glaring at the boy. The boy glared back at him and gave the tiniest shake of his head before he looked up at Hutch and said, 'Yeah, anything.'

'Have you told anyone else about this man Zarghun?' India said from behind the screen.

'No,' I said. 'We're keeping quiet about everything.'

'Even about coming to see me?'

'Yes.'

She came out from behind the screen wearing faded jeans and a soft white jumper, pinning up her hair. 'Would you mind waiting here? I just have to get my notes from the director. I won't be long.'

'No problem,' Connor said.

Hutch followed her out, stopping on the steps to glance over his shoulder. 'If it's OK, I'll lock the door. We don't want anyone barging in and getting funny about unauthorized visitors. You all want tea with those Danish?'

'Sure,' the boy said.

Connor barely waited for the door to shut before he turned on him. 'What the hell did you punch me for?'

The boy reached up to the window and rattled the lock. 'So you wouldn't tell them we've got a car. Come on, we can be halfway to London before they stop searching round here.'

'What are you on about?'

'You heard her. She said "Arif Rahman".'

'So?'

'Did you mention Arif's second name?'

'What? I don't know . . . maybe.'

'Take it from me. You didn't. And neither did Aliya.'

'No,' I said. 'I couldn't have. I didn't know what his second name was.'

'Quick,' the boy said, 'see what they're doing.'

Frightened and confused, I peered through the blind. 'They're walking towards the food vans. Both on their phones.'

The boy grabbed India Lambert's handbag and pulled out lipsticks, letters, a hairbrush and her purse. Connor flew at him and wrestled the bag out of his hands. 'What are you doing?'

'Get off me.' The boy gave him a push. 'Don't you get it? She's in on it. Her and her muscle-man boyfriend.'

'You're crazy!' Connor said.

The boy lifted a handful of charred paper out of the bin. 'So why did she burn Aliya's note and why didn't Hutchins take us through security?' He snatched a nail file from the mess on the dressing table and jabbed it at the lock on the back window. 'You stay if you want. I'm out of here.'

'You're insane,' Connor said. 'Tell him, Aliya.'

I didn't want to believe it, but as I watched India and Hutch through the window I could feel the doubt growing inside me. 'I . . . I don't know. She takes aid to Afghanistan all the time, she meets powerful people who could have got Zarghun out of prison and . . . and I think it's true that none of us said Arif's second name.' There was something else, something worrying me, like a sharp little splinter working its way to the surface of my mind.

'Yeah, see.' The boy's face was scrunched up, concentrating on the window lock. 'Miss Butter-Wouldn't-Melt, travelling round the world for her charity, and all the time

I bet she's checking out suppliers and finding new officials to bribe. It's the perfect cover.'

I wasn't listening, I was thinking about my grid, the facts we knew and the blanks between them. 'Look, Merrick was killed on Wednesday afternoon, Arif disappeared on Wednesday evening and Behrouz was blown up on Wednesday night.'

'So?' Connor was shaking his head, running his hands through his hair.

'The last call Behrouz made was on Wednesday morning. To India Lambert. Maybe he told her that Merrick and Arif knew about Zarghun and maybe she was the one who ordered them to be silenced.'

The boy spun round. 'She's right, Connor, and I bet it was some of Hutch's army mates who arranged Merrick's "accident".' He went back to digging at the lock. 'And if we don't get out of here fast, they're going to arrange an accident for us too. What are they doing now?'

'Still talking on their phones,' I said. With trembling fingers, I took a hairpin from the dressing table and offered it to the boy. 'Try with this.'

Connor, whose face had turned the colour of sour milk, grabbed it from my hand, elbowed the boy out of the way and slipped it into the tiny keyhole, twisting his oil-stained fingers delicately from side to side until it gave a click. He pushed up the lower half of the window, which opened like a flap. 'Come on, then! Hurry up.'

As I scrambled on to the padded bench I snatched one

of India Lambert's letters from the dressing table and slipped it into my pocket. I was a thief now, as well as a liar. We wriggled backwards through the narrow gap, almost falling on to the track, and ducked into the undergrowth, creeping along the bottom of the high stone wall. Connor let us step on to his cupped hands to climb over it before he scrambled up after us. We dropped on to the wooded lane on the other side, running around the curve of the road to where we'd left the car. The boy was in a lot of pain, his injured foot kept giving way and he was gasping for breath. In the end Connor almost had to carry him to the car. Now I was glad he hadn't brought a minicab. The bright-orange Khan's sign would have screamed through the trees and given us away.

Connor started the engine, hit the accelerator and swung into the lane. His hands were moving fast, slipping the gears, spinning the wheel to avoid the bumps and holes. I tried not to think about Merrick driving us out of Kabul and turned round to peer through the darkened windows. A glitter of silver was coming down the lane behind us, Hutch's car screeching to a stop. I saw the flash of his white shirt as he jumped out, crashing through the undergrowth, calling my name. He came nearer. I wriggled lower in my seat. He was looking past us, casting up and down. My heart stopped. He was staring as if he could see right through the blackened windows. Suddenly he began to run towards us, yelling into his phone. Connor speeded up, shouting, 'Lock your doors!' He let out a string of bad words as two huge trucks came lumbering towards us down the lane, blocking our escape. A man got out of the first one and stood in the road, holding up one hand to guide the drivers through the narrow space and the other to tell Connor to back up so they could get past.

Hutch reached our car and grabbed the handle of Connor's door. When it didn't open, he swung back his fist, punched out the cardboard on the broken side window, plunged his arm through the hole and made a grab for the lock. The boy flung himself across the seat and sank his teeth into Hutch's fingers while Connor hit the accelerator, threw the wheel sideways and swerved off the lane into the woods. Hutch yelled and stumbled back. Connor hurtled past the trucks, zigzagging through the trees. I flinched as branches bounced and scraped along the windows and turned to see Hutch pelting back to his car, ready to come after us as soon as we'd by-passed the trucks. But Connor didn't go back to the lane. He plunged deeper into the woods, where Hutch's high wide car couldn't go. The wheels churned the leafy mud, catching and spinning, crunching twigs and rocking the little chassis. Tree trunks loomed as we crashed through the branches. I ducked my head right down, afraid they would smash the glass and spear us in our seats, but Connor kept his nerve, swerving, skidding, lurching, until without warning the trees thinned and we burst out of the woods into a field full of cattle. The grass was lush and as green as the velvet dress in India Lambert's trailer. Connor headed for the far end, jolting us over the bumps and only slowing down when he came to a patch of mud scored with deep rain-filled ruts leading up to the gate.

'Open it!' he shouted. 'Quick, before Hutch comes round the other way.'

I threw myself out of the car and splashed towards the gate. There was a metal lever on a spring. Listening out for Hutch's car, I pulled it and pushed it, not knowing how the mechanism worked. The cattle were circling the car, closing in on it, some of their heavy wedge-shaped heads so near to me that I could hear their puffing breath and the suck of their hooves on the mud. I yanked at the lever and glanced back. They weren't cows. They were young bulls. Plump, well fed and bigger than any cattle I'd ever seen. Thirty or forty of them, twitching their tails and nostrils and staring at me with threatening, long-lashed eyes.

I wrenched the lever. It gave with a snap. I pushed the gate, yelling at the bulls to get back. They didn't budge, not even when Connor blasted the horn. The boy got out, stumbling forward, unsteady on his feet. He waved his arms, shouting feebly, 'Go on! Move it!' For a moment they switched their stares to him, tilting their heads, jostling each other as if they might charge at him and the car. He stood there pale and swaying. I thought he would fall and get trampled. I ran towards the bulls, trying to head them off. The lead one stared at me with eyes like black marbles, then turned away. Slowly the others followed, their muscles rippling beneath their mud-spattered hides. I pushed the boy into the car and ran back to the gate. Connor revved the engine. I was sure the wheels were going to sink into the mud, but he rammed the car into reverse, got up some speed and shot forward across the mud, sending up an arc of black spray. I rammed the gate shut and scrambled back into the passenger seat, expecting him to turn and race off up the hill. Instead, he rocketed across the road, swerving through a gap into the field opposite, sped along the hedge and pulled up in a grassy dip.

Was he mad? 'What are you doing?'

He cut the engine, pointed up at the road and said, 'You watch. He'll be coming past any minute.'

We gazed up through the hedge. I flinched with fear as first a yellow truck then a blue van sped past. Out of sight, brakes screeched. We heard a car door open. Someone had stopped to look into the field opposite. I closed my eyes. Seconds later the car door slammed. I opened my eyes to see a rush of silver flicker past the hedge as Hutch drove on up the hill.

The boy grinned at Connor. 'Nice one. What do we do now?'

'We go to the colonel and tell him everything,' I said. I waved the envelope I had taken from India Lambert's dressing table. 'I have the address. It's in London, in Highgate. We must watch his house and wait until he comes.'

The boy rolled his eyes. 'How can you even think of trusting him after what just happened?'

'I don't believe he knows that India Lambert is working with Zarghun.'

'What? You think he hasn't noticed that his wife's an evil, scheming, drug-dealing, murdering liar?'

'She is an actress. It is her job to lie. That is why she is so good at it. Look how she is deceiving him with this man Hutch. But the colonel is a good man. You heard what Behrouz said on the video, "Seek out Colonel Mike Clarke so that justice can be done."'

'There's two ways you can take that,' Connor muttered.

Why didn't they understand that I had no choice? 'If you won't come with me, I will go on my own.'

'You can't take the risk,' the boy said, 'not till we've thought this through.'

'Risk?' My throat grew hoarse with frustration. 'What is the risk if you have nothing to lose?'

'The risk is, you could end up dead.'

'Without the colonel I am dead anyway.'

'Don't be stupid, we'll find some other way . . .'

'If you believe that, then you are the one who is stupid. If the colonel does not help me, either Zarghun's people will kill me here or I will get sent back to Afghanistan and the Taliban will kill me there.'

Connor started the engine, flung his arm across the seat and backed out of the field. 'Do what you like. I'm going to lay low at Arif's while I work out what to do. You can come if you want, it'll be safe. No one knows I'm staying there.'

'I'm up for that,' the boy said.

I was furious that they wouldn't listen to me. Especially the boy. Who was he to tell me who I should and should not trust? I pulled out my phone.

'Who are you calling?'

'India Lambert said the colonel is coming back to his house today. If I speak to him, maybe I will know if I can trust him.'

Connor rolled his eyes. 'If he picks up, you keep me out of it.'

The boy slumped back in his seat. 'Yeah. And me.'

I left a message on the colonel's voicemail and rather than talk to either of them I turned on the radio. Connor speeded up. I watched him from the corner of my eye. He was a different person when he drove. No longer shy and awkward, but expert and fearless, like Behrouz, as if the wheel and the gears had become part of him.

I turned my face to the window and closed my eyes, a childhood memory flooding back; a time in the mountains when Behrouz was only nine. We were visiting my grandparents and a huge slick of grey-black mud from the swollen river brought boulders crashing down the slopes on to their village, ripping out trees, tearing through houses, and everybody was running and panicking, trying to round up their children and their livestock and get out of the valley, all except for one old blind man who wouldn't budge. He stood in the middle of the street beside his son's brand new truck, waving his stick and yelling that someone must drive it to safety. Our family got separated in the chaos. I was with my mother and she was frantic that she couldn't find Behrouz. My father came running, yelling Behrouz's name, and then we saw the truck lurching past us down the winding track with Behrouz at the wheel, perched on the lap of the old blind man, who was working the brakes and the gears. I smiled, remembering how Behrouz and I used to roll around laughing when my father told that story. The sound of Behrouz's name from the radio dragged me back to the moment.

'Police have released CCTV footage of a man they believe to be Behrouz Sahar getting off a bus in Highgate at ten forty-five a.m. on Wednesday morning and walking towards the home of Colonel Mike Clarke. The colonel was not at home at the time and the police believe that Sahar was doing a recce of the area, preparing to return later to plant his bomb.'

I scrabbled for my grid, trying to make sense of this new information.

The boy leant in between the seats. 'That's weird. Didn't Merrick text him Wednesday morning saying he couldn't get hold of the colonel's address?'

'Yes.' I ran my finger down my notes for Wednesday. 'The text came at 9.22. It said, ". . . got Clarke's home number, no luck with address or mobile". Then Behrouz called the colonel's house at 9.25 and spoke to India Lambert for seven minutes.'

Connor half glanced at the grid. 'So how did he

manage to find the address and get to Highgate by a quarter to eleven?'

The boy punched a fist into his palm. 'Because India Lambert gave it to him! That must be where he was heading when me and . . . when I saw him coming down the stairs.'

He had managed to avoid mentioning his father but I still felt a pang of fury at the reminder of that man.

'I don't know,' Connor said. 'If he went to her house and she wanted him dead, why did she let him leave?'

That was the biggest blank on my grid. I had no idea what Behrouz had been doing between the time he was in Highgate and the time he was snatched from Meadowview that night.

'What if she didn't let him leave?' the boy said into the silence. 'What if he escaped?'

Connor shot me a look. 'In that case he was a bloody idiot to go back to Meadowview. No offence, Aliya, but he must have known they'd be watching your flat.'

I thought of our last night in Kabul and all the risks Behrouz had taken to save us from the Taliban and in that moment I knew exactly why my brave, daredevil brother had gone back to Meadowview. Hot tears slid down my face. 'He came back to save us,' I said. 'He thought Zarghun's people would hurt us to punish him for getting away.' The tears flowed faster. 'But they caught him in the car park before he could get upstairs. If it hadn't been for us, he wouldn't have been there. He would have got away.'

DAN

It took us nearly three hours to get back to London. We knew India Lambert would have her mates in the police on the lookout for us, so Connor had his eyes glued to the windscreen, searching for ways to avoid the main roads, doubling back down farm tracks and criss-crossing half of Kent. I was watching the back window, waiting for Hutch to come screeching up behind us, and Aliya had the colonel's house on redial. When she wasn't calling it or leaving messages, she was staring into space.

All I could feel was this bone-numbing exhaustion, a hopeless desire to flip a switch and make everything stop, and a desperate need to throw up. What with the fear, the guilt, the movement of the car and Trent's drugs still swilling round my system, by the time we got to Stoke Newington I was sweating like a pig and about to hurl any minute.

'Where's Arif's?' I groaned. 'Is it far?'

Connor was idling at a crossroads, waiting to turn left. He pointed down the road. 'Down there. Over the newsagents.' I followed his finger along a row of manky shops and scanned the street, hoping there'd be a parking space right outside Arif's flat. My eye caught a shiny black BMW squatting opposite the building like a waiting panther. Its number plate ended AUA. Same as Hamidi's.

'Back up!' I yelled.

'What?'

'It's Hamidi.'

'Where?'

'In the black BMW.'

Connor swung right and rocketed away in the opposite direction. 'Where to?'

We were out of options. My house, Aliya's hotel, Meadowview – they'd be watching them all, waiting to pick us off the minute we went near. My mind was spinning on empty, my skull was tightening. 'I don't know. Keep driving.'

'Go to Highgate. To the colonel,' Aliya said. 'We have to!'

'No way!' Connor snapped. 'I told you I'm not going anywhere near him.'

'Yeah, me neither, Aliya,' I said.

We got to a main road, Connor driving fast, jerking his head up every couple of seconds to look in the mirror, trying to put as much distance between us and the BMW as he could, burning left past a disused cinema, down an empty stretch of one-way road built up either side with dingy flats. A kid on a bike shot out from an alley. Connor slammed on the brakes. The car slid into a skid and slewed out of control, missing the kid by a couple of inches. The kid carried on across the road, trailing an arm behind him, flipping us the finger.

'Jesus!' Connor said. 'I could have killed him.' He dropped his head on the steering wheel and sat still for a few seconds before he reached forward and turned the ignition. The engine grunted, refusing to fire. A horn blared. I turned around. A lorry was heading towards us, bearing down, flashing his lights. Connor turned the key, pumped the pedal and with a jerky splutter the engine started.

I don't know how she did it. One second Aliya was sat up front and Connor was jamming the car into gear, the next she'd thrown open her door and jumped out. By the time I realized what was happening, Connor was moving, pushing the accelerator to get out of the lorry's path. I looked back. Aliya was running fast, disappearing between the buildings. I snatched up the envelope she'd left on the seat.

'She'll be going to the colonel's, we've got to stop her.'

Connor hurtled on to the next junction, swung left, and

chucked me his phone. 'Call her. Tell her she's crazy. I'll go round the block and pick her up.' We drove around – must have been nearly half an hour – doubling back, taking every side road. No sign of her. I kept calling, getting her voicemail, until the battery died.

I stuffed the envelope in my pocket and felt around, looking for coins.

'You got any money?' I said.

'A bit.'

'See if you can find a phone box.'

'OK. And we're going to need petrol soon.'

We'd ended up somewhere east, going towards the Lea Marshes – takeaways, pawn shops, warehouses, the sky darkening, street lights and civilization thinning out ahead.

We drew up at a set of lights. Connor glanced in the mirror and let out a yell. I flipped round just as Hutch's silver Range Rover rammed into the back of us, throwing me forward like someone had cracked a baseball bat across my back. The car lurched again, the same horrible sick-making thump came from behind and my head bashed into Connor's headrest. There was a terrible sound of screeching metal as he floored the accelerator. The back of the car must have been pushed right in and the back wheels were jamming against the wheel arches. We lurched on for a few metres, then both of the back tyres blew, letting the wheels turn free but they were shuddering and banging on the bare rims.

I turned my head, saw Hutch's radiator grill drowning in a spray of sparks whenever we hit a dip and our ruined back end scraped the surface of the road. Connor was shouting every swear word under the sun but he kept the car on the road and took a right. Someone had parked a boat – some sort of cabin-cruiser – on a trailer at the kerb. Connor braked, but too hard, sending the back of our car swinging out. It slammed into the trailer, skewing the back of the boat round to block the road. The trailer tipped and the boat slid on to the road in front of Hutch. A squeal of rubber as he tried to brake, but he was going too fast and went straight through the bow, drilling through the cabin. Then a horrible crunch as he hit the solid metal of the trailer.

Our poor battered car took one juddering leap over a bump in the road and slewed to a stop beside a concrete bollard.

ALIYA

I kept running and didn't look back, through a maze of tall gloomy warehouses, ducking along the fence around a building site, squeezing through a gap by a sign saying 'One Hundred Luxury Homes' with a picture of a smiling family sitting in a sunny kitchen eating a meal. The picture was nothing like the muddy mess on the other side of the fence. I slipped behind stacks of bricks and pallets, staying low so the men in yellow hats wouldn't see me. My feet kept sinking into the thick red clay, and once I got to the other side I had to kick some loose fence panels apart to get out. I crawled into a half-deserted street of run-down houses and litter-blown pavements. I stopped a woman with a little boy in a buggy eating chips from a paper bag. The rich smell made me almost faint with longing.

'Please, where is the nearest station for the Tube trains?'

The woman leant into the buggy and took one of his chips. 'It's a thirty-minute walk, love.' She bit off the top of the chip and pointed the rest of it down the street. 'You're best off going right to the end of this road, turning left and getting a bus on the High Street.'

'Thank you.' I stumbled away, wary of the passing traffic and the scowling strangers lolling against boarded-up shops, smoking cigarettes and checking their phones, convinced they were India Lambert's men waiting to hustle me into a waiting car. The sky was darkening and the weather was getting worse, damp wind blowing in sideways. I'd been walking for about fifteen minutes – cold, miserable and frightened – when my phone vibrated in my pocket. I checked the screen and shook my head to clear it, unable to believe the name I was seeing. I sniffed back tears. It was the colonel.

'Aliya? Aliya Sahar?'

'Yes.'

'You've been calling my house. I've just picked up your messages.' A lorry thundered past. I pushed my finger into my ear, trying to hear him. 'You shouldn't be phoning me, the police will . . .'

'I have to see you.' I couldn't stop my sobs. 'It's about my brother . . . and your wife.'

'My wife?' His voice cracked. 'What's happened? Is she hurt?'

'No . . . not hurt but . . . Colonel Clarke, Behrouz is innocent and your wife . . . she . . . she is not.'

'What are you talking about?'

I backed into a doorway. 'It's hard to explain. Farukh Zarghun, the warlord who sold drugs in Afghanistan. He's here. In London.'

'Zarghun? He died last year. In prison.'

'We've got proof he's alive. Behrouz took photographs of him. That's why Zarghun's people tried to kill him. Please, Colonel . . .' The sobs were tearing up my voice. 'You have to help me. They are trying to kill everyone who knows about Zarghun.'

'Look, you did the right thing coming to me.' His voice had sharpened. 'Sit tight and I'll get my secretary, Martin Chivers, to pick you up. Where are you?'

'If I tell you, I have to be sure you won't tell your wife.' My voice rose in panic.

'What is all this about my wife? She's filming in Kent. I won't be seeing her until next weekend.'

'All right.' I spun round looking for a street sign. 'I'm in Amhurst Road, opposite a shop called Palmer's that sells newspapers and sweets.'

'Are you alone?'

'Yes.'

'I see . . .'

I strained to hear his voice. 'Colonel, are you still there?'

'Yes, yes, I'm here. Look, Martin should be with you in

about forty minutes. I'm on my way home from the airport now, so I'll meet you at the house.'

'What car should I look for?'

'A black people carrier.'

DAN

I sat there for maybe a minute just listening to the silence. I wanted to stay there for ever – not get bashed or drugged or drowned or chased by Range Rovers with killers at the wheel. I might have done too if Connor hadn't grabbed my arm and yanked me out of the car.

'Come on, mate, we've got to get out of here.'

He pulled me up the road towards the Range Rover. Hutch was slumped at a weird angle, pushed back by a corner of the boat trailer which had crushed into his shoulder, his face criss-crossed with cuts from the glass of the windscreen, blood oozing down his front. Connor hardly glanced at him and moved on. With a hazy thought that I should call an ambulance, I leant in through the passenger door and clipped his phone out of the hands-free. There was shouting from down the road and the sound of sirens. Hutch's eyes opened a slit. He looked at me. He must have been hurting a lot but the only thing in his eyes was fury. I limped past the wreckage of the boat. My head was pounding and my back felt like it had been smashed with a hammer and stuck together with pins. Connor was on the other side of the road behind the wheel of an old Honda. I bent painfully into the passenger seat and saw he'd ripped off a bit of the dashboard and twisted a load of wires together.

'What the—?' I said, still stupefied. The sirens were getting louder, screeching towards us.

'Just get in!'

I flopped on to the seat, still holding Hutch's phone. I looked at it, dazed. Connor stuck the rickety little Honda into gear and drove. The phone vibrated in my hand. Voicemail. As if on automatic, I clicked on the message.

ALIYA

Martin Chivers, the colonel's assistant, was the opposite of Hutch: fair-haired, pasty and skinny, with small serious eyes. He was dressed in a smart grey suit, a blue shirt and a striped tie. Although he was very polite to me, holding the door of the car open and saying it didn't matter at all when I apologized for the mud on my trainers, he hardly said anything else on the way. I didn't mind. I needed time to think what I would say to the colonel and how I would know if I could trust him.

I leant back, letting the warmth of the heater soak into my skin and watching the bustle of London slip past. It wasn't long before grubby back roads gave way to long tree-lined streets, shiny little shops and cafes and neat, old-fashioned houses and I saw signs saying Hampstead and then Highgate. Martin Chivers left the main road and drove down a secluded lane, curving around the back of a vast overgrown churchyard full of tall trees and crumbling monuments. It was so leafy and deserted it felt more like the countryside than the city. He pressed something on his key ring. A set of tall iron gates swung open. He turned into a long driveway leading to a large three-storey house built of faded pink bricks, with tall stone pillars on either side of the front door. He opened it with a key, held up a hand for me to wait while he pressed buttons on a complicated alarm, and took me across a wide hallway, the polished floor scattered with beautiful silk rugs from Afghanistan, past rooms filled with china and glass and delicate old furniture, to a door at the far end. 'The colonel said you're to wait in his study,' he said. 'I'll bring you something to eat. He shouldn't be long.'

'Thank you.'

The colonel's study was lined with books, most of them bound in leather with gold writing on the spines. There was a big old desk at one end and small lamps throwing out pools of soft warm light. I thought it was the most welcoming room I had ever seen until I noticed a portrait of India Lambert hanging above the mantelpiece. I stared at it for a moment, then I turned my back on her, glad that I had prepared myself as best I could for whatever was to come.

Too jittery to stay still, I wandered around the room,

picking up framed photos of the colonel shaking hands with people I half recognized from the news, running my fingers over a brass sculpture of his head that stood on a black marble plinth, touching the embroidered silk cushions on the chairs. Even the curtains were made of silk. I gazed out across the massive garden overflowing with rose bushes, through windows sealed behind double layers of thick glass. I think it might even have been bullet-proof; it certainly kept out the sound of the wind and rain lashing the gnarled trees outside. It was so quiet in there that all I could hear was the tick of the big brass clock on the mantelpiece and the growl of my empty stomach, which was why I had no idea that the colonel was back until the door burst open and he strode towards me, hand outstretched. I felt my body tremble and tears of relief prick my eyes. He gave off such an easy, good-natured feeling of power that I wanted to trust him completely, but the lying eyes of India Lambert kept me on my guard.

'Aliya.' He clasped my hand in both of his. 'I'm so sorry you've had such a difficult time getting hold of me. I was in Scotland. Please, sit down.' He pointed to a high-backed chair covered in worn brown leather.

'Thank you for letting me come. If you hadn't called me back, I . . . I don't know what I would have done.'

He brushed away my thanks and sat down opposite me. 'To be honest, I've been praying that something would come to light to exonerate Behrouz. So come on, you said he took some photographs of Farukh Zarghun here in the

UK. Do you have them with you?'

I took the picture of Zarghun and Hamidi outside Hardel's out of my backpack. The paper was crumpled but the faces were clear. He studied it carefully. 'Good grief, it's Zarghun all right. Beard or no beard. God knows how he got out of prison and into the UK, but if he thought Behrouz was about to expose him, I imagine he'd go to any lengths to stop him. This man with him, he's Tewfiq Hamidi, Zarghun's former commander.'

'I know.'

'These are dangerous men, Aliya, but you can stop worrying now. I called the police as soon as I spoke to you. They're on their way.'

'No!' I jumped up. 'There are policemen working for Zarghun, that's why Behrouz didn't go to them.'

'It's all right.' He leant forward, his voice firm and calming. 'I spoke directly to the commissioner. He's sending over a couple of very senior detectives from the anti-corruption unit, who I guarantee you can trust. They'll need to take a detailed statement, so I suggest you use the time until they get here to relax.' He looked at his watch. 'They shouldn't be long.'

He sat back and stretched out his long legs. 'What I can't believe is that you managed to piece all this together on your own.'

I looked down at the red-patterned rug on the floor.

He said gently, 'If anyone helped you, Aliya, they'll be in danger too. Just tell me where they are and I'll send

Martin to pick them up.'

I was torn. I wanted to get the boy out of danger – he was my witness, my only proof that Behrouz had been kidnapped – but I had promised him and Connor that I wouldn't tell the colonel about them. I looked up at the portrait of India Lambert and decided I would say nothing about them until the detectives came. That way there would be no risk. I nibbled at my cuff and said quietly, 'You don't need to pick anyone up.'

I could feel his eyes on me. 'Are you sure?'

I got out my grid and said quickly, 'I used this. It helped me to keep track of all the things Behrouz did so I could work out what had happened.'

'All right, my dear, you know best.'

He smiled and I smiled back; he was being so kind and understanding. Hopefully the detectives would talk to me in private and then I could tell them about India Lambert and they could break the terrible truth about his wife to him. My stomach made a rumbling noise. I couldn't stop myself looking at the door, hoping that Martin Chivers would come quickly with the food he had promised.

The colonel had wandered over to the window. 'You know, I love this room. The combination of wood panelling and books makes it so soundproof that I can play my music as loudly as I like, or just sit and yell at the injustices of life, safe in the knowledge that the outside world can't hear a thing.' He pressed a button on a silver remote and closed his eyes as the room filled with beautiful music. He let out a deep sigh and waved his hand as if he was conducting the musicians, jerking his fingers faster as the music got quicker. 'Did Martin show you around the house?'

I shook my head.

'It's quite wonderful. Full of history, some parts of it date right back to the sixteenth century.' He smiled as if he was about to tell me a secret. 'I don't usually show people this, but I think you've earned special treatment.' He beckoned me over. 'Come and see.'

I wobbled towards him, faint with hunger. The music was getting louder, drums thundering, cymbals clashing, the colonel humming along as he slipped his hand under one of the bookshelves. I heard a click. Slowly the book-case swung back on some kind of pivot and a waft of cool stale air came out at me from a dark stone-lined space.

'It's a priest's hole,' he said proudly.

'What is that?'

'A hiding place for Catholic priests who were being persecuted for their religion.'

I leant in to get a better look.

'It was constructed by a builder called Nicholas Owen, who was famous for creating secret spaces that no one could ever find. Such craftsmanship. Look at the neatness of the stonework, the thickness of this old oak door. But he refused all payment, and ended up getting tortured and executed because he wouldn't betray the men he'd helped.'

I felt the pressure of his big gentle hand on my shoulder.

'Owen was a fool, you see, an idealist. His persecutors would have paid him well to inform on his clients and no one need ever have known he was working for both sides. Behrouz was just the same.'

I twisted round and looked up at him, embarrassed that I'd lost the thread of his meaning.

A strange look had come over him, a sort of tight excitement. 'Your family could have had it all, Aliya, a comfortable house, the best doctors for your mother, the best schools for you and your sister, and all we asked in exchange was a little cooperation from Behrouz. I explained to him that trading in narcotics was a business just like any other and that no one need ever know he was working for us. But the fool refused.'

My head emptied. My body froze. All I could do was stand there dumbly while his meaning exploded in my brain.

DAN

There were six voicemail messages on Hutch's phone, all from the same number. I clicked 'play'. A man's voice blared in my ear, angry and panicked. I recognized the Geordie accent – it was Trent. 'Where the hell are you? The girl's at Clarke's and he wants the boys there now! He's going spare. Call me.'

'They've got her!' I rocked back, still dazed from the crash. 'Clarke's in on it and he's holding her at his house.' Every fibre of my battered body was screaming that I had to get her out of there.

'I told her!' Connor said. 'I told her not to go near him.'

'Yeah, all right, you told her. But we've got to save her.'

'You and me? Against that lot?'

I looked over at Connor and saw how scared he was,

chalk-white. I was scared too, petrified, but what did that matter?

'Yeah, Connor. You and me.' I pulled out the crumpled envelope. It was ripped but you could still read the colonel's address. 'And if you haven't got the bottle, then just me. But at least you can bloody well get me to Highgate.'

ALIYA

I tried to twist out of the colonel's grasp but his fingers were on my neck, holding me like iron pincers. 'Where did they go, Aliya?'

'Who?'

He shook me hard. 'Dan and Connor. You were with them when you left the film set. Where did they go?'

'I don't know, I swear, I don't know.'

The door swung open. The shock waves running through my body got fiercer as the freckled policeman, Mark Trent, walked in with his phone to his ear. The colonel glanced round. 'Have you found them?'

'Not yet.'

'What about Hutch?'

'Still not returning my calls.'

Clarke ripped my backpack off my back and threw it to Trent. He caught it with his free hand, unzipped it with his teeth and shook out my things, kicking at my purse, my headscarf and the flurry of folded printouts as they tumbled to the floor. Clarke spun me round, still gripping my shoulder, and searched my pockets. 'Where's your phone?'

'It . . . it was in my backpack.'

'Turn that music off,' he shouted. 'Is he answering?'

Trent seemed worried. He gave a shake of his head and flicked a wall switch. In the sudden quiet Behrouz's video looped through my head. 'I have a plan . . . to seek out Colonel Mike Clarke so that justice can be done!' My brother had been sending me a message but I'd been so taken in by the colonel's power and his show of kindness that I'd totally misunderstood it. I struggled to shut off the fear and the fury, determined, somehow, to carry out Behrouz's plan. I hunched forward, pushing my wrist to my mouth, plucking and fumbling with my chewed cuff, and in a thin, frightened voice I stammered, 'Are you going to kill me, Colonel Clarke?'

'Not until you stop being useful.'

'I . . . I won't help you! It doesn't matter if you kill me. When Behrouz is well, he will tell everyone the truth about you and Farukh Zarghun and your drug ring.'

He sighed as if he was genuinely saddened. 'I'm afraid not. We put a little pressure on one of the orderlies and we've finally got him on side. He assures me that your brother will be dead by the morning.' He glanced at the clock. 'In fact he should be coming on shift in about an hour.'

I could feel the room whirling, my heart juddering, my hopes dying.

'No, please, no.'

Clarke snapped impatiently at Trent, 'For Christ's sake, where is he?'

Trent was sweaty, pale, wiping his forehead. 'I don't know. One minute he says he's got them cornered, the next, nothing.'

'Then Aliya's going to have to help us out.' Clarke relaxed his grasp just a little. 'You're going to call your friends Connor and Dan and tell them that you're here, that anti-corruption officers are on their way and that I'll send a car to wherever they are to pick them up.'

'No!' I bucked and wriggled. 'I won't.'

He snatched my arm and twisted it behind my back. The strength in his hands was paralysing, like steel clamps stopping my blood, tearing my muscles, ready to break my elbow. I crumpled forward, reaching my other hand to my mouth to stifle a sob. 'I can't remember Connor's number and . . . and Dan lost his phone when Mark Trent tried to drown him!'

'That's not a problem. We've got Dan's phone right here, with Connor's number in the contacts.' He called over to Trent. 'Block the caller ID and give it to her.'

Through a haze of agony I saw Trent pull a second phone from his pocket and walk towards me, thumbing the keys. 'There's another message from his dad, asking where he is.'

'Ignore it,' Clarke said.

It wasn't just that I was desperate to delay making that call, there was something I needed to know. I blurted it through the waves of pain, 'His father . . . does he know what you did to Behrouz?'

'Abbott?' Trent gave a dismissive snort. 'Nah, he's just Jez Deakin's runaround, but he comes in useful, now and then. Just like you.' He rammed the phone to my ear and his voice hardened. 'Talk!'

He'd put it on speaker and as the connection went through my thoughts swarmed and buzzed, trying to work out how I could warn Connor without alerting Trent and the colonel to what I was doing. My heart tripped when a voice came on the line. But it was a woman. 'The number you have dialled is unavailable. Please try later.'

Trent snatched it away and Clarke growled at him angrily, 'Keep trying until you damn well get through. This is your fault for not checking the barge properly.' I could almost feel the fury coming off him.

Trent hit the keys again and, for all his attempts to hide it, I could see he was terrified. The same message crackled out of the phone. Relief gave me strength.

'The hospital will know Behrouz was murdered,' I hissed. 'They will find out who did it and they will trace the killer to you.'

Clarke shook his head and pushed his face so close to

mine I could feel his spittle on my skin. 'No one's going to look further than Al Shaab, not once they've claimed responsibility.' His gentle voice was a shocking contrast to the venom in his eyes. 'They'll say they did it to stop him cracking under interrogation. The press will love that.'

I didn't understand. 'Why would they say this when Behrouz has never worked for them?'

Trent was trying Connor again, looking increasingly worried, and I think to mask his panic he sneered at me, 'Because we've just shot the video. Same deal as the one with Behrouz, only this time it's his friend Arif on camera.'

'Arif?' I whispered. 'He's alive?'

'For Christ's sake, Trent, get a move on!' the colonel snapped.

I pressed my cuff to my mouth. 'Al Shaab! It's you!'

Clarke said genially, 'Let's just say that my wife isn't the only one with a taste for the theatrical.'

His eyes slid back to Trent, who was pressing the phone to his ear, frowning hard and shaking his head. 'Sorry, boss. I still can't get through.'

'Then we'll just have to keep our guest safe till you do.'

A twist of his grip, a powerful jerk of his wrists and I was pitching forward into that dank stone-lined hole. I reached out to stop myself falling, slammed my hands against the rough wall and whipped round to catch a narrowing wedge of light. Then there was nothing. Just silence and total, utter blackness.

DAN

The drive was a dark blur of terror. Rain pounding the windscreen, engine straining, chassis rattling and groaning, pain shooting through every bone in my body, nerves jangling, Connor yelling that we didn't stand a chance against Clarke, me panicking that we wouldn't get there in time or we'd get pulled over by bent cops, or worst of all that Hamidi was going to come burning out of nowhere and run us off the road. Trent's voicemails were coming every thirty seconds, his voice thick with clamped-down fury. I'd have chucked Hutch's phone out the window if I hadn't been using it for directions. What was it Aliya always went on about – having a plan? Good idea. Trouble was, I didn't have one.

ALIYA

I slithered to the floor, hands clasped over my head, trying to hold down the roaring panic. The blackness was like nothing I'd ever known and the air was so musty and still it felt like the breath of a tomb. If priests really had been hidden in here, how long had they lasted? Hours? Days? Months? Did they pray and eat and dream in darkness, or did they share this cold dead air with candles? Terror flooded my mind. I pushed it back, forcing myself to stay calm. The boys had been right about the colonel and I had been wrong. But at least I had stayed on my guard.

I still had the grid in my hand. I slipped it into my pocket and fumbled for the phone nestling in the torn cuff of my hoodie and hit the buttons. No signal of course, just a pale glow from the screen that eased the darkness and fed my hope. I crawled across the stone floor, pressed my ear to the handleless slab of wood that served as a door and listened to the muffled bark of Clarke's angry voice and Trent's low jerky mumble as he tried to calm him down. I couldn't make out any of the words but that's not what I was listening for. I turned off the phone to save the battery and, dazed with hunger, fear and cold, I leant against the door and waited, praying for one particular sound. It could have been ten, fifteen or even thirty minutes later when it came, snapping me out of a halfway world between nightmare and waking. There it was: the slam of the study door. I forced myself to wait some more, listening for footsteps, taps, coughs, anything that would betray a human presence in that room, and then, counting slowly to twenty to quieten my nerves, I got up from the floor. I switched on the phone and in the spooky glow from the screen I felt in my pockets for my grid, folded the paper into a narrow strip and ran it carefully down the hairsbreadth gap between the stone wall and the wooden door. It caught on the locking mechanism. With my eyes fixed on that vital spot I reached deep into my sock for Behrouz's gun and slid back the safety catch, the way I'd seen so many fighters do in the streets of Kabul. But I wasn't a fighter and I clasped it in my hand, doubting my courage to pull the trigger. A ghostly image crept into my mind of that hospital orderly leaving to go to work and kill Behrouz. A deafening bang and a blinding flash threw me back against the wall. Light punched a jagged hole through the door. I fell back, hitting the stone floor, cordite burning my nose and my ears ringing so badly it was like a hundred sirens going off inside my head.

I dragged myself up, pocketed the gun and rammed my shoulder against the door until it opened. I sprinted across to the window and pulled the catch on the glazing panel. It fell back on a hinge. I rattled the window. It was locked. I spun round, grabbed the sculpture of Clarke's head from its plinth and slammed it through the glass. A piercing alarm shrieked through the house. I scrambled over the window ledge, ripping my leg on the broken pane, stamping on the head lying in the mud, and ran blindly, slashing through rose bushes and stumbling round tree trunks. Halfway across I turned and through the screen of foliage saw faces peering from an upper window. I ducked low, trying to shake the ringing from my skull.

The slam of the front door echoed through the darkness. I kept running till my lungs tore with pain, scrambling through flower beds, squelching through rows of vegetables, swerving round the back of sheds, thorns tearing at my hands and face as I dived through the thick hedge on to the lane. Behind me on the drive cars were starting up, engines revving, tyres squealing. I cringed back into the hedge, stabbed by a hundred tiny knives, head pressed on to my knees, heart stopped as Trent's pale-blue hatchback turned right out of the drive and crawled past me, then Chivers' black people carrier shot out of the driveway, turned left up the hill and moved slowly into the darkness, searching for me. Shouts rang out behind me. Torch beams criss-crossed the trees, coming closer, forcing me out of the hedge. Hands and face sticky with blood, I ran on to the darkened lane, feeling along the fences on the other side. No gaps to slip through, no ditches to hide in, just endless railings like prison bars, trapping me in the open. All I could do was run as I had never run before. A pair of headlights blazed towards me, blinding me with their brightness. I threw myself flat, like my teachers had told us to do when foreign missiles rained from the sky, and I prayed that this car held a stranger. The tyres screeched to a halt. A black figure leapt out and ran towards me through the light. Shielding my eyes from the glare. I fumbled for the gun, raised it with quaking fingers and screamed out, 'Get away from me!'

DAN

pulled the gun from her hands and yanked her to her feet. She was sobbing and gasping, her face bloody and scratched. Her legs buckled and I had to prop her up and drag her to the car. I pushed her across the back seat and jumped in the front.

She jolted upright, her eyes opened wide and she screamed, 'Hospital! Go to the hospital. They will kill my brother tonight!' She shook Connor's shoulders, her voice rising way off the register. 'Behrouz! They will kill Behrouz!'

Connor slammed the Honda into reverse, made a sharp turn in the narrow lane and thumped the accelerator to the floor.

I stuck my head out the window and looked back.

'There's a car turning at the top of the hill and people with flashlights running down Clarke's drive.'

'Don't worry about that,' he yelled. 'Just tell me where to go!'

I punched the keys on Hutch's phone, searching for directions, panicking when I looked up and saw the blue hatchback roaring back up the lane towards us. I ducked down.

'That's Trent. Did he see me?'

'I bloody hope not.' Connor looked back, didn't see the bump, the front wheels took off and the undercarriage landed with a horrible crunch. For a second he lost control, banging along the sides of a couple of parked cars, somehow managing to steady us again as we shot on to the dark spooky road by the cemetery. 'Where now?'

'Down there!' I kept shouting and pointing, zigzagging a route to Highgate Hill.

'Quickly, quickly!' Aliya gripped the back of Connor's seat. 'They will guess that I will go to the hospital. That I will try to save him.'

'Calm down,' Connor said. 'They don't know we switched cars.'

The Honda rattled and wheezed but Connor drove like a crazy man, pushing up tight behind buses and cars, running lights, dodging in and out of bus lanes. My heart juddered as we weaved between cyclists and drunks, beating boy-racers through gaps the width of a wheelbarrow, flashing past shop windows, the street lights blurring into one until I saw a sign saying 'Hospital' and the entrance a hundred metres ahead of us. The traffic slowed, held up by roadworks – too thick for any of Connor's tricks, and one-way only, so he couldn't even turn around. It didn't matter. It was only a hundred metres. We were going to make it. I turned to see how Aliya was holding up. Her eyes were swivelling in their sockets, her lips drawn tight in pain and panic. But she'd seen the entrance and there was hope there too, just a glimmer.

And then I saw the raindrops on the back window flash blue. Probably an ambulance. The light was threading its way through the traffic thirty metres back. The cars were shifting to give it space. It gained ten metres. We slowed right down again as the lights ahead turned red. A howl came from behind me. It was Aliya.

I swung round. I could see now that it wasn't an ambulance – it was Trent's blue hatchback with one of those magnetic lights they stick on top of plain-clothes police cars. Luckily the cars were jammed too tight to let it pass and maybe, if the lights changed quickly, we could still make it without him seeing us. Connor revved the engine. I gripped the broken dashboard, willing the lights to go green. 'Come on, come on.'

Then suddenly Trent swung on to the pavement and squeezed past the side of a white van six vehicles back. In the wing mirror I could see him coming, scanning the faces in every car he passed. Searching for us.

I still had Aliya's gun in my hand. I waved it towards the back seat.

'Is this thing loaded?'

Aliya shook her head. 'There was only one bullet. I used it.'

Connor grabbed the gun out of my hand, threw it on the floor and glanced in the mirror. Trent's car was fifteen metres back, alongside a Mini.

'Now . . .' Connor said, his face and his voice very calm. 'Aliya, move across to the seat behind me and get a hold of the door handle, and you, Danny boy, climb in the back, nice and quick . . . and when I say "now", we're going to jump out and run like hell.'

My body wasn't up to gymnastics but I squeezed myself over the seats and landed beside Aliya. I glanced back. Trent was moving on, level with our rear bumper now.

Pumping the accelerator, Connor wrenched the wheel to his left, yelled, 'Now!' and cut the Honda straight across Trent's front wheels. We were off through the traffic as Trent piled into the passenger side of the Honda, stoving in the door where I'd been sitting, crushing the rusted old metal almost over to the gear stick.

And, just like Connor said, we ran like hell.

ALIYA

We raced into the hospital car park, past the vans with satellite dishes on the roof and the clumps of journalists chatting and sipping coffees. I made for the entrance, saw Hamidi with two hard-faced men standing beside the doors and swerved back.

The news reporter with the long black hair and red lipstick was standing in front of a camera talking into a microphone. I ran towards her. Her eyes flickered nervously but she kept talking, expecting me to join the little crowd of onlookers who had gathered to watch her. I didn't stop. I ran right up to her. A voice rose from my belly and screamed into the camera, 'I am Aliya Sahar, the sister of Behrouz. He is innocent!'

Strong hands grabbed me from behind and tried to wrench me away. I took strength from desperation and clung on to the microphone. 'The guilty ones are Colonel Mike Clarke and a man called Farukh Zarghun.' I flung one hand towards the hospital. 'And Tewfiq Hamidi, who is standing there by the entrance.' Lights flashed, people were shouting, running with cameras, jostling to get a better view of me. 'They sell drugs. They kill people. They bribe policemen, and they've paid an orderly to kill Behrouz tonight.'

The reporter threw her arm around me, shouted over my head and shoved the microphone into my face. The hands fell from my shoulders.

'Can you prove this, Aliya?'

I pulled out my phone, pressed 'play' and held the screen to the camera. A picture appeared on the little monitor at the cameraman's feet, a blurry hand, a shirt, a chin, a cheek, an eye, but you could see they were the colonel's, and though the voices were tinny and thin, the words were clear enough.

'Are you going to kill me, Colonel Clarke?'

'Not until you stop being useful.'

A wall of microphones, cameras and journalists yelling my name closed in. I'd had a plan, not much of one, but somehow I think it had worked.

DAN

Two weeks later

They played it over and over for days. Every time I turned on the TV, there it was. Sometimes they showed the whole scene from different angles, using footage from the CCTV and all the other news cameras in the car park: Aliya running through the cars, me and Connor rushing after her and freezing in shock when she veered away from the entrance, grabbed the reporter's microphone and started yelling into it. I thought she'd gone mad till I realized what she was doing. Smart move, when you think about it. But then she's one of the smartest people I've ever met.

They also played the photos from Behrouz's phone. When they showed the one at the Meadowview fundraiser, they highlighted the faces of the policeman at the cake stall and the man lobbing balls at coconuts. I don't know why I never realized it before – they were Mark Trent and Jez Deakin.

When I look back on it the rest of that night, it's a blur. I remember Dad coming to the police station to get me. What an idiot. They arrested him there and then, but next morning they let him out on bail, unlike the rest of Clarke's people, who look like they'll be staying on remand for months while the cops dismantle his empire. Every day there's another big-name arrest in the papers, some investigator from the Drug Enforcement Agency flying in from the States or Afghanistan, or an announcement from the Prime Minister about smashing high-level corruption.

Mum's chucked out all the nicked appliances Dad got her for her birthday and now there's three big holes in her perfect kitchen. Things at home are pretty weird. One minute Mum's crying and shouting at Dad, the next she's crying and hugging him. Dad doesn't say much. Now and then he puts his hand on my shoulder and says, 'I'm proud of you, son,' and I nod and duck out of his way, feeling terrible. Turns out that Jez had laundered thousands of pounds of drug money through Abbott & Co's books. Dad's admitting to fencing stolen appliances but he says he had no idea about the money-laundering, and though he kind of knew Jez was involved with drugs, he'd turned a blind eye to it. The recording of Trent telling

Aliya he was just Jez's runaround should go some way to helping Dad's defence. Anyway, his lawyers are hoping if he testifies for the prosecution, they can swing some kind of deal, and we've just got to hope it'll work out. Jez's mum Eileen won't talk to us. Sticks her nose in the air every time she walks past. Snotty cow. Her darling son deserves everything he gets. And he's going to get plenty.

The good news is the police found Arif trussed up in Hamidi's attic along with a tape of him claiming it was an Al Shaab operative who'd killed Behrouz. He was bruised and battered and really pissed off, but now he's sold his story to the tabloids, he's cheered up a lot, even though they won't be able to print it until after Clarke's trial. He's buying a flat and Connor's moving in. I see Connor a lot, he's a good mate. Good driver too. Maybe one day I'll find a way to pay him back for what he did.

The bad news is that Aliya won't speak to me. Even when we're at the police station, going over what happened, looking at mug shots of people they think might have been working for Clarke, she insists on sitting in a separate room. I don't blame her. I know there's nothing I can ever do to make up for what I did. Or rather what I didn't have the guts to do. I miss her, though. Sometimes I play the clips of her in the hospital car park just to see her face.

ALIYA

've had my hair cut very short and spiky, like a boy. I did it to stop people recognizing the wild, dishevelled girl they'd seen on their television screens shouting accusations about Colonel Clarke. Sometimes I wish I could take scissors and cut away the anger too. It doesn't ease, even when it says on the news that they've arrested more of Clarke's network. Businessmen, immigration officials, detectives, soldiers, van drivers. It's as if we've dropped a stone in a pool of fetid water and the ripples won't stop spreading. But there is also anger at the boy. Wherever I go, whatever I do, it's always there inside me, like a lump of hot black tar.

The policemen at Behrouz's door still watch me as I come and go, but they're there to protect him now and they smile at me and call me by my name. I've got to know some of theirs: Keith, Brian, Jim and Phil – short, blunt English names. They bring my mother tea sometimes and try to make her go home to rest or go down to the canteen to eat, but she refuses to leave Behrouz's bedside unless I am there. That's all right, because I come every day while Mina is at nursery. For the first few days after Clarke's arrest I would push open the door of Behrouz's room, see his empty eyes and nervous, blistered smile and know I was still a stranger to him.

After a while I began to bring him things that I hoped might stir a spark in the ashes of his memory: a hot *bolani* with pepper sauce, DVDs of his favourite films, a bowl of *banjaan*, and then, one day, the photo of our family picnicking by the river which I printed off the internet. When he focused on the image of my father, something flitted across his face like the shadow of a startled bird and gave me hope. I propped the picture beside his bed and for the next three days I talked to him about Baba and our life in Kabul, and on the fourth day it was as if someone had cracked open the shutters in his head and let in the thinnest shaft of light. The memories were patchy, but every day a few more filtered through the darkness and the day he finally smiled at my mother and called her Mor-jan, I thought she would swoon with joy.

Gradually, with the help of the photos from his phone, we began to fill in the blanks on my grid and work out exactly how he'd come to be in that lock-up. It broke his heart when I told him that Captain Merrick had been killed, but it made him even more determined to make his own statement to the police.

Today he is ready. He sits up in bed and beside him, resting against the jug of water, is the picture Mina has drawn for him of the new house the council is going to give us. As I tell him about the patch of garden, the shiny tiles in the kitchen and the hot water that is always there when you turn on the tap, the room fills with important men and women, some in uniform, some not. They lean against walls, squash into chairs and talk in hushed whispers. I recognize Inspector McGill, the officer who interviewed me for eight long hours after the explosion. He nods at me. I do not nod back. My mother gazes at them all, then tightens her scarf and leaves the room.

The policeman called Keith switches on the video recorder, murmurs the date and Behrouz's name and tells him, 'In your own time.' Behrouz glances at me, I smile at him. He takes a sip of water and in the raw, rustling whisper that is all the sound his burnt throat can make, he begins to speak.

'On the morning of the Meadowview fundraiser PC Mark Trent asked to search my cab because he'd been tipped off that I was using it to transport drugs.' His eyes wander a little as he reaches for the memory. 'He found a package in the boot and made me open it. It was full of white powder. He tasted it and said it was heroin. I denied it was mine but by then my fingerprints were all over the packaging. Then he told me about a gang with links to Afghanistan who were moving drugs around London on the canals and using the Meadowview loading bay as a holding depot.' The listeners shuffle their feet and exchange glances. 'He said if I helped them out, I would make a lot of money and he wouldn't pursue the charges for possession. But if I didn't cooperate, he would arrest me, and my whole family would be deported.'

Behrouz takes another sip of water and shakes his head when the doctor leans in and asks him if he's getting tired.

'I decided my only hope was to gather enough evidence to prove he was corrupt. To buy myself time, I told him I'd have to think about it. He gave me five days. Later I saw him talking to a plumber called Jez Deakin, who sometimes does work at the flats. I could tell from the way they were looking at me that Deakin was involved.'

Slowly and painfully, between sips of water, he tells them how he followed Jez Deakin and saw him and Tewfiq Hamidi unloading suspicious parcels from a Hardel Meats van. The boy and I had been right: Behrouz had gone to Hardel's to get a better photo of Hamidi, and was shocked and terrified when he recognized Farukh Zarghun and realized that Zarghun had recognized him. His voice is already beginning to fade but everyone is so quiet it doesn't matter. His eyes sweep the room. 'I knew that only a top-level conspiracy could have got Zarghun out of jail and into Britain, so I tried to get hold of Colonel Clarke. He was the only person I trusted to protect me and help me to expose the truth.'

When Behrouz describes how he asked Merrick to get him the colonel's private number, he swallows hard and plucks at the bandage on his hand before he finds the strength to go on. 'As soon as he sent me the colonel's home number I called it and told his wife everything – who I had talked to and what I knew. She told me to come to their house immediately and she would arrange for me to speak to the colonel in the States. Before I went I hid my old phone so there would be a copy of the photos if Zarghun's people caught up with me on the way.' Outside in the hallway someone coughs and a trolley rumbles along the floor.

'India Lambert set up a Skype call with the colonel. Very calmly he told me that he was the one who had arranged Zarghun's fake death and organized his entry to the UK under a false name. He said it had been necessary because Zarghun still controlled the Afghan end of the drugs supply chain. He said he'd backed my asylum claim so he could take me into the heart of the business and he'd got my family housed at Meadowview so I could oversee the storage of some big drug shipments that were coming in via the canal. He'd planned for Trent to ease me into the business and, once he was certain of my loyalty, he would have revealed his own involvement and moved me up the ranks. But my investigations had forced his hand.'

'Why did he pick you?' asks a voice that sends a quiver through my flesh. It is Inspector McGill. Behrouz's eyes seek him out in the crowd before he answers.

'Clarke said my reputation as a decorated hero, my language skills and my clean-cut looks . . .' Behrouz croaks out the ghost of a laugh and touches his bandaged face. Who knows how he will look when those bandages come off? '. . . would make me an ideal goodwill ambassador for Hope Unlimited, and that my foreign trips for the charity would provide the perfect cover for meeting useful officials and international dealers.'

'How did you respond to this proposition?' McGill asks.

'I pretended to agree to it. But he demanded more than assurances. He asked me to go with Tewfiq Hamidi that afternoon and prove my good faith by killing a courier he suspected of double-crossing him.'

I gasp and raise my hand to my mouth. Behrouz has kept this from me and for a long moment he refuses to meet my eyes.

'Hamidi took me off in his car but I managed to make a run for it. I was certain they'd go after my mother and sisters to punish me, so I waited until after dark and went back to Meadowview, disguised as a woman, to try to get them out. But Hamidi and his thugs were waiting for me. They beat me up and threatened to kill my family unless I made a video claiming that I was a member of Al Shaab. I added some words of my own to the ones they made me read out. I hoped that my sister would get the message that Clarke was a criminal and responsible for what had happened to me.' He looks over to where I am standing. His voice is almost gone. With the last of it he wheezes, 'If it wasn't for her, I would be dead, the world would believe I was a terrorist and Mike Clarke, Farukh Zarghun and all their corrupt cronies would be walking free.'

Keith clicks off the tape and the silence in the room grows thick and uncomfortable. The doctor lifts his hand and insists that Behrouz must rest now. One by one the men and women leave. He gives Behrouz an injection. Within minutes he falls into an exhausted sleep and I run from the hospital because it hurts too much to stay. The hot black anger weighs me down and tears fill my eyes, distorting the buildings and the cars and the outline of the elderly man coming towards me, leaning heavily on his walking stick. He is red in the face and struggling to breathe. As we draw level, he trips and catches hold of my arm.

'Are you all right?' I say.

'Just a little dizzy. I think I need to sit down.' He keeps hold of my arm and dabs his face with a handkerchief. When his breathing is steadier, he points to a wide white building and says, 'I was on my way to take afternoon tea in that hotel, would you mind awfully helping me inside?'

Something inside me recoils from the tightness of his grip. I hear WPC Rennell's words in my head: 'London's a big city and the people in it aren't always what they seem. There's some you can trust and some you can't.' But I tell myself he's a sick old man and I let him lean on me as I guide him into a red-carpeted reception area full of spindly gold-painted chairs, tables with marble tops and palm trees in pots. He points to an archway. 'Through there, my dear, if you would be so kind. It's the table in the corner.'

The table is laid for two; thin white china on a starched white cloth, pale-pink flowers in a silver vase. He sits down heavily. 'Thank you, my dear.' He waves his upturned hand over the cakes and the little pots of jam and butter. 'Please, do join me.'

'Me? Oh, no. Thank you.'

'I insist. It's the least I can do.'

'You're expecting someone.'

He smiles. 'I asked them to lay for two, just in case I had the pleasure of a companion.'

The waitress appears with a silver teapot and sets it down on the table.

It would be rude to hurry away and I'm tired and thirsty, so I hang my bag on the back of the chair and sit down. He smiles again and pours tea into my cup.

'Forgive me. I should have introduced myself. George Woodcote.'

I shake the plump pink hand he offers. 'Hello, Mr Woodcote, I am—'

'I know who you are.'

My face burns. I look down.

'Don't be alarmed, my dear. I'm afraid I rather bumped into you on purpose.'

Fear prickles my skin. I look up slowly. 'Why?'

'I wanted to congratulate you on the excellent job you did exposing Colonel Clarke's drug ring.'

'Oh.'

'May I offer you a scone?'

He takes a small brown cake, slices it in half, spreads it carefully with red jam and white cream and hands it to me on a plate. 'This is called a cream tea. It's a very English treat.'

I bite into the crumbly little cake he calls a scone and store these new words away.

'I have to say, it's not often that we come across a young woman with your . . . language skills . . . intelligence and . . . tenacity.'

I don't like the change in his voice. I don't like the way he says 'we'. 'Are you from the police?'

'Not exactly. However, my organization does work in tandem with them on occasion and we certainly took a close interest in your brother's case and your activities after the explosion.'

The kindly twinkle in his eye has dulled to a glimmer of steel.

A close interest? My activities?

'You had me followed, didn't you?' I say. 'All those people who kept brushing past us, walking where we walked, sitting where we sat. They were working for you.'

He chuckles as if we are playing a game, but it's a hollow sound and it makes me angry. 'We thought you might lead us to Al Shaab, but it wasn't easy. You and your friend Dan proved very elusive.'

'Why have you brought me here?'

'Don't look so concerned. I have a proposition to make to you.' I say nothing and he keeps on talking. 'There's an organization that we've had our eye on for a while. It works with young refugees but we think it's a front for something a little more sinister.' He folds his napkin to a point and dabs a blob of cream from his lip. 'We were rather hoping you might be able to find out what's happening from the inside. There would be a payment of course. A substantial sum.'

I stare at him as his meaning sinks in. 'You want me to spy for you?'

'Well . . . yes, if that's what you want to call it.'

I feel a ridiculous urge to laugh. Why do people keep offering my family these horrible jobs? Behrouz didn't want to run drugs for Colonel Clarke and I certainly don't want to spy for the British government.

'You thought I was a terrorist. You thought I would lead you to Al Shaab.'

'Only at first. Do have another scone.'

I push my plate away. He drops his napkin into his lap and reaches for my arm to stop me leaving. 'There are many things you learn as you get older, my dear, especially in a business like mine. One of the most important is that it's deeds not words that prove a person's worth. You've been through a lot – uncertainty, fear, pain, threats – but you stayed loyal, kept going against all the odds and risked your life to help someone you cared about. People capable of that sort of selfless loyalty are pretty thin on the ground. Gold dust, you might say.'

Gold dust.

It all comes back to me: the running and hiding, the barge, the black water, the fear and the pain the boy suffered to help me without betraying his father, trying as best he could to do the impossible and stay loyal to us both. I stand up. 'I have to go.'

'My dear, what's the problem?'

I run out of there. As I hurry down the street I get out my phone and call a number. My heart is heavy. Then I hear the boy say quietly, 'Hey, Aliya,' and the sound lifts my anger away.

'Hello, Dan,' I whisper. 'I think I owe you a ride on the London Eye.'

ACKNOWLEDGEMENTS

I would like to say a big thank you to my editors Rachel Leyshon and Bella Pearson and my agent Stephanie Thwaites at Curtis Brown for their guidance and support, I would also like to thank Detective Constable Laura Hynes for her help with my research and for being so patient about my endless questions and Nasir Ahmadi for his insights into life in Afghanistan. And, of course, a very special thank you to my husband, James, for his endless patience, enthusiasm and encouragement.

CHASING THE DARK by Sam Hepburn

Mum's gone. Killed in a hit-and-run car crash. Her last words a message for someone I've never heard of.

What happened that night? All I've got is a trail of secrets and lies, but am I just chasing the dark?

Properly pacy, smart and intriguing . . .
a fast-moving and cleverly structured plot . . .
it all builds to a suitably thrilling climax.
BOOKS FOR KEEPS

Paperback, ISBN 978-1-910002-80-3, £6.99 • ebook, ISBN 978-1-909489-01-1, £6.99